PRAISE FOR CAF

Hummingbird Lane

"Brown's (*The Daydream Cabin*) gentle story of a woman finding strength within a tight-knit community has just a touch of romance at the end. Recommended for readers who enjoy heartwarming stories about women overcoming obstacles."

—*Library Journal*

Miss Janie's Girls

"[A] heartfelt tale of familial love and self-acceptance."

—*Publishers Weekly*

"Heartfelt moments and family drama collide in this saga about sisters."

—*Woman's World*

The Banty House

"Brown throws together a colorful cast of characters to excellent effect and maximum charm in this small-town contemporary romance . . . This first-rate romance will delight readers young and old."

—*Publishers Weekly*

The Family Journal

HOLT MEDALLION FINALIST

"Reading a Carolyn Brown book is like coming home again."

—*Harlequin Junkie* (top pick)

The Empty Nesters

"A delightful journey of hope and healing."

—*Woman's World*

"The story is full of emotion . . . and the joy of friendship and family. Carolyn Brown is known for her strong, loving characters, and this book is full of them."

—*Harlequin Junkie*

"Carolyn Brown takes us back to small-town Texas with a story about women, friendships, love, loss, and hope for the future."

—*Storeybook Reviews*

"Ms. Brown has fast become one of my favorite authors!"

—*Romance Junkies*

The Perfect Dress

"Fans of Brown will swoon for this sweet contemporary, which skillfully pairs a shy small-town bridal shop owner and a softhearted car dealership owner . . . The expected but welcomed happily ever after for all involved will make readers of all ages sigh with satisfaction."

—*Publishers Weekly*

"Carolyn Brown writes the best comfort-for-the-soul, heartwarming stories, and she never disappoints . . . You won't go wrong with *The Perfect Dress!*"

—*Harlequin Junkie*

The Magnolia Inn

"The author does a first-rate job of depicting the devastating stages of grief, provides a simple but appealing plot with a sympathetic hero and heroine and a cast of lovable supporting characters, and wraps it all up with a happily ever after to cheer for."

—*Publishers Weekly*

"*The Magnolia Inn* by Carolyn Brown is a feel-good story about friendship, fighting your demons, and finding love, and maybe just a little bit of magic."

—*Harlequin Junkie*

"Chock-full of Carolyn Brown's signature country charm, *The Magnolia Inn* is a sweet and heartwarming story of two people trying to make the most of their lives, even when they have no idea what exactly is at stake."

—Fresh Fiction

Small Town Rumors

"Carolyn Brown is a master at writing warm, complex characters who find their way into your heart."

—*Harlequin Junkie*

The Sometimes Sisters

"Carolyn Brown continues her streak of winning, heartfelt novels with *The Sometimes Sisters*, a story of estranged sisters and frustrated romance."

—All About Romance

"This is an amazing feel-good story that will make you wish you were a part of this amazing family."

—*Harlequin Junkie* (top pick)

The Sawmill Book Club

ALSO BY CAROLYN BROWN

Contemporary Romances

Meadow Falls

The Lucky Shamrock

The Devine Doughnut Shop

The Sandcastle Hurricane

Riverbend Reunion

The Bluebonnet Battle

The Sunshine Club

The Hope Chest

Hummingbird Lane

The Daydream Cabin

Miss Janie's Girls

The Banty House

The Family Journal

The Empty Nesters

The Perfect Dress

The Magnolia Inn

Small Town Rumors

The Sometimes Sisters

The Strawberry Hearts Diner

The Lilac Bouquet

The Barefoot Summer

The Lullaby Sky

The Wedding Pearls

The Yellow Rose Beauty Shop

The Ladies' Room

Hidden Secrets

Long, Hot Texas Summer

Daisies in the Canyon

Trouble in Paradise

Contemporary Series

The Broken Roads Series

To Trust

To Commit

To Believe

To Dream

To Hope

Three Magic Words Trilogy

A Forever Thing

In Shining Whatever

Life After Wife

Historical Romance

The Black Swan Trilogy

Pushin' Up Daisies

From Thin Air

Come High Water

The Drifters & Dreamers Trilogy

Morning Glory

Sweet Tilly

Evening Star

The Love's Valley Series

Choices

Absolution

Chances

Redemption

Promises

The
Sawmill
Book Club

CAROLYN
BROWN

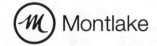

Published by Montlake, Seattle

www.apub.com

Amazon, the Amazon logo, and Montlake are trademarks of Amazon.com, Inc., or its affiliates.

ISBN-13: 9781662514333 (paperback)
ISBN-13: 9781662514340 (digital)

Cover design by Lesley Worrell
Cover image: © the_burtons / Getty Images

Printed in the United States of America

To Letha Clark,
for all the love, encouragement, and support

Chapter One

"Desperate times," Libby O'Dell muttered, but she couldn't remember the rest of the saying.

"What was that?" Amanda asked as she folded clothes and boxed them up for Libby to put into her SUV for the trip the next day.

Call for desperate measures. Victoria O'Dell's voice popped into Libby's mind so loudly that she jerked her head around to see if her grandmother had been resurrected and was standing right there beside her. Not once in all the years that Victoria had been gone had Libby heard her voice, so why was she hearing it now?

"You look like you just saw a ghost," Amanda said.

"I didn't see one, but I heard one. I said, 'Desperate times,' and Victoria, my grandmother, popped into my head to finish the saying," Libby answered.

"My granny does that pretty often," Amanda said. "I'll be washing dishes or folding clothes, and she'll say that I need to do the job a different way. She was always bossy. Is this the first time you've heard Victoria's voice?"

Libby sat down on the edge of the bed. "Yes, it is. We didn't have the best relationship, but she did raise me and teach me the antique business. As hard as I ran away from that, I can't believe that I'm leaving tomorrow to interview for a job right back in the same thing. Guess your past *will* catch up to you."

Amanda sat down beside Libby and gave her a sideways hug. "Hey, girlfriend, you don't have to take this job if it doesn't feel right. You can always come back to Austin and live with me for a couple of months while you look for something here."

"Yoo-hoo! Y'all girls about to get all packed up?" Dolly's high, thin voice floated across the small apartment's living room and into the bedroom.

"We're back here," Amanda called.

"Looks like you're going to have to store some stuff," Dolly said as she made her way through the maze of belongings.

"Yep, maybe a few boxes," Libby said with a nod. "But Amanda has offered to loan me some space in her garage until I can get settled. Then, when I have an address, she will ship them to me."

"I couldn't help much, so I made y'all some sandwiches and brought over some chocolate pie. It's all on the table. Why don't you take a few minutes to rest and have some supper?" Dolly led the way out of the bedroom.

Libby felt like a giant when she stood up, but that wasn't anything new. She had always been the tallest kid in class, towering above most of the boys at her high school graduation in Jefferson, Texas. Amanda barely came up to her shoulder, and Dolly was even shorter. She'd met Amanda when she moved into the dorm at the University of Texas in Austin. They had been roommates for two years and had become best friends. Just thinking about moving away from Amanda and striking out on her own put a lump in Libby's throat.

"I haven't eaten yet, either," Dolly said as she moved a box marked For Libby to the floor. "So we can have a last supper together."

"You can take that one home and burn it," Libby said to Amanda.

"What, this box? Why would she do that?" Dolly asked.

"Because I don't want it," Libby answered as she eased down into one of the mismatched chairs around an old yellow chrome table.

"I can't trash something that might be important to you someday. I'll just ship it to you when you have an address, and you can burn it yourself," Amanda said.

"Ugh, fine," Libby groaned, but she didn't intend to ever open the thing. It was the only item she had been given when her grandmother passed away. Everything else—the business, Victorian Antiques in Jefferson, and the house, with all its contents—had been sold to pay Victoria's gambling debts. So, no, that box probably had leftover stubs and hot tips that would never pay off. She had no qualms about burning it.

"Well, that's settled. Let's finish our sandwiches," Amanda said. "I can't wait to get into that chocolate pie."

"Where's my manners?" Libby placed a hand on Dolly's bony shoulder. "Thank you, Dolly, for bringing us food. I was going to suggest that we grab a taco when we get done, but BLTs are so much better."

Dolly smiled so big that the wrinkles on her octogenarian face deepened. "I don't know about that. I sure do love me some tacos, but this is what I had in my apartment to work with. Now, let's talk about this interview. Ever since you got laid off three months ago, you've been saying how you want to get out of the city. 'Course, you'll have to drive a long way just to get a pizza, but maybe Madam Fate is working a miracle of some kind."

"I'll miss you both," Libby said around the lump in her throat. "Am I doing something totally insane? I don't even know if I'll get the job or if I want it. Should I change my mind?"

Dolly laid her veined hand on Libby's. "I feel like this is right for you. You do need a change and an adventure, darlin' girl. The man who owns the antique store is an old soul. I knew when I was shopping at that store that you'd like him. Did he send off any bad juju when you talked to him on the phone?"

Libby shook her head. "No, he seemed nice enough—and was really interested in hiring me because I have both bookkeeping and antique experience," she replied. "I said that I would never set foot in another antique store or have to smell lemon-scented furniture polish again. I feel like I'm going back on my word to myself, and that I'm disappointing the little kids at the women's shelter."

Amanda shook her head so hard that her long blonde hair flopped around her face. "You only said that when you found out that your grandmother had gambled away your college funds. I hate to see you move away, but we can FaceTime every day, and it's only a five-hour drive. We can visit each other on long weekends. You need this, Libby, so stop second-guessing yourself. Dolly's been there and talked with the owner. She wouldn't let you go if she didn't feel like you should give it a chance. Besides, didn't your grandmother always say that you were too backward to do anything risky?"

Victoria's voice butted into the emotional conversation: Stick-in-the-mud *were the words I used.*

"Don't worry about your work at the women's shelter," Dolly said. "I went down there today and volunteered to take your time slot. The little kids all flocked around me like I was their grandma."

"Oh, Dolly!" Tears pricked Libby's eyes. "That is so sweet of you. Those kids need positive attention so much."

"You are welcome, but honey, I'm doing it as much for me as I am for them," Dolly said. "I love little kids, and being around them keeps a person young—at heart, if not in the body."

Libby forced a smile. "If it doesn't feel right, I can always come back here, even though I'm sick of the city, or . . ." She paused. "I might just use up my savings and do some impromptu traveling. I can always work as a waitress for a few weeks and then move on to something else."

I'll show you I'm not a stick-in-the-mud, she thought as a picture of her grandmother's face flashed through her mind.

You won't make it at this job any more than you did the last one, Victoria's voice taunted Libby the next day as she drove north toward the little community of Sawmill, Texas, not far from the Oklahoma border.

Libby stomped on the brake and came to a screeching halt right beside a road sign that said she was entering Powderly,

Texas—population: 935. She stared across the console for several seconds, even though Victoria wasn't floating above the passenger's seat.

"What did you say to me?" she asked but did not expect an answer, since Victoria had been dead for more than a decade. "I was laid off because the company sold out to a bigger corporation."

If you had finished your education, you might have had a better job in a better place.

Maybe it was leaving that cursed box behind that had raised her grandmother's spirit up out of the grave to haunt her. Victoria's best friend had given Libby the box when she drove to Jefferson for the simple but weird memorial, and there had always been an eerie aura around the thing. She had taken it to her apartment in Austin; shoved it back into a dark corner of her closet; and for the most part, forgotten about it. Until Amanda had helped her pack almost everything she could get into her SUV and head northeast for a job interview.

"I'm not so sure I want to talk to you after all these years, and I may not even take the job if it's offered to me," she grumbled.

Maybe the box had brought about the reverse of *Gremlins*: Victoria had left whatever gambling hall was in the afterlife to fuss at Libby in daylight.

People didn't converse with the dead—not even those who were prone to talk to themselves, like Libby did all the time. She shook thoughts of her grandmother from her head, pulled back out onto the two-lane road, and concentrated on her driving as she passed through town. An old man coming out of a diner waved at her. On the other side of the road, a young woman with two little kids in tow threw up a hand and smiled. Libby acknowledged them both with a nod. A little farther down the road, she noticed a convenience store, and then a church with one of those old wooden signs. The paint was peeling off it, but its message caught her eye: STOP! SALVATION INSIDE.

Libby instinctively moved her foot from the gas pedal to the brake when she read the first word. Tires screeched. Horns blasted.

This place isn't going to be my salvation, she thought. People leaning on their horns—or even two people waving at her—didn't erase all the fears that had burrowed down deep in her soul; the trust issues and the fear of commitment were merely a few. Just a few more miles, and she would have a job interview—nothing more nor less, in spite of what Victoria had whispered in her ear.

Did she really want to live in a town so small that it didn't even have a post office?

Her grandmother had always warned her that she would grow up to be a stick-in-the mud. As a child, Libby hadn't been sure what that meant, but the tone in Victoria's voice all those years ago and the expression on her grandmother's face definitely suggested that sticking in mud was something that would send a person straight to hell. Do not pass go. Do not collect any money. Just pick up your horns and sunscreen on the way down.

Libby shook the memory loose and tried to erase that box she had left behind with Amanda from her mind. Before daylight that morning, she had thrown her last tote bag in the passenger's seat and driven out of Austin. That was definitely a risk, so Victoria could crawl back into whatever gambling place she had been playing blackjack in since her passing and keep her opinions to herself.

She shot another blast of stink eye across the console. "If I get this job, I'll find a spot for you in a dark corner. I don't need or want your advice."

"Turn right onto Farm Road 906 and continue for three miles," Matilda, the mechanical voice on her GPS, said.

Libby slowed down and made the turn. There were very few houses, not a single vehicle on the road, and no one to wave at her. She felt like she had fallen off the face of the earth, so she turned on the radio to be sure there was civilization in the area. A few minutes later, Matilda told her to turn left onto Sawmill Road in one mile. Libby tapped the brakes, but then she started thinking about the song "Wait in the Truck." Lainey Wilson had taken home all kinds of awards for that song, and it was on Libby's playlist. The lyrics talked about a whole different situation from Libby's experience of waiting in the vehicle, but every time she heard it, the memories surfaced from those years ago when she was a little girl.

Libby had spent a lot of time waiting in an old station wagon while her grandmother hit the poker tables at the casino. She was told to keep the doors locked, not roll down the windows any farther than a one-inch crack, read her books, and enjoy the food in the brown bag that Victoria had packed for her.

Why drive seven hours for an interview for a job that you aren't sure you want when there are dozens of positions open in Austin? the aggravating voice in her head asked. This was definitely not Victoria's gravelly smoker's voice, but the one that often popped up when she had doubts about something.

"I need a change of scenery," she answered. "And it won't be a forever job. It's just a little layover until I can figure things out. Besides, I haven't gotten the job yet, so I don't have to worry about the *why* or *where* of things until I do. And I'm tired of big-city traffic and the constant rush."

"Reroute, reroute, reroute," Matilda repeated over and over again when Libby breezed right past a narrow gravel road.

"I hear you!" Libby said and slapped the steering wheel of her ten-year-old SUV, then whipped an illegal U-turn in the middle of the two-lane road.

She focused on the signs and Matilda's voice until she saw a small sign at the corner of a side road that said ONE MILE TO SAWMILL ANTIQUES.

"Turn right," Matilda said.

"You could say *Good job* once in a while," Libby grumbled as she made the turn.

She hadn't driven down a gravel road in so long that she had forgotten about the dust that boiled up all around her. Was she silly to drive more than three hundred miles from Austin to interview for this job?

Answers didn't suddenly appear; no airplane wrote letters in the clear blue sky. The gray cloud of dust surrounding her on three sides filtered through the air conditioner vents and made her sneeze. He had said that Sawmill was basically a community, not a town, but who in their right mind would live this far out in the boonies? Or better yet, who would drive all the way out here to buy antiques?

"No one with a lick of common sense!" she said, raising her voice and answering her own question. "Benny said that it was a full-time position with benefits and even a free apartment if I wanted to live in an old service station."

Though she had never met the man in person—and didn't even know what he looked like—her elderly neighbor, Dolly, had assured her many times that he could be trusted. Her words came back to Libby as she slowed down so she wouldn't miss the turn again.

"You've wanted out of the city life for a while," Dolly had reminded her in the pep talk she had given Libby more than once. "You got nothing to lose. Your rent is up. You've been looking for work since you got laid off, and the job doesn't have to be a forever thing. Try it for a few months, and if you don't like it, move on. You are young and smart. You can find a job anywhere. At the very least, you'll be out of the city. I knew that going on that road trip with my girlfriends to look at antiques was a good idea, and now look at what our adventure produced."

Adventure was the word that Libby couldn't shake from her mind. In retrospect, she might be driving for hours to show her grandmother that she wasn't a stick-in-the-mud. The next sign she saw told her that she was traveling on a dead-end road. That was the gospel truth, she decided with a nod. Angels walking on a barbed wire fence and singing her favorite song couldn't make her work in an antique store for the rest of her life—especially not in this godforsaken place. At best, this was simply a stopover until she figured out exactly what she wanted to do with her life. She had lived her entire life in three ruts—the first one in Jefferson, Texas, until she finished high school; two years in college, where all she did was study; and then at a boring job in a little cubicle for eight hours a day because she thought it was secure.

"I *am* a stick-in-the-mud," she whispered. "No wonder I can't hold on to a relationship. I'm as boring as yesterday's news."

Knee-high weeds and scattered waist-high saplings had sprung up around defunct oil wells on either side of the narrow-rutted road. The gray cloud of dust still followed behind her—blotting out the past and chasing her toward a hopeless future.

When she had left Jefferson, Texas, for college, Libby had promised herself that she would never work in an antique store again or allow a bottle of lemon-oil furniture polish in her house. Imagining the smell of the spray her grandmother had made her use to dust the antiques gagged her so badly that she cracked the window for a breath of fresh air. She would rather have a little gray dust on the shoulder of her dark blue shirt, she thought, than a green cast around her mouth.

Even after her grandmother's friend June had called her to say that Victoria had dropped dead of a heart attack in one of the casinos she frequented, Libby had not changed her mind, nor had she ever regretted the way she had felt at her passing. Some folks got all emotional over the death of a loved one—but then, maybe they'd been close to the one who had passed on. Libby had figured out years ago that she and Victoria were more like roommates. Had she inherited her grandmother's business, which she had not, she would have sold it—lock, stock, and barrel—to the highest bidder.

She slowed down more for a curve, and then right ahead of her was an enormous warehouse with SAWMILL ANTIQUES written in red block lettering on a sign hanging on a false front that extended upward at least fifteen feet from the store's true roof. Two elderly women wearing bibbed overalls and floppy straw hats worked in a flourishing vegetable garden between a couple of white frame houses to her left. They both looked up and waved and then went back to hoeing weeds. *Is this the entirety of the Sawmill community?* Libby wondered.

9

From the looks of the dirty windows on the old service station on the other side of the road, the business had been closed for years. Surely this wasn't the apartment Benny had offered her—rent free and utilities paid—as a bonus. She parked in front of the store and removed her sunglasses. The faded sign in the window said that, at one time, Sawmill Antiques had been the Sawmill Git and Go.

Was the name *Git and Go* an omen telling her that she should *git* back in her truck and *go* away as fast as she could? Perhaps she shouldn't even turn off the engine—just make a U-turn and head back to Paris. She'd passed several cheap no-tell motels where she could hole up for a day or two until she figured out whether she wanted to go east or west. Either one would prove that she was out for an adventure—even if it took every last dime of her savings.

Don't run from a challenge, Victoria scolded her.

"You have reached your destination," Matilda said.

"Which one do I listen to?" Libby asked herself out loud. "'Git and Go' or 'reached your destination'?"

She opted for the latter, even if only for an hour or so. She shut off the SUV's engine, took a deep breath, and put her hand on the door handle. The style of the single gas pump to her left proved that the station had been built before she was born. The hose was gone, and the bottom half, which she imagined had been bright red, had faded to a strange shade of pink. Bright afternoon sunrays bounced off a silver travel trailer parked right close to the place. A huge gravel parking lot sat between the defunct service station and the antique shop. Libby couldn't imagine ever seeing vehicles filling the space, not with millennials throwing out everything that belonged to their ancestors. More than that, she wasn't sure she wanted to live in such a desolate community.

Practically everything you own is in the back of this car. Even though you are thirty, you are acting like a classic millennial, aren't you? I knew the day would come when the world would turn upside down, and it has. Victoria's voice sounded angry.

Before she could argue with her grandmother, a big yellow, three-legged dog ambled off the service station porch. Libby opened the door, hoping the whole time that his wagging tail was a sign he was friendly and didn't intend to blame her for whatever had taken one of his front legs off. She held out her hand, and the dog shoved his head against it to be petted.

"That's the strangest thing I've ever seen," a deep masculine voice said, getting louder as it drew nearer and taking her attention away from the dog. "Elvis has been here ever since I have, and he's never even let the two ladies across the street pet him."

She turned toward the voice and the tall man walking in her direction.

He stuck out his hand when he was only a couple of feet away from her. "I'm Benny Taylor. You must be Libby. You are a little early."

She shook with him, dropped his hand, and took a step back. "Yes, I am, and it's nice to meet you in person. So, the dog's name is Elvis, and he doesn't like most people? Where did he get his name?"

With a name like Benny, she had expected him to be an older man and had drawn a mental picture of him wearing bibbed overalls and maybe having only a rim of gray hair around an otherwise bald head. She had not expected Benny Taylor to be Mr. Tall, Blond, and Handsome, all wrapped up in a bright smile. Good-looking guys like the one standing in front of her, wearing snug-fitting blue jeans and a T-shirt that hugged his ripped abdomen, usually managed gyms or maybe quarterbacked for a pro football team. They did not own and operate a dusty old antique store.

He motioned toward the porch. "His name is Elvis because he can sniff out drugs as fast as Elvis Presley could get a woman to swoon over him. He doesn't like most folks—but evidently, you are an okay person. Let's get out of the sun and have a bottle of water before we go out to the shop for the interview."

She followed him up the wooden steps. A gentle breeze set the leaves in motion on a huge pecan tree that shaded the porch and stood between the trailer and the old store. The beat-up yellow chrome table with four mismatched chairs that filled the space between the door leading inside and the end of the porch reminded her of the one she'd left behind in her apartment. A thick layer of road dust covered all the chairs. She pulled a tissue from her purse and dusted one off before she sat down.

Elvis had followed her to the steps but then deserted her and went to sniff all the tires on her vehicle. When he'd finished, he hiked a hind leg and watered the front wheel on the driver's side. She stared, mesmerized, watching the dog balance himself on one front leg and one back one.

"Water, sweet tea, or apple juice?" Benny asked. "There's beer in the refrigerator in the store. I'll be glad to get you one if you would rather have it."

"Water is fine. Is this the apartment you said I could have?" She tried to keep a neutral expression, but disappointment filled her heart.

Benny opened an antique Coke machine that sat on the other side of the door. He pulled out two bottles of water and handed one to her before he sat down.

"Yes, it is, but don't judge the book by the cover." He chuckled. "The apartment in the back is small and simple, but it's not as bad as what you are probably thinking. Did you have a good trip?"

She twisted the top off the bottle and took a drink. If the apartment wasn't that bad, then why wasn't he living in it instead of in a fancy trailer?

"I don't know that I'd call it a 'good trip,' but I can say it was a long one. I allowed a little extra time for traffic. That's why I'm a few minutes early." She didn't say that she had almost kept going when she missed Matilda's instructions. She was more than a little superstitious, and for a split second, that simple thing had seemed like a sign to her.

"I know what you mean by a long trip. I drove up here pretty often from Houston, but that last journey seemed to take forever. Probably because in the previous ones, I was coming to see Grandpa. The last one was to handle his funeral and his final wishes. It didn't seem nearly as bad when I was moving here, though. At that point, I felt like I'd been set free from prison." He took a sip of his water and went on. "You are seeing all of Sawmill right here. Even though I knew the place and wanted to be here, I still suffered from culture shock at first, so if you take the job, you can expect it to take a while to feel at home. It wasn't long, though, until wild horses couldn't have driven me back to the city."

"I'm sorry about your grandpa," Libby said. "Who are those ladies? Do they work at your store?"

Benny took another long drink of his water. "Thank you. It's been two years, and I still miss him. Those women are Opal and Minilee, and they are kind of like my surrogate grandmothers. They work at the store when they feel like it. Mostly dusting and cleaning, but no regular hours. They did bookkeeping there when my grandpa was alive."

Libby wished she could say that she missed her grandmother. When it came to Victoria O'Dell, the raw emotional edges hadn't softened much with the passing of time.

"I'm told that good memories help ease the pain," she told him, repeating the words her grandmother's friends had told her when she drove back to Jefferson for the memorial.

"I've heard the same thing, but I'm not sure I believe it," Benny said and then changed the subject. "So, when we talked on the phone a couple of days ago, you mentioned that you grew up in an antique store?"

"That's right," she answered. "Over in Jefferson, a small town that's known for its bed-and-breakfast places and its many antique stores."

"Then you have some idea of small-town living. The résumé that you emailed me says that you have computer-slash-bookkeeping experience—and what with growing up in an antique shop, you are basically what I'm looking for." He hesitated and frowned. "Tell me a little about the shop where you were raised."

"That's right," she answered. "My grandmother owned Victorian Antiques in Jefferson. She raised me from the time I was born. That's a story for another day, but I literally grew up in the shop. Last time I was there, my baby bed was still in the corner of the office."

"My grandfather and I visited the stores in that area several times," Benny said. "I worked here at Sawmill Antiques in the summer while I was in high school and college. I don't remember the names of the places, but I might have been in your shop. How did you even hear about the job opening here?"

"My neighbor Dolly suggested I apply. She loved your store when she visited here last weekend. When she saw the Help Wanted sign on your door"—Libby shrugged—"she knew I was looking for a job, so she convinced me to call."

"With your bookkeeping experience, you could probably work anywhere. Why would you apply for a job here?" he asked.

"I'm tired of Austin, and . . ." She paused and took another drink. It had been ten years since she had applied for a job, and Amanda had put in a good word for her at the agency back then, so that hadn't been much of an interview. Everything she had researched said to be forthright and honest but not talk too much, especially about personal things. "And I have experience in both areas—bookkeeping and antiques."

"Tell me more about your grandmother. Did she inherit the shop or just start it up?"

Was this a personal or professional question? If he wanted to research her story later and see if there really was a Victorian Antiques in Jefferson a few years ago, her answer could back her up.

"My grandmother, who was really Victoria, inherited the building from her folks. They had run a grocery store in it for years before they passed away. She loved antiques, so she bought out all the antique stock in a place in town that was going out of business and started her own. She taught me well, and it's like riding a bicycle: I may wobble a little at first, but I know my antiques."

"Then why didn't you keep the store when she passed away?"

"Victoria never met an antique she didn't like—or a blackjack table she didn't love," Libby replied, reminding herself to keep her answer short. "When she died, she owed more money than her house and business was worth. The banks foreclosed, and the loan sharks had to eat a big loss. I wouldn't have kept the store, anyway, or the house where I grew up."

Benny nodded a couple of times as if he understood, but he was just being nice. No one could feel what another person's past had been. "I'm sorry—your grandmother was Victoria, right? What made you leave your last job?"

"The insurance company was bought out by a huge corporation that wanted certified accountants to do the job I had been doing. I was not certified, so I was laid off. Like I said, I'm tired of the big-city life, and I'd like to try something other than just working with numbers all day, in a cubicle where I seldom talk to anyone," she answered and then shrugged. "My grandmother was always Victoria to me. She declared that she was too young to be a grandmother, so I was taught to call her by her name."

That was as close to the truth as she could get without delving into the fact that she still hadn't gotten over her grandmother's betrayal—and probably never would. The insurance money from Libby's father's death was supposed to have been put aside for her college education fund . . . but when Victoria had died, it was all gone.

"Then you came to the right place." He reached down and scratched Elvis's ears for a minute when the dog got tired of sniffing the new vehicle before he stood up. "Let's walk out to the store. I'd like you to see it and the office. We open at seven in the morning and close at seven in the evening on Friday, Saturday, and Sunday. That's thirty-six hours of work a week."

She was smart enough to know that such a small company was under no obligation to offer even a basic benefit package. If he had pulled a bait and switch, had offered her a place to live and insurance on the phone and was now reneging, she might be tempted to baptize him with what was left of the water in her bottle.

"Elvis and I are usually scouring the country for more stock from Monday morning till sometime on Thursday." He pointed at a moving van parked beside the building. "How much you work on those days is up to you. I would like you to at least put in a couple of hours a day doing the bookwork. I'll pay you what you were making at the insurance company, and time and a half for anything over forty hours," Benny said. "Like I told you on the phone, you are welcome to the apartment at the back of the service station. The Sawmill Book Club meets twice a month in the front part of the building. But Grandpa set up the little efficiency apartment in what used to be the storeroom, for times when he was too tired to travel back and forth to Paris. That would save you from having to commute." He used a key to open the door for her.

"Why doesn't Elvis like those ladies who were working in the garden?" Before she stepped through the door, she drew in as much fresh air as she could get into her lungs and held it there as long as possible so she wouldn't have to smell lemon furniture polish mixed with dust and a little mice urine. Benny flipped on the lights, and she breathed in the fresh scent of cinnamon.

She raised a dark eyebrow. "Are you making snickerdoodles in here?"

"I don't like the scent of that lemon polish, so I buy a special formula with no scent for dusting the furniture, and dish soap works fine for the glass pieces," he explained. "I use scent cubes in half a dozen warmers—that's what you are smelling. I started melting them this morning. The aroma sticks around all weekend. Cinnamon is my favorite, but sometimes I use gingerbread or vanilla. Do you like it?"

"I love it," she answered and tried to take in the whole place in one quick scan.

"To answer your question, I think maybe one of Opal or Minilee's visitors smokes a little pot. He's a former drug dog and has been trained to lay down wherever he gets a whiff of the stuff. He lays in one of their yards when I go over to visit them. It's kind of like he's telling me that there's drugs over there."

"Are you kidding me?"

"No, ma'am. I love them, but Elvis is trained, so I can't ignore the signs. Now, on to the history of this place," he said. "Years ago, this was a sawmill." He led the way through the huge warehouse with high ceilings. "My grandpa and his brother built it, and it was a big business for a while. They put in the little gas station and convenience store to help the folks out who had to drive from a distance to work here. Those two small houses across the road were where they lived until they got married and moved down to Paris. Then they gave the houses to the day and night supervisors as a bonus. Later in his life, Grandpa got interested in antiques, and the lumber business was on the downhill slide, so the rest is history. Tell me, what would you change about this place?"

The question came so abruptly that it startled Libby. She wondered if her answer would be the yea or nay as to whether she got the job. She'd been unsure about taking it, even if Benny offered to hire her, but when she'd walked into the store, something had changed. Call it fate or God or even the universe, but something was tugging at her heartstrings. She wanted to work here for some strange reason—and more than that, she wanted to live in the community. At least for a little while.

Closure, her grandmother's voice whispered. *You could find what you've been looking for right here in this godforsaken place if you just open your eyes.*

She ignored the voice in her head and ran her hand across a maple four-poster bed a lot like the one that had been in her bedroom as a teenager. She had loved that bed, and then one day, she came home from school to find an old iron bed sitting in the place where her pretty one had been. Her grandmother had sold her entire bedroom outfit to a dealer and replaced everything with discards from the store. That night, Victoria took the money she had made from the sale and went to the casino.

At least she was happy the next day since she had won a couple thousand dollars, Libby thought.

"Well?" Benny asked.

"I'm sorry. I was thinking about your question," Libby answered with a tiny white lie. "I like the way it's set up like a furniture store, with living room stuff in one area, bedroom in another, and so on—but I would put shelves along the walls to display small items for each particular room. Vases in the living room; old cookware, rolling pins, and that kind of thing in the kitchen. But it's your business, and with all the little stuff scattered on the tops of buffets and end tables, folks *will* tend to wander through the whole place."

"I like your idea," Benny said with a nod. "It's something to consider for the future."

You passed that test, but why didn't you ever mention that notion to me? Her grandmother's tone reminded Libby of the times when she had fussed at her for some small infraction—mostly on the days following nights she had lost money at the poker table.

Why on earth had Victoria waited until now to pop in with all kinds of advice? If the woman was in heaven, she could pull up a gold brick or two from the streets to cash in for poker money so she'd never be broke again. And if Libby needed closure—and she wasn't sure that she did—it certainly wouldn't come from Victoria O'Dell or this place.

Libby took a deep breath and let it out slowly to clear all the thoughts from her head. "What did you do before you took over this business?"

"I was a lawyer in a big firm in Houston," Benny answered. "I woke up one morning, called in sick—which was not a lie, because I was certainly sick of my job. I spent the whole day wandering until I realized that I was just going from one antique store to another. I had put this place up for sale when my grandpa died and hadn't had a single offer in a whole year. As I meandered, memories came back of all the good times I'd had with my grandpa right here in this tiny community. It was like the universe was telling me that I belonged in

Sawmill, not working eighty hours a week at a job I had come to hate. I resigned the next day, bought the trailer, and Elvis and I moved up here. He's happier than he was in the city, and so am I. That was a year ago, and my dad still thinks I made a big mistake. Don't get me started on what my mother thinks."

"Regrets?" She reached the back of the store, circled around, and walked up the other side.

"Not a single one," he answered. "The restrooms are on your left. There's a janitor's closet next to them, and then the office. We can finish visiting there if you've seen enough of the store, but first, tell me what you think of that secretary to your right. I just bought it at an estate sale in Mena, Arkansas, last week."

Libby ran her hand across the wood. "Burled oak. Curved glass is original, and makes it even more valuable." She bent to get a better view of the hardware. "This isn't replacement. You can tell by the way it has worn down the wood." She straightened up and opened the drop-down door to see the cubicles inside. "I'd say it was manufactured at the beginning of the 1900s, sometime in that first ten years. Was that a test?"

"Yep, and you passed. The bill of sale is tacked to the back—it was bought in 1907 and shipped to Jacob Coppenhaver." He opened the door into a small office.

The room was an unsightly mess, with stacks of paper all over the desk, dust thick enough to write your name covering every one of the filing cabinets lining the back wall, and an overflowing trash can—a far cry from the rest of the well-organized store.

Benny gathered up an armload of papers from one of the two chairs and set them on the other end of his desk. Then he circled around to sit in a worn leather office chair. "Have a seat. I have drawn up a contract that is good for six months. It simply states your wages and says that if at the end of the allotted time you want to stay, we will negotiate a new contract. I don't want you to sign it just yet, but look it over carefully, and give me an answer this afternoon."

"No need. I want the job, and I'm glad to live in the old service station," Libby said as she slid into the freshly emptied chair. "So why don't I just read over it and sign now?"

"Because there's one more little test. Remember those two ladies who were working out in their garden? Minilee and Opal?"

Libby nodded.

"They are in their eighties, and they grew up around this area. They will be your neighbors, and they like to meddle," he said.

"What does that have to do with me?" she asked.

"Did you hear that last part?"

"About meddling?"

He bobbed his head.

"Remember me telling you about my neighbor who told me about this job? She's eighty-four. She still drives, works part-time as a secretary in her church, and she and a couple of her friends go on at least one road trip a month. I lived beside her for ten years. I've learned all about the fine art of handling meddlers," she told him.

"We're going to Opal's house for dinner today so they can meet you," he blurted out. "I want you to get to know them before you sign the contract, because, for the most part, that's who you'll have around through the week while I'm out on the road."

"That sounds great." Libby picked up the folder and stood. "I expect you mean the noon meal and not the evening one. It's almost twelve o'clock. If Opal and Minilee are like Dolly, my former neighbor, they don't like to be kept waiting."

Benny pushed his chair back and got to his feet. "You are so right. Opal's house is the second one down from here, and I'll be willing to bet that the table is already set and the sweet tea poured. Do you always accept invitations to a meal with strangers?"

"No, but I've got a feeling this is another test, and I need—no, I *want*—this job. I saw those ladies when I drove up, and neither of them looked like serial killers." She smiled. "And I am starving. I ate a breakfast biscuit in the car on the way, but I haven't had anything since then."

"You really drove all this way with intentions of taking the job?" Benny asked.

"Not in the least," Libby replied as they walked out of the building. "I came here to make my neighbor happy. Her psychic told her that if she did a good thing for someone, then she would be lucky all week. That's how she put things together for me and your store after her trip. I don't want to be the cause of her getting hit by lightning, not winning the lottery by one number, or some other horrible thing. But after I arrived, I got this gut feeling that I should stick around and work for you."

"Then I'm glad for your gut," Benny said with a grin.

"I might as well get to know the neighbors now if I'm going to live here. You do realize that I'm increasing the population thirty-three and a third percent just by moving to Sawmill, don't you? I *should* get a free meal for that alone." She was amazed that she could joke about something so serious—but then, she was determined to show Victoria that she could be adventurous and take risks.

"With that kind of negotiating power, you'll be running for mayor in the fall," Benny teased.

"Or for school board, at the very least," Libby shot back.

"Those are high expectations since we don't have a school and are just barely considered a community." Benny winked at her. "But you might get elected to be president of the Sawmill Book Club if you agree to join."

"Of course I'll join if I'm asked. I love to read." She was amazed at how easy talking to Benny was and how much she had already changed her mind about living in a place so small that even calling it a community would be stretching the definition.

Elvis ran ahead of them and flopped down in the shade of a tree with flowers of every color spilling out over the edges of a truck tire that encircled the trunk. Libby studied it as they passed the first house and the garden, and stopped to walk around it when they were close enough.

"I don't see a cut in the tire. How did it get there?" she asked. "Using it for a flower bed is a good idea, but . . ."

"Opal planted the tree the first year she and her husband, Ernest, moved into the house," Benny said with half a chuckle. "I asked the same question when I was just a little boy. Ernest was the gas station's day supervisor at that time. Minilee's husband, Floyd, was the night manager at the sawmill. That's got nothing to do with your question— but anyway, Opal told me that she planted a little sapling, and she was afraid Ernest would mow it down, so she put the tire around it for protection. That would have been over fifty years ago, long before either of us were born. Now it produces a crop of pecans every few years."

Just like Victoria planted the knowledge of antiques in me, and even though it's lain dormant for years, it's still there and growing, Libby thought.

Then Victoria's voice was back in her head: *Too bad I didn't plant a seed of adventure in you. I tried, but you were too serious all the time.*

"I take chances," Libby muttered.

"What was that?" Benny asked.

"Just me arguing with the voices in my head," Libby answered.

"I do that a lot when I'm out on the road by myself," Benny said. "Who was in *your* head?"

"My grandmother. She's been gone for more than a decade and hasn't come back to haunt me until the last couple of days."

"Why do you think she's popping into your head now?"

"I have no idea." That was the second little white lie of the day. Victoria was back to gloat, like she had when she had won big at the casino. Was there a limit on how many lies Libby could tell in one day without them all adding up to one humongous black one?

"I hear from my grandpa pretty often. His spirit is probably immortal," Benny said with a smile.

"Not your dad or mom?" she asked.

"Nope. Dad and I don't see eye to eye on very many things, and he thinks I should follow in his footsteps instead of Grandpa's. Mother—well, that's another story. She left when I was a little boy."

"I wouldn't have believed such a thing was possible, but my grandmother would have proven me wrong today," Libby agreed. "Her spirit was probably off somewhere in a casino, and she forgot all about me for a few years."

He liked Libby's confidence and was glad that she wanted the job, especially because he wouldn't have to train her in either the business of antiques or bookkeeping. The latter was what he really hated. Computer work reminded him of those eighty-hour workweeks. Days and days of being cooped up in an office with no windows, hoping that someday he would have a place with a view. Yes, sir, he would be glad to turn all that over to Libby.

Are you sure you aren't drawn to those pretty blue eyes and the fact that she's easy to talk to? His grandfather's voice sounded like it did when he teased Benny.

When Grandpa Walter fussed at him, he usually talked back, but today he kept his silence and just shook his head. Sure, he'd always been a sucker for blue eyes, but that had nothing to do with hiring someone. Neither did her long brunette hair, or her chiseled cheekbones, or the fact that she was close to six feet tall and he'd always liked tall women. At six feet, four inches, he had to bend double just to kiss a short woman.

If things didn't work out with Libby in the next six months, he could always put out feelers for another person to help him. When she talked about growing up in an antique shop, her eyes held a haunted look. Something seemed not quite settled in her life. But he was not a knight in shining armor who rode in on a white horse to rescue the damsel in distress. He just needed someone to work for him, not a woman to fall in love with.

"Hey!" Opal stepped out on the porch and waved. "Dinner is ready and on the table. We thought y'all might be comin' around about now. Come on in, get washed up, and let's get acquainted while we eat."

Benny had spent most of his summers with his grandfather. His father was often traveling out of the country with his oil business, and his mother had lived in England for years with one of her many husbands. Opal and Minilee always had a full cookie jar, cold sweet tea, and stories to tell him, most of the time while they sat outside on one front porch or the other. He had felt more at home in their small company houses than in the big, fancy house where his grandpa had lived in Paris some twenty miles south. Back when Benny was first out of law school, he'd pointed out to his grandpa that a block of C-4 couldn't get him to move away from the Paris, Texas, estate. His grandfather had laughed at the joke and replied that he was right. Other than the few nights a month he spent in the service station apartment, his grandpa loved his home. His memories of his precious wife and son were in the big house, and the only way he was leaving it was feetfirst in a body bag.

Besides all that, Naomi and Claude, the two overseers at the estate, would miss him if he didn't go home every night. Benny figured that his grandfather felt a little guilty when he stayed at Sawmill even a few nights a month.

"You can both wash up in the kitchen sink," Opal said as she stood to the side to let them enter the house.

"Feel like you are a kid again?" Benny whispered.

"Yep, and I like it," Libby answered.

Chapter Two

Opal's living room was straight out of the seventies, with ivy wallpaper, an orange-and-brown-plaid sofa and armchair to match, crocheted doilies on the coffee table and end tables, and not a speck of dust anywhere. The kitchen was through an archway straight ahead. A table for four was set with floral dishes and covered with bowls of food that smelled so good, Libby's stomach growled loudly.

"I hope you're not one of those picky eaters that counts every calorie," Opal said.

"No, ma'am, I am not," Libby assured her as she washed her hands. "I'm not a bit bashful when it comes to good home cooking."

Neither of the women came up to Libby's shoulder. Opal might have been ten pounds heavier than Minilee, and her face was a little rounder, but they both had light brown eyes and a touch of black still in their gray hair. Minilee's faded bibbed overalls hung on her thin body, and her red T-shirt had seen better days. If she or Opal had applied makeup that morning, sweat had wiped it all away. Opal's jeans had patches on the knees, and her T-shirt had a picture of daisies on the front.

"I like anyone who doesn't turn up their nose at home cooking." Minilee pointed to a chair on the left side of the table. "You sit right there. Benny will sit at the head."

Libby pulled out a chair and took a seat. "Are y'all sisters?"

"Nope," Opal said as she eased down into a chair. "Our husbands were cousins, so that makes us cousins-in-law. Ernest was my husband, and Floyd was Minilee's. But we might as well be sisters. We've lived right here in Sawmill for more than sixty years." Opal bowed her head. "It's your turn to say grace, Minilee."

"I prayed at breakfast, so it's your turn," Minilee argued.

"I said it last time we had company around the table," Opal informed her without looking up.

"All right, but I'm going to write it down on the calendar," Minilee growled, but then her tone changed, turning sweet and soft when she started the simple prayer. Evidently, she didn't want to test God's patience by talking to Him in the same voice she used on her cousin-in-law.

As soon as Minilee said, "Amen," Opal raised her head and passed a platter filled with thick slices of ham to Benny. "I miss the days when me and Ernest raised our own hogs. I made the best rub to put on the hams and then smoked them for days. My poor husband died two days after he retired. Just sat down in his chair one Sunday after church and was gone before I got dinner on the table."

"I'm so sorry." Libby took the platter from Benny and put a piece of ham on her plate.

Minilee started a bowl of fried okra around the table. "My Floyd passed away three weeks before retirement. Me and Opal been widows for up near twenty years now. We don't try to raise our own meat anymore, but we do keep up a garden. Except for the meat, everything on the table came from there."

"And we can or freeze a lot of what we can't use or give to the book club girls," Minilee said as she passed a relish tray with fresh tomato slices and two kinds of pickles to Benny.

"Book club? That sounds really nice. How many members do you have?" Libby wondered if there were just the two elderly ladies or if others came from down around Paris, or maybe that little town she had passed through on the way to Sawmill.

"There used to be ten of us, but only four are regulars these days. At our age, folks have aches and pains, and family issues. But the two of us and a couple others hold down the fort for the most part. We'd be glad to have you join us, if you like to read," Minilee said.

"I love to read, and I'd be honored to join you," Libby said. "Thank you so much for inviting me. And thanks also for this awesome meal."

"We're glad you and Benny can join us today. And happy to get to know you since you *might* be our neighbor," Opal told her.

Libby didn't miss the emphasis put on the word.

"Tell us a little about yourself," Minilee said.

"I was born in Jefferson, and my grandmother raised me in her antique shop. She died my second year in college, so I had to either take out student loans or quit classes and get a job. I chose the latter one because I do not like the idea of being in debt. I've been working as a bookkeeper in an insurance firm for the past ten years," she told them, keeping her answer as short as possible.

"That's what you do, not who you are," Minilee said. "I want to know something about you personally."

"Well, my name is Libby O'Dell, but my birth certificate name is Elizabeth Victoria O'Dell. There's not much to tell that I didn't already say. I used to volunteer at a shelter for abused women before I left Austin." She hoped that was enough to satisfy Minilee's curiosity.

Quietness settled over the room. To Libby, it seemed as if everyone had even stopped chewing. Finally, she broke the silence. "My neighbor in Austin used to go to the farmers' market and bring tomatoes home, but they weren't as good as these."

"We only use organic fertilizer," Opal said.

"That means we like manure, not chemicals. We've got a guy from up around Grant, Oklahoma, who brings us bags of horse manure. That stuff is like vitamins for roses and for tomatoes. It's high in nitrogen, phosphorus, and potassium. You don't have high blood pressure, do you?"

Libby frowned. "No, but why would you ask?"

"It's also high in salt," Minilee explained. "Me and Opal are healthier than most women our age. Heck, we're even better off than most women *your* age. We don't use much store-bought food. That stuff is filled with preservatives, and I personally think that's what's wrong with the world today. It messes with their minds. But if you've got blood pressure problems, you'd need to be careful with too much salt."

Opal and Minilee had managed to draw more information—little that it was—out of her than she'd ever told anyone the first time she met them. If that wasn't enough, she hadn't signed the contract yet. She could always start driving whichever way the wind blew her and find work—even if it was stocking shelves at a local grocery store.

When she tuned back in to the conversation, they were talking about putting in a compost pile. She finished her food and listened with one ear until Opal changed the subject abruptly. "Y'all ready for dessert? Minilee made a blackberry cobbler yesterday. We picked the berries a couple of days ago. Me and Ernest discovered the patch out behind what was the sawmill back in them days, and we been pickin' them ever since."

"At least, on the years when they produce," Minilee added.

"When they don't, we rely on the ones we have canned and stored down in the storm cellar." Opal pushed back her chair and headed across the room toward the oven. "The cobbler has been warming up in the oven. It's so much better with just a little heat on it. We made real whipped cream this morning, too. When we can, we buy cream from a dairy farmer over near Powderly."

"Y'all should put in a café or maybe a little food wagon to run on the days the store is open," Libby suggested.

"Honey, we're too old for that, but we have thought about making a cookbook and calling it *The Sawmill Book Club Cookbook*." Minilee stood up, went to the refrigerator, and brought out a bowl of whipped cream.

"That sounds awesome," Libby said. "Can I help with anything?"

"Nope, we got it covered," Minilee answered. "And when y'all get done, you don't have to worry about helping with cleanup today. You need to look at the apartment across the street and figure out if you really want to live in Sawmill. Don't pay any attention to the windows in the front part. We always clean them once a month before the book club meeting. That'll be next week. I imagine you'll have your hands full getting moved in if you decide to stay here. It hasn't been touched since Walter died."

"Hope you ain't afraid of spiders and mice," Opal said.

"Not one bit," Libby answered. For free rent, she would have a standoff with a rattlesnake.

Chapter Three

"So, Libby is a nickname?" Benny asked as they walked across the street.

"Yep, and I was glad that I didn't go by Elizabeth when I started to school. With *Libby*, I only had to learn four letters to spell my name."

"Me too," Benny chuckled. "Walter Bennington Taylor the Fourth is my full name."

"Will there be a fifth?" Libby asked.

Elvis had been sleeping under the table on the front porch, but he awoke when he heard them. He raised his head, seemed to smile, and made his way over to Libby. She reached down and petted him while Benny unlocked the door.

"You didn't answer my question," she said.

"I'm sorry. I want a family someday, but if I had all girls, the answer would be no. I wouldn't saddle a sweet little baby girl with that name," he said with a chuckle. "Would you name a child Elizabeth or Victoria?"

Libby rose up and took a step toward the open door. "Nope."

Benny motioned her inside. "Point proven."

Libby stepped into a big open room—the sort a person would expect in a convenience store. A countertop where a cash register most likely used to sit. Shelves behind it that had probably held cigarettes in the beginning but now bore hundreds of books. A glass-front cooler on the wall to the left with a couple of cases of beer, at least six gallons of sweet tea, two plastic jugs of milk, and five pounds of dog food. From the marks on the black-and-white-tile floor, there had been a couple of display cases in the room at one time, but they were gone now. A table with several chairs around it took up space to her right.

"I keep extra stuff in the cooler," Benny said. "The refrigerator in my trailer is really small. Feel free to store whatever you want in there if you decide to stick around."

A lot of *ifs* had been floating around Sawmill in the last couple of hours. Was that an omen that she should be giving this idea some extra time and thought before signing on the dotted line?

Benny motioned toward all the books. "You'll have plenty of reading material."

"Are you a member of the book club?" she asked.

He shook his head. "They meet on the first and third Mondays of each month. Normally, I leave that morning to go scavenging for more stock. And . . ." He lowered his voice to a whisper. "I'm not one bit interested in joining the club, so that's a good excuse. I'm going to leave you to look around by yourself. I've got some inventory to get logged into the computer out in the store. Besides, Opal and Minilee will be out there soon to work a few hours. I like to be there in case one of them tries to crawl up on a ladder. The apartment is right through that door." He nodded to his right.

"What do they do at the store?" Libby asked.

"They dust and wash up whatever glassware needs it. They both tell me that they need to stay active, and I learned a long time ago not to argue with them."

Libby thought of Dolly and nodded. "There were four apartments on the ground floor of the building where I lived. Elderly folks lived in the other three. Dolly was the one I knew best since she'd lived there longer than I had. She had actually been the first one to move into the complex when it was built. I didn't argue with her . . ." She paused and smiled. "But then, no one ever crossed Dolly. I will miss her popping over to bring leftovers or give advice."

"I understand completely. Take your time inspecting the place. I'll look forward to getting the contract back when you've had time to look it over." Benny waved over his shoulder as he left with Elvis hobbling along behind him.

Libby stood in the middle of the floor and turned around several times. She tried to psych herself up about having a completely free apartment before she stepped into the back room. She told herself that no matter what it looked like—if she had to sleep on the floor and use a crate for a table—she could do anything to save money. Finally, she crossed the room, put her hand on the knob, and closed her eyes. She flung the door open in a quick motion, and the smell of vanilla wafted out to meet her. She glanced around the one-room place and found the source: a three-wick candle burning brightly beside the kitchen sink.

"Thank you, Benny, for this welcoming present," she muttered and turned around slowly to take in the rest of the apartment. An old iron bedstead that had been painted turquoise was over against the wall—not a queen or king, which was good since her only sheets were for a full-size mattress. A blond dresser that looked like it had come out of a 1970s furniture store and matching nightstands completed that area. The living area had a love seat and a wooden rocking chair covered in dust. The coffee table was an old flattop steamer trunk that was still in excellent condition.

The bedroom furniture reminded her of what she'd had during her junior and senior years of high school—after Victoria had sold off her beautiful maple bedroom set and given her the store leftovers that no one had wanted to buy. Was there some kind of universal sign in this?

A wooden thread spool attached to the end of a cord slapped her in the forehead when she took a step forward. She reached up, pulled on the spool, and a bare bulb lit up the whole room. Before moving on, she tied a couple of knots in the cord to shorten it.

"Evidently, Walter was shorter than Benny," she said as she wandered over to the kitchen area, which was across from the bed.

A small two-burner stove, a microwave, and a mini fridge lined a six-foot space that had a tiny sink in the other corner. She pulled back the floral curtains covering the cabinets to find mismatched dishes, glasses that had once had jelly in them, and coffee mugs. Beyond the kitchen area, the walls were lined with bookcases and cubicles, much like the storefront.

"I can easily use these for storage," she said.

She saw an open door at the end of the room and followed the footprints on the dusty floor to a fairly good-size bathroom with a wall-hung sink, a toilet, and a claw-foot tub. She closed her eyes and imagined sinking down to her neck in warm water later in the evening.

"Everything I need and more." She wandered back to the other room, sat down on the sofa, pulled the contract out of her purse, and read through it three times. The salary was good, especially when she considered overtime—and a free apartment with no utility bills would allow her to save a lot of money. A nest egg to move on after six months would be a good thing.

She glanced at all the dust in the apartment and remembered her grandmother fussing at her about being a neat freak. She hadn't really had much choice in the matter. Victoria had hated cleaning the house as much as or more than she loved gambling. It was a wonder that her grandmother had kept her office as neat as she had.

By the time Libby was six years old, she had learned to pick up after her grandmother and use the microwave to make herself something to eat.

She wanted to sign the contract, go out to her vehicle, and bring in her things—especially the box of cleaning supplies, so she could get the dust off everything and really scrub the bathroom. But until Benny put his name on the dotted line under hers, that might not be the smartest thing to do.

Benny leaned back in the office chair, laced his fingers behind his neck, and propped his feet up on the desk. A loud squeaking noise from the front door told him that Opal and Minilee had arrived, but he didn't budge. However, the sound of two pairs of boots coming across the wooden floor made him take his feet off the desk and sit up straighter. The verdict was on the way, and he wasn't sure he was prepared for it. Would he argue, negotiate, or refuse to accept it altogether?

Opal came in first, folded her arms across her chest, and sat down in one of the chairs on the other side of the desk. Minilee followed her lead, but she held her hands in her lap.

Opal took a deep breath and blurted out, "You are a grown man, so you can make your own decisions."

"Do I hear a *but*?" Benny asked.

"Yes, you do," Minilee replied. "More than one out of Opal, but only one from me."

"I'll go first," Opal said without hesitation. "She's too sweet. That tells me that she's trying too hard to be what we want instead of being herself. There's a kind of blank look in her eyes when she talks about herself. She might do for an employee, but there's no way you can think about having a relationship with her."

"My turn," Minilee chimed in. "Her bookkeeping experience will help you a lot, but I agree with Opal that she's not relationship material. We'll need those six months to ferret out what's keeping her from having a light in her blue eyes. None of us know anything about her—"

Benny shook his head. "I called all the references on her résumé. Her workplace said that she had never been late a single day and had only used a week of sick days back five years ago. One lady said that Libby was a private person but seemed to get along with everyone. She had three personal references—all of them told me the same story: she was a bit of a loner, always serious about her job, and had an excellent work ethic."

Minilee shook her finger at Opal. "I told you that she's not a serial killer. She's going to work for him, not seduce him into marriage just to get his money. But there has to be a reason anyone would want to live in Sawmill, or even in that small apartment, right?"

Opal gave Minilee a dose of stink eye. "She might have heard that you have a lot of money from the inheritance that Walter left for you, and she's just playing you—acting all secretive and sweet natured." Then she jerked her head around and glared at Benny. "If she knows about the money, then others do, too, and pretty soon, so many gold diggers will be coming down the road that the dust won't ever settle."

"It surprises me that more women haven't come around flirting with our boy," Minilee said.

"I'm not stupid. I can spot a gold digger a mile away," Benny protested. "Someday I want children, but only with a woman that I love."

Opal butted in. "You better find that woman soon. You'll be thirty-five in two years, three months, and two days."

"How many minutes and seconds?" Benny chuckled.

"We don't need to figure that out," Minilee told him. "Time goes fast, so you need to get serious. Walter will be singin' on the golden steps of heaven when you have a couple of kids."

"I am very serious about my life," Benny assured them. "I want a relationship, and I want a family—a whole yard full of kids. But it will either be for love or not at all."

"Said like a true romantic," Opal said after a long sigh. "Just remember it takes nine months to cook a baby, so you really don't even have the full three years if you want to start a family by the time you are thirty-five."

"Where did that number come from, anyway?" Benny asked. "What about it makes it so magical?"

"Because after you have that first baby, it will take eighteen years to get him or her through high school, and another four to eight to put the kid through college. Added up, that is about twenty-six years, and you'll be an old man," Opal declared.

"And if I had a whole houseful, then I'd be in my seventies when they were all grown, and you might not even be around to rock the babies." He chuckled again.

"Don't tease us," Minilee fussed. "If we didn't love you like a grandson, we wouldn't be concerned about you."

"The feeling is mutual, but y'all need to realize that I only met Lizzy—I mean, Libby—this morning. Heck, I can't even get her name right, so I won't be dropping down on one knee and proposing before supper. Besides, I don't believe in that love at first sight stuff, and I'm looking for an employee, not a wife."

"Well, thank God for that!" Opal exclaimed. "I still think my greatniece, Tatum, would be a good match for you."

"And she's just getting out of the military, which will give you plenty of time to get to know her and start a family *before* you are thirty-five," Minilee added.

"Okay, then." Benny didn't need their approval to hire Libby, and he really didn't like them meddling in his love life—not that he'd had one since moving out of the city the summer before.

His grandfather chose that moment to impart a little advice. *It's complicated, as all you kids say these days.*

You got that right, Benny agreed with a slight nod, then glanced across the desk to see broad smiles on Opal's and Minilee's faces. He shook his head. "Not 'okay,' as in I'm agreeing to go out with Tatum, but that I have decided to hire Libby if she agrees to take the job. She has more skills than I ever thought I'd find, and she's willing to live out here in the boondocks. I'm not interested in anything other than a working relationship, so put your fears in the trash."

"That's good," Opal said, and her smile faded but only slightly.

It didn't take the brain power of a neurosurgeon to know that neither she nor Minilee were going to give up on Tatum—not yet, anyway. But Benny took his small victories where he could get them when it came to those two.

"We can live with that—and on a positive note, Libby will make a good neighbor since she's not a picky eater," Opal declared.

Minilee frowned. "What does her liking fried okra have to do with anything?"

"Just everything," Opal argued.

Benny took a deep breath and let it out slowly. At least the old gals were bickering about food instead of his future, and that was a good thing.

Libby wasn't sure if she was supposed to take the contract to the store, but if she had the job, she had a lot to do to get the place cleaned up by bedtime.

Just a few hours ago, you weren't even sure you wanted this job, and now you are so eager that you are wanting to unpack and make this crazy apartment a home. What changed? Victoria was back in her head.

"Valid question," Libby whispered.

The answer was simple. She felt totally at peace in this little backwoods community, and she could save a lot of money by not having to pay rent. She would have six months to think about where she wanted to go next—maybe back to school to get her accounting degree. She had checked out an online course that she could finish in two years and still hold down a job.

She scanned the apartment once more and shoved the contract down into the side pocket of her purse. The door to the outer room opened, and voices, in tones that sounded like Opal and Minilee arguing, penetrated the walls of her apartment.

It's not yours until two signatures are on that paper, Victoria's voice growled in her head. Libby wished her grandmother would find a blackjack table and leave her alone so she could make out the words being said on the other side of the wall.

She slung her purse over her shoulder, opened the door, and stepped out into what had been the front part of the service station. "Hello, again."

Opal threw up a hand to wave. "We came over to get the books we're supposed to read for Monday's club meeting. I knew we had two copies, and here they are." She pulled a couple of paperbacks from the shelf. "Ilene and Sally will be the only other club members here this week. That's pretty normal for these days. We're all getting older, and it's tougher to get out and about."

"We've been so busy with the garden and our part-time jobs at the store that we're just now getting around to reading the books and answering the study questions," Minilee said. "We apologize for just barging in. We're not used to anyone living here, but if you take the job, we'll share phone numbers so we can call before we arrive."

If you take the job. Victoria had left her blackjack table—again. *Sounds to me like they have more doubts than you did when you drove up here.*

"I've signed the contract," Libby told her and headed across the room, but turned around when she reached the door. "Would it be all right if I borrow books from the shelves, too? I love to read when I have time."

"Sure thing," Opal answered. "Sally and Ilene bring books to us when they are finished with them. We're glad to share."

"Sally is Opal's sister," Minilee explained, "and Ilene is my youngest sister."

"And I thought the entire Sawmill world was just y'all and Benny," Libby said.

"Only from Monday until Friday morning," Opal told her. "Then it becomes a whole nother world."

"Do lots of people really drive all the way back here for antiques?" Libby asked. "I thought the younger generation was taking over the world and giving away everything their grandparents owned."

"This week might only get us half a parking lot full of cars, trucks, and trailers since it's the end of the month. But rest assured, the next one—the first weekend of the month—will make up for it. You'll be dog tired when Sunday evening rolls around," Minilee warned. "The first Friday of every month is always hectic. Folks get paychecks then, and they're eager to spend some of that money."

"We usually get everything put to rights on Monday morning, but after a big weekend, it takes a little longer to get everything put back in order. People ain't got no sense these days. They pick up a vase in the living room area and carry it back to the bathroom or kitchen part of the store," Opal added. "I expect you'll be busy most days just catching up on the bookwork here at first. Since me and Minilee retired, that office looks like a dump ground."

Time and a half is always good! Victoria butted into Libby's thoughts again.

Libby imagined her grandmother thinking about taking the extra money to the casino and started to smart off out loud but clamped her mouth shut for a few seconds. "Looks like I won't have time to do much reading after all."

"You'll always have the evenings," Minilee called out.

"I guess I will, at that." Libby smiled and headed for the door. "See y'all later."

Libby stepped out into the bright sunlight. She had been so focused on her new job that she hadn't realized how hot it was outside until a blast of hot wind hit her in the face. Sweat beaded under her nose, and a tiny dust devil whirled out in the middle of the street.

"I haven't seen one of those since I left Jefferson," she muttered and started toward the store. Elvis came out from under the table on the porch and walked along beside her. "What do you think, old boy? Are you escorting me to a new job, or are you walking with me to a rejection?"

Elvis wagged his tail but didn't offer any answers.

"Some help you are," Libby fussed as she entered the store.

"Hey!" Benny yelled from twenty feet away. "I was on my way to see what you thought of the living quarters and if you had time to go over the contract."

Libby bit back a sigh of relief when she met him halfway and pulled the papers from her purse. "Signed and ready for you to put your name on the dotted line. I like the apartment fine, and I'd like to get busy cleaning it and unpacking."

He took it from her and began to make his way to the back of the store. "Let's go to the office. I'll sign and make a copy for you to put in your files."

"I'm guessing that Minilee and Opal gave their approval?" she asked and followed his lead.

"They did, but only as an employee," he answered with a chuckle.

"What does that mean?" She frowned and followed him into the messiest office she had ever seen.

He crossed the floor to a desk piled high with paperwork, picked up a pen and scribbled his name at the bottom of the top sheet of paper, and then made a copy of the entire contract. "They have been trying to fix me up with either one of their relatives or a friend of a friend for years. I warned you about their meddling."

"Good Lord!" Libby gasped. "Are you serious? I'm not interested in a relationship with anyone—no offense—so they sure don't have to worry about that. Besides, I've only known you for a few hours."

"They want me married and starting a family before too long." He stapled the copies together and handed them to her.

"Why?" Libby almost choked on the one word.

"They think people are too old to start a family after they're thirty-five. I keep telling them that kids keep a couple young. Right now, this minute, I'm just glad that you have agreed to work for me," he said with a grin. "Be here at seven in the morning, ready to hit the floor running."

Chapter Four

*L*ibby sat up in bed—heart pounding and pulse racing—when she opened her eyes. She thought she must have had one of her recurring nightmares, but no matter how hard she tried, she couldn't remember what it was. She checked the time on her phone—5:28 a.m. She shut off the alarm she'd set for five thirty. The old metal springs squeaked when she pushed back the covers and threw her legs over the side of the bed. The sound reminded her of what had greeted her every morning when she wiggled in her bed at the Jefferson house.

She crossed the shiny, clean tile floor in her bare feet and put on a pot of coffee. While it dripped, she made the bed, got dressed in her running clothes, then poured a cup and sat down on the edge of the sofa to drink it. A flash of the nightmare came back to her, but it was gone so fast that she had trouble hanging on to it. Then another one hit, and cold chills chased down her spine.

She'd had bad dreams since she was a kid, when Victoria started leaving her alone in the big old two-story house while she went to the casino. She had imagined all kinds of monsters and bad people coming to kidnap her and would often sleep on the sofa until she heard her grandmother opening the front door. She would race upstairs and jump into her bed and pretend to be asleep. Sometimes Victoria would check on her, but most of the time, she just went on to bed without even peeking inside Libby's bedroom.

The worst of the recurring dreams started the night she had watched a scary movie—at least, it was terrifying to her—about a ten-year-old girl who had been abducted from her house when her parents were away. They had never found her or her body. That movie had stayed with her for three decades, and she still couldn't shake it.

"For goodness' sakes, I'm thirty years old," Libby fussed at herself. "You'd think I'd outgrow these scary dreams. Sure, I was only ten when Victoria started leaving me alone—and in spite of her warnings not to watch scary movies, I did. But that was in the past."

Libby remembered one night in particular, when she had actually gone to sleep in her own bed. She was fourteen that summer and should have been used to staying alone, but she had had another case of night terrors, and it was so real that she screamed out in her sleep. Evidently, Victoria had just gotten home from a late night, because she was really angry at Libby for yelling.

"For God's sake, girl, what is the matter with you?" Victoria had asked.

"There was a man in the house," Libby had declared.

"Bull crap!" Victoria had huffed. "It was just a bad dream. You've been watching those scary movies again, haven't you? I told you not to watch anything that wasn't PG rated, and now you have to pay the price."

"No, it was real," Libby had protested.

"It couldn't be real, Libby. How do you know that someone was in the house? Did you leave the doors open?"

Libby hadn't been able to shake the very real dream. "He was here."

"Holy smokin' hell!" Victoria's voice had gone all high and squeaky. "You might be right. A convict *is* on the loose. I heard it on the radio on the way home. Did he go into my room? Did he find my stash of winnings?"

Libby shook the memory from her head and finished off her first cup of coffee. The nightmare varied from time to time. This time, she had run from the faceless man and made it out the front door before he tackled her and dragged her back into the house.

"Someday I'm going to win—even if it's only in my dreams," she said. Not today, though. Today she planned to run a couple of miles, come home, and take a shower before she went to work. Amanda had advised her to go to therapy to get past the nightmares, but she couldn't bear to tell another person about her life.

In her opinion, talking about her past would make all the memories rise to the top.

She had her hand on the doorknob when her phone rang. She jogged across the floor and answered it without even looking at the caller ID.

Amanda rattled off questions. "Did you take the job? Do you like it there? I need pictures."

"I got the job. I think I'm going to like it here, and I will send pictures today," Libby answered. "And I will send an address so you can ship the things I left behind. I'll have to ask Opal and Minilee how they get their mail out here. Counting me and Benny's dog, this place has a population of five."

"Well," Amanda giggled, "you did say you wanted out of the big-city life, and I can hear excitement in your voice. Got to get ready for work now, but I'll look for pictures of the whole population—including your boss—very soon. Dolly told me that he's quite a handsome guy. What do you think?"

"No thoughts yet." Libby crossed her fingers behind her back. "Talk to you this evening?"

"It's a date," Amanda said and ended the call.

Rays of orange peeked over the eastern horizon, turning the dark blobs into trees, abandoned oil wells, and a few cows while she kicked up dust on her morning run. Running outside in the fresh morning air was a whole new experience for Libby. In Austin, she had gone to the small gym located in the middle of the apartment complex and run three miles on the treadmill each morning. Today her watch beeped when she had gone a mile, and she spun around and started back.

She could see the convenience store ahead when a car passed and sent up a cloud of dust that settled over her. Just great. Now she'd have to wash her hair and blow it dry before she could go to work. Forget about making oatmeal for breakfast. She would have to make do with an energy bar. Even if she had to go hungry, she was determined not to be a minute late on her first day on the job. And since the car that passed her hadn't come back, she figured there was already one customer who wanted to check out the merchandise.

"Good morning!" Benny fell into step beside Libby. She looked downright cute in dark slacks and a silky-looking shirt that matched her crystal clear blue eyes. Her almost-black hair smelled faintly of coconut with a hint of vanilla.

"Looks like we've already got potential customers." He nodded toward the parking lot, which was already half-full of vehicles.

"I figured we'd have one person at the very least waiting for the doors to open, because a car passed me when I was out for my morning run," she told him.

"If I'd known that you ran every morning, I would have advised you to keep off the road—especially on Friday, Saturday, and Sunday. The dust seldom settles from morning to evening," he said as they crossed the parking lot. His hand brushed against hers, but he was careful not to let it happen again. "Behind your place and my trailer, there's an old logging path that makes for good running. If you reach the Red River, you've gone about a mile and a half, so there and back makes for a three-mile run."

"Thanks. I'll do that tomorrow," she said.

"I leave at five thirty every morning, if you want a partner." He opened the door, flipped on the lights, and headed back toward the office. "Welcome to your first day. Let me show you the easy way Grandpa taught me to do things."

"Keep a few Sold tags, complete with numbers on the back, in your hip pocket," she said. "Write the name of the person buying the item on the bottom in the white space, along with the number on the price tag attached to the piece. When they load their merchandise, they have to show that bill of sale to show that the item is paid for, right?"

"Your grandmother taught you well." Benny gave her a wink and opened a file cabinet drawer, then handed her a stack of tags plus a roll of tape.

She shoved the tags and the tape into the pocket of her slacks, picked up a pen from his desk, and headed out of the office. "Where do they pay for their purchases?"

"Right here in the office. The tags on the items have a tear-off at the bottom with an inventory number on it, so tape or staple that to the Sold paper," he answered. "I enter that number into the computer and get all the information for payment; then I print out a receipt. They can either carry their small items out or back their trucks or trailers up to the doors and load up the big ones."

"We don't provide loading?" she asked.

"No, ma'am, but we do let them borrow our dollies to help them get them out. They're responsible for their own packing quilts."

"Okay, then, I'm going to go wait on customers," she said and headed out of the office.

"Now there goes one classy lady," Benny whispered under his breath.

Chapter Five

A hot breeze blew Libby's hair back when she stepped outside the shop on Sunday evening, but she was just glad that it wasn't rushing so fast that it felt like she had opened an oven door. She glanced up at the sky to see dark clouds shifting back and forth across the setting sun and caught a whiff of rain in the air. She was a little surprised that the last vehicles leaving hadn't wiped away any bits of the sweet smell of the approaching rain. She had sure been wrong about no one driving out into the boondocks to look at or buy antiques. For the past twelve hours, she hadn't had time to sit down for even a couple of minutes between customers. And it had been like that all three days.

"Think it will rain?" she asked Benny after he had locked the door.

"I hope so," he answered and fell into step beside her. "It will settle the dust and cool the air. Was this anything like a day at your grandmother's shop?"

"Good lord, no!" she gasped. "We didn't sell this much merchandise in a *week*—but then, there are several antique shops in Jefferson, so there was a lot of competition."

Elvis made his way out from under the shade tree at Opal's house and walked with them the last few yards before leading the way up onto the old station porch and stretching out in front of the door.

Benny took two bottles of water from the cooler, sat down at the table, and offered her one. "This was a slow day compared to what will most likely happen next weekend. The first one of the month is always hectic."

She took the water from him, eased down into a chair, stretched her long legs out in front of her, and twisted off the top. "The ladies mentioned that. If I was more graceful, I would seriously consider buying roller skates. How did you ever manage it alone?"

"It wasn't easy," he answered and drank down half his bottle of water before coming up for air. "I just kept moving as fast as I could, and folks had to be patient. Having some help helped even more than I ever dreamed possible. And what makes you think you're not graceful?"

"Experience," Libby said. "I can stumble over air. I grew so fast that my balance couldn't keep up—I was always the tallest kid in the classroom."

"Were both your parents tall?"

Libby shook her head. "Nope. From the little my grandmother told me about my mother, she was a short girl, and my dad was just average."

"Well, you've surely outgrown that clumsy stage now," Benny said with a yawn. "And even if you hadn't, I'm glad you are working for me." He stood up and rolled his neck to get the kinks out. "Elvis and I will be leaving early in the morning. What're your plans for the days I'm gone?"

"I'm going grocery shopping tomorrow. What y'all or Benny stocked for me in the kitchen is about gone. Got any suggestions as to what store to go to in this area?"

"You can find a fairly good one in Powderly, and that's about five miles from us. Or you can drive down to Paris or up to Hugo, Oklahoma. It's maybe fifteen miles to either of those."

"You're not much help," she said. "Which one do you use?"

"I buy what I need on the way home from my trips," he answered with half a shrug and headed toward his trailer. "Minilee and Opal go shopping about once a month. You could ask them where they like to go."

"Anything in particular you want me to do while you are gone?" she asked.

He stopped at the bottom of the steps and looked back over his shoulder. "Keep track of your hours. Payday is each week on Thursday evening."

"Then my first job is to get that office in order. Have a safe trip," she said and went inside to find Minilee and Opal sitting at the long table in front of the books.

A quart jar full of wildflowers and two empty vases sat in the middle of the table. The clouds parted in the sky outside, and a few minutes of light flowed through the sparkling, clean windows.

"That sunset is almost as beautiful as those flowers," Libby whispered.

"We gathered them for book club tomorrow evening." Minilee gestured to a green antique vase with pink flowers painted on the sides. "I think the bouquet would look best in my vase."

"I'm better at arranging flowers," Opal declared. "And my crystal vase would show them off better. Which one do you think is best, Libby?"

Libby hesitated for a moment, not wanting to take sides this early in the friendship. Then she noticed the array of colors created on the far wall when the sunbeams passed through the water in the jar.

She pointed. "Hurry up and look at the wall behind you before the clouds cover up the sun again."

"Well, would you look at that?" Minilee said with a smile.

"Looks to me like that is a sign that you should use the quart jar," Libby finally said.

Opal pursed her thin lips and eyed the flowers. "We could put a ribbon around the top. And use my fancy lace tablecloth. We should think of using quart jars at Benny and Tatum's wedding. We could have a country wedding and use burlap for ribbons."

"Benny is getting married?" Libby wondered how that would affect her job. Was that the reason he wanted her to sign only a six-month contract?

"Of course he is," Opal answered. "He doesn't have much choice in the matter. Once Tatum sets her mind to get something done, it's as good as finished before she even starts, and she's had her eye on Benny since they were just kids."

Isn't that just the way my luck runs! Libby thought. She could be booted right out of her new job early by a woman who wanted to get hitched to Benny.

"But back to our book club," Minilee said. "We always have supper before, so don't plan on cooking for yourself on the nights that we all meet up. We eat at five, and then we talk about the book until about seven and catch up on all the local gossip. That way Ilene and Sally can get home before dark. After the time change in the fall, we have our meetings at lunchtime rather than supper." She pushed back her chair and picked up her vase before she stood. "We realize you haven't had time to read the book, but this can be a trial run for you to see if you want to join us while you are here."

While you are here? Did they already know that this was a six-month job?

"I would love to," Libby replied and wondered how she kept her voice so calm when she wanted to scream. "What can I bring? I'm going to do some grocery shopping in the morning—"

"Which way are you going?" Opal butted in.

"I don't know yet. Do you have a favorite place?" Libby asked. "Would y'all like to send a list or maybe go with me?"

"We would love to go along," Minilee answered. "We usually just go to Powderly since it's closer, but every few months, we drive up to Hugo to the Walmart store. We were both raised between Grant and Hugo, and it's nice to drive up through that area every so often."

"Then Hugo it is," Libby said. "What time do you want to leave?"

Minilee started for the door but then turned back. "You are the driver, so you tell us. We have our morning coffee on my back porch every morning at six. If the weatherman is right and it rains tonight, then we won't have to water the garden. We just need time to fix supper before club starts, so we need to be home by midafternoon."

"How about we leave at eight o'clock?" Libby suggested. "We can do our shopping and maybe have ice cream as a midmorning snack afterwards. We'd be home before noon and have plenty of time to get ready for the book club meeting."

"That sounds great," Minilee answered.

"We'll be ready," Opal added. "Just honk and we'll come running."

"You can run," Minilee giggled. "I'll walk."

"You know what I meant," Opal fussed.

Libby could still hear their banter when she went inside her apartment and closed the door behind her. She eased down onto the sofa and kicked off her shoes, then leaned her head back and closed her eyes. Her phone rang and jerked her awake a few minutes later.

"Hello," she answered groggily, and then saw Amanda's bright smile on the screen.

"Hey, girl, how did the first weekend go?" Amanda asked. "You look like you just woke up."

"I did, and the time went fast. And it was hectic." Libby covered a yawn with her hand. "How are things going there?"

"Fantastic! That means you aren't bored. I loved the pictures of your apartment. I can't believe that you are getting it free, even if it is in the back of a service station. And you've got a trail to run on in the morning. Man, you must be in love with the whole thing. Plus, you get to work with a sexy guy every day . . ." She stopped to take a breath.

Libby jumped in and tried to turn the conversation. "All is good. Tell me about you and John."

"Things are so good!" Amanda's eyes sparkled, and her smile broadened. "We are going to move in together. My house is bigger than his apartment, so we've decided to live here. You still haven't given me the address for your boxes—do you have it yet? He'll need to use some of the garage."

"First of all, congratulations. You and John are perfect for each other. And yes, I have an address." Libby rattled off the one Opal had given her. She would have to weed out some more things before these six months were up. Her SUV had been jam-packed when she left Austin. There was no way she could cram what was in the extra boxes into her vehicle.

You might as well let her keep them. You'll get tired of living in the boondocks, Victoria whispered in her ear.

"Hush!" Libby growled.

"What was that?" Amanda asked.

"I had to cough," Libby lied. "I'm so happy for you and John. This is just the first step, you know. Before long, you'll be looking at big white dresses."

"Or maybe booking a trip to Las Vegas," Amanda said with a giggle.

"That sounds even better." Libby hit the speaker button, laid the phone on the table, and fixed herself a glass of sweet tea while she talked.

"It does, doesn't it? No fuss or planning. Just go to one of those chapels and come out married—but that's a ways down the road. John will be home in five minutes, and I need to freshen up. We're going out to dinner tonight."

Libby opened a can of gumbo and poured it into a saucepan to heat. "We'll talk again soon. Except for Monday, my evenings are free until Friday."

"One more thing before I go," Amanda said. "How are things with the sexy Benny? Have you been flirting with him?"

"I learned today that a woman named Tatum has set her eye on him and that she always gets what she wants," Libby answered.

"Ha! She sounds like fun." Amanda chuckled. "But I *was* hoping he might be the one for you. Maybe Tatum—I never have liked that name—won't get what she wants this time. After all, Benny does have a say-so in the matter. Maybe he will be the first one to not give Tatum what she wants, and he will be the one for you."

"Not a single chance of that. I'm still too busy trying to figure out who I am," Libby said and quickly ended the call.

Chapter Six

"Opal, did you remember your list?" Minilee asked when they were crossing the bridge over the Red River into Oklahoma.

Opal patted the pocket of her chambray shirt. "Got it right here. Without it, I'd get home with half of what I needed and too much of stuff that's not good for me."

"Well, rats!" Libby slapped the steering wheel as she caught what Minilee had said.

"Where's a rat?" Minilee squealed.

Opal reached up from the back seat and patted her on the shoulder. "She's just Sunday school cussin'. What she meant to say was 'Dammit.' I imagine she forgot her list."

"I did," Libby admitted. "I didn't mean to scare you."

Minilee shivered. "I'm terrified of mice. They're only slightly smaller than Bigfoot in my mind."

"And I'm just as afraid of a spider, so when I see one, Minilee kills it for me," Opal added.

"It don't matter if it's two o'clock in the morning," Minilee said with a nod. "If I see a mouse, she comes runnin', and I do the same if she finds a spider. What makes you scream for help, Libby?"

"Snakes," she answered, not willing to tell them that she checked the locks on doors and windows at least three times every night before she went to bed because of the scary movie she watched when she was a kid. Or that she slept with a night-light on, pepper spray on the stand beside her bed, and a Taser under the mattress. Staying behind while Victoria was away had set patterns she didn't think she'd ever shake.

"I don't like them, either, but I'll face off with a rattler before I will a mouse," Minilee declared. "Just thinking about those evil critters makes me cringe. But if one gets into your apartment, honey, you just call us or else run across the road. I'll grab the hoe, and we'll send him off to wherever those devils go in the afterlife."

Opal giggled in the back seat. "I was sixteen years old before I learned that you could kill a snake with a .22 pistol. Mama always chopped their heads off with a hoe before Daddy got her a little gun for protection when he had to be gone. He went to work for the railroad, and sometimes he didn't come home for a week at a time. You're going to want to take the next exit onto West Jackson Street and just follow it all through town."

Libby shook the visions of any kind of creeping critters from her head and slowed down to shift lanes and make the exit. After a couple of traffic lights, she noticed an ice-cream store on her left and made a mental note to stop there after they'd gotten their shopping done.

"Just ahead on your left," Minilee told her.

Libby turned into the lot, drove up to one of the entry doors, let Opal and Minilee get out, and then found a parking spot. She took a notepad from her purse, closed her eyes, and tried to remember everything on the list she'd left at home. She blinked a couple of times and then wrote down as much as she could remember. That would be a starting place, and hopefully, she wouldn't buy too many snacks and not enough real food like Opal had talked about. When she'd finished her list, she got out of her SUV, grabbed a cart that had been left beside her vehicle, and pushed it inside the store.

Minilee and Opal were nowhere to be seen, so she started toward the beauty aisle for shampoo and conditioner. She heard their voices before she even turned the corner and saw both of them talking to a young woman—likely someone they knew, based on their smiles.

"Oh, here's Libby now." Opal motioned her over.

She tossed one bottle of shampoo and one of conditioner into her cart as she pushed it down the aisle toward them.

"This is Tatum, my great-niece who just left the service on an early out. Tatum, this is Libby," Opal said. "She started working for Benny this past week."

Libby extended her hand. "Pleased to meet you. Thank you for your service."

Tatum had a firm but brief handshake. "Likewise. Are you a veteran?"

"No, but once upon a time, joining the air force crossed my mind," Libby said.

Tatum eyed her from the toes of her sandals to her ponytail and then shrugged. "You are too old to join now," she said, then turned back to Opal and Minilee. "Like I was saying, I talked to Bennington this morning. He was on his way to one of those god-awful antique things, but he'll be back on Thursday. We're going out to dinner that evening."

Libby frowned at Tatum's comment about *god-awful antique things*. She might have had the same opinion, but she never used words with that kind of venom.

Maybe he'll hire you to manage the store after six months, Libby's grandmother whispered in her ear.

Opal's smile deepened all the wrinkles in her face. "That's wonderful. Where are y'all going?"

Tatum pushed a strand of her chin-length blonde hair back behind her ear. "Some place in Paris—Texas, this time . . . Hopefully, before long, we can honeymoon in the real Paris. But don't tell Bennington that I said that," she said with a smile. "A girl doesn't give away all her secrets on the first date."

She does not have her eye on the man but on his bank account. Libby could have sworn Victoria had been reincarnated as a six-inch person with tiny little wings who had flown across time to sit on her shoulder.

"Why do you call him Bennington?" Libby asked, shaking off the thought.

Tatum turned her head toward Libby and frowned. "Because Benny sounds like someone who fixes a car."

Minilee narrowed her eyes. "*Benny* fits him just fine. That was downright rude."

"Well, pardon me," Tatum said, turning back with a head wiggle as Opal elbowed Minilee. "It's good to see you, Aunt Opal, and you, Miz Minilee." She nodded toward Libby. "I'm sure I'll be visiting y'all more in the next few months."

"My door is always open, and if you give me a couple of hours' notice, I'll have dinner on the table or maybe even your favorite chocolate pie made." Opal threw up a hand and waved as her great-niece disappeared around the end of the aisle.

"Minilee!"

The high-pitched voice right behind Libby startled her so badly that her body tensed. She whipped around to see a tall, thin woman with her arms open wide for a hug. Minilee crossed the short distance between them and hugged the lady.

"I wasn't expecting to see you until this evening. What are y'all doin' in Hugo?" the woman asked.

Minilee took a step back. "We're doing some shopping. Let me introduce you to Libby. She's our new neighbor, and she drove us up here. Libby, this is my sister Ilene Dalley. She's one of our book club members, and she'll be there tonight."

"Pleased to meet you," Libby said. "Let's meet back at the car when we're all done. I'm the third vehicle in aisle D."

"Sure thing." Minilee waved her away with a flick of her hand.

Luck was not with Libby. She backed her cart out and headed toward the greeting card aisle with the intention of picking out a couple of cute "thinking of you" cards to send to Amanda and Dolly. She had just picked up a funny one when Tatum T-boned her cart with so much force that Libby dropped the card.

"What the . . ." Libby started. She picked the card up and put it back on the shelf.

"Sorry about that," Tatum said with a saccharine smile to the person she was talking to on the phone. "I didn't see you."

Liar, Libby thought. There was no way the woman hadn't seen her.

"No problem," Libby said. "Shall we call the police and exchange insurance information?"

"That's a stupid thing to say," Tatum snapped and went back to talking on her cell phone. "That woman that works for you just stopped dead in front of me in the middle of the aisle and caused me to ram into her cart. I hope she pays more attention to the expensive things in your store than she does when she's shopping. Now, what were you saying about your favorite vacation spot?"

Libby glanced down at her cart, which was so far to the side that a bulldozer could have gone around her, and then gave Tatum a dirty look. The woman raised a shoulder in half a shrug and went on with her conversation.

Not worth it. Libby headed on toward the back of the store to get milk, butter, and cottage cheese. Benny could have the curvy blonde with the big brown eyes if he wanted her—that was his business—but Libby hoped the woman stayed away from the antique store. If you looked up *bitch* or *jerk* in the dictionary, Tatum's picture would be right there. Libby hesitated at the candy aisle but forced herself to go on when she saw that Tatum had stopped midway down it. She hadn't gone but a few yards farther when someone tapped her on the shoulder.

"Hello, again," Tatum said from right behind her. "I was hoping I'd cross paths with you a third time."

"Why's that?" Libby asked, her bullshit meter suddenly registering off the charts.

"I could use some advice concerning Bennington," she said in a silky-smooth voice.

"Not sure I could be much help there," Libby told her.

"You've been around him more than I have lately, so I believe you can. He and I were young kids together in Sawmill, but I haven't seen him in years," Tatum said.

Victoria was back. *You are being played.*

Maybe the player becomes the one who is played in this case, Libby thought.

Libby shook her head. "I've only known Benny a few days."

"What can you tell me about him? Aunt Opal sings his praises all the way to the moon. I want to know what an outsider thinks before I get involved and possibly waste my time."

The word *outsider* blazed through Libby like a double shot of cheap whiskey. She didn't expect to build a work family, but *she* was shopping with Opal and Minilee. Didn't that give her a little bit of an edge on friendship?

And having ice cream with them later, she reminded herself.

"I'm sorry, but like I just told you, I've only known Benny for a little while. He left this morning on a buying trip, so I can't give you any kind of opinion other than he's a hard worker," Libby said. "So, you guys aren't together?"

"No, but it's just a matter of time. We're going on our first date in a few days, and from there . . ." Tatum sighed. "But, *dearie!*" She dragged the word out like it tasted bad on her tongue or she wanted Libby to feel like she was sixty years old. "I don't care about his work ethic. Tell me something personal about him."

"Don't know anything personal about him except that he likes fresh tomatoes and fried okra . . . *honey.*" How dare this woman treat her like something she had walked through out in the pasture?

"Would you tell me more if you could?" Tatum asked.

"Probably not," Libby answered. "You need to take care of that yourself, especially since y'all were so close as children. You have a good day, now." She left the woman standing there glaring at her and pushed her cart on toward the back of the store. Poor Benny! Even though she didn't know him all that well, she dang sure felt sorry for any guy who got caught up in Tatum's web.

Libby awoke from one of her recurring nightmares with a start when she heard the hinges of a door squeak. Sweat streamed down her face and got into her eyes, and she blinked several times. She wiped the moisture away with the back of her hand and glanced over at her phone lying on the nightstand.

Good Lord! The book club meeting was due to start in ten minutes. She sat up so fast the room took a couple of spins before it settled down enough that she could stand up. She quickly washed her face, ran a brush through her hair, and grabbed the dessert she had made from the refrigerator. Nothing fancy or that had to be cooked—just a cheesecake mixture in a graham cracker crust, topped off with a can of cherry pie filling.

The aroma of something spicy wafted across the room when she opened the door into the front area. Evidently, there had been lots of paper goods left over from the club's Easter meeting—or from a recent baby shower—because the table was set with pink paper plates, blue disposable cups, and yellow napkins. And they all matched the wild-flowers in the quart jar in the middle of the table.

"That pie sure looks good," Minilee said. "I haven't made one of those in years, and it'll be good after the chicken casserole I whipped up for this evening."

"Something light and sweet to go with our coffee while we discuss the latest book," Opal said with a nod. "I just got a text from Sally. She's picking up Ilene, and they'll be here in about five minutes."

"Which is a surprise." Minilee pulled a coffeepot out from under the counter, filled the reservoir with water, and scooped coffee grounds into the basket. She hit the button to start it dripping and then walked away. "Ilene is always late to everything. She's been slower than molasses in the winter since we were little girls."

"That's why Sally picks her up on club night," Opal explained. "It kind of works out because Sally would show up in the middle of the afternoon if she didn't have to bring Ilene with her. She's one of those people that think you go to hell in a handbasket if you are two minutes late to anything and an hour early is a good thing."

"So, two very different ladies?" Libby asked.

Minilee folded paper napkins and laid one on each of the plates. "Yep, just like me and Opal."

Libby didn't say a word, but she couldn't help but think that the two were like twins. She looked around at the big room, then noticed the six-foot table had only five place settings. "Why don't y'all have your club in one of your houses since there's only a few of you?"

Opal set a pitcher of lemonade and one of tea on the table. "Used to be, there was ten of us—sometimes even more—and we needed the space. Now it's just the four of us most of the time."

"Did you ever think about inviting others, maybe from your church or old friends?" Libby asked.

"We thought about lots of things," Opal answered, "but we're so comfortable with the little group we have that . . ." She shrugged.

"We even considered asking the author of whatever book we were reading to join us on Zoom but decided against it," Minilee said.

"Why?"

Minilee giggled. "After a lengthy discussion, we decided that our favorite authors might disappoint us. We want to keep them on pedestals."

"What happened to all the rest of the members?" Libby asked.

"A couple passed away, and two or three went into assisted living, and it dwindled down to just four of us. Dorothy comes about once a year, but she's got her daughter back living with her now, and by the end of the day, she's plumb worn out from taking care of her great-grandbaby."

"And"—Minilee filled five blue cups with crushed ice and set them around at each place setting—"Cora Mitchell still makes it a few times a year, but her husband has dementia, so she has to get someone to stay with him in order to get away. But we call her and Dorothy after the club meeting and tell them all about it."

"Where do they live?"

"Both of them live in Paris," Opal answered. "I hear car doors slamming. Ilene and Sally drive down from Grant, Oklahoma. We kind of bypassed that area this morning on our way to Hugo."

"Yoo-hoo, we are here," a thin voice called out as the front door opened.

"They can see that, Sally," a huskier voice that sounded like it belonged to a lifetime smoker said right behind her.

Libby had thought that Ilene reminded her of someone when she met her in Walmart. Now it became clear that she was a ringer for Blanche from *The Golden Girls*, and Sally looked like she could be Marie's sister from *Everybody Loves Raymond*. Then they stepped into better light, and she could see the differences . . . but it was still more than a little uncanny.

"Libby, this is my sister, Sally." Opal pointed to the lady who could have been Marie's long-lost cousin and then swept her finger over to the taller woman. "And you met Ilene this morning at the Walmart store."

"And this is Libby," Minilee butted in, "the woman we told y'all about who's working for Benny out in the shop."

"Welcome to Sawmill and to the club," Sally said.

"Ditto. Nice to see you again," Ilene added with a nod. "We're glad to have a new member. Can we please eat now? I'm starving. I knew there would be chicken casserole tonight, so I just ate a bowl of cereal for lunch."

"You are always hungry," Sally fussed. "She ate a Moon Pie and a bag of chips on the way up here."

"Those little individual bags of chips are mostly air with just five chips inside, and the Moon Pie was a mini, not a full-size. That was just my appetizer," Ilene argued.

The bickering reminded Libby of what had gone on just before her grandmother and her gambling buddies left the house. When she was a little girl—younger than ten, anyway—she thought they were angry with each other and was glad to see them go play the slots or blackjack.

Mary Lou Ritter would babysit her on nights when it was too cold for Libby to stay in the car alone, and she always played games with Libby or colored with her, and sometimes she even had a craft project all planned out for the two of them.

For some reason, Victoria never left Libby in the car after dark or when it was bitter cold. She always said that was asking for trouble, and Libby understood the reason now. Her grandmother at least cared enough about her that she didn't want her to be abducted. But in the summertime, it stayed light until nine o'clock, so Victoria would go earlier and leave at dusk. Then Mary Lou had graduated from high school when Libby was ten years old, and Victoria decided that since Libby was taller than Mary Lou had been at eighteen, she could stay in the house by herself.

Opal jerked her out of the past and back into the present when she asked, "Libby, are you all right? You look like you just saw a ghost."

"Sorry, I was just lost in la-la land," Libby said with a quick smile.

Minilee pointed to the chair at the head of the table. "We all do that from time to time, but now we need to sit down so Ilene can say grace. The rule is, whoever brings the food does not say the prayer."

Libby eased down into her designated chair. Opal and Minilee were to her right, and the other two were across the table. They all bowed their heads, but Libby opened one eye to study the four ladies while Ilene thanked the heavenly Father for what seemed like everything but the kitchen sink. She caught Opal's eye, and the elderly lady smiled and slid a sly wink her way.

"Amen!" Ilene said in a loud voice, then stood up. "Lizzy, pass me your plate, and I'll do the honors. This casserole is too hot to pass around."

"That is Libby, not Lizzy," Opal corrected her.

"Sorry about that," Ilene said.

Libby handed her plate to her. "No problem. I get that all the time. You'd think that my grandmother would have nicknamed me Lizzy instead of Libby since my birth certificate name is Elizabeth."

Ilene put two big scoops of food on Libby's plate and handed it back to her.

"My birth certificate name is Virginia Lee," Minilee said.

"How did they get Minilee out of that?" Libby asked.

"When I was first born, my daddy said I was a little mini of my mama. Her name was Lee Anna. Everyone started calling me Minilee. I didn't even know that wasn't my name until I went to school and Mama had to produce my birth certificate," Minilee answered. "So it's always been Minilee, except on legal papers."

"Speaking of names, I heard that Tatum has a date with Benny," Sally said. "Now, wouldn't it be something if they got serious?"

Amanda's voice popped into Libby's head. *Let the gossip begin.*

"That's right." Opal beamed. "I'd like to see the first date turn into something serious. Tatum has always been a go-getter, and she'd be good for Benny."

From Libby's first impression, Tatum was more than a little over-bearing. She didn't like antiques—or tiny communities—so Benny would have to change drastically in order to live with her.

Or else be miserable. Amanda's voice was right on the money.

She tuned back in to the conversation when Minilee passed the basket of hot rolls to her. Now the four ladies were talking about the weather. Evidently, the weatherman had called for severe thunderstorms over the next two days.

"It'll be a great day to spend dusting and straightening up the shop," Opal said. "We'll take the leftovers up there tonight after the club meeting in case it rains tomorrow morning. That way, we won't have to get out in the weather until the end of the day."

"That's my sister." Sally's tone had an edge to it. "Always thinking ahead."

Opal shot a cold look across the table. "Someone had to organize things. Mama was scatterbrained, and I was the oldest kid, so the lot fell to me."

For the first time, Libby wondered if the reason that Victoria had been such a poor housekeeper was because she was scatterbrained. Maybe she'd had her mind set so solidly on having fun that she didn't think about important things, like keeping a neat house or making food for her granddaughter. Libby might have gotten a heart-condition gene from her father, but she had not gotten the messy gene from Victoria. That was a blessing.

She realized that the ladies had all stopped talking and every eye was on her. The silence was deafening, and Libby felt like she did back in elementary school when she had to stand in front of the class and give a book report. "This is a wonderful meal—almost as good as the dinner I had with Opal and Minilee the other day. These sweet potatoes remind me of the ones that we had when I went to Thanksgiving dinner with my friend, Amanda, and her family last year."

"I always make the turkey at Thanksgiving," Opal said, "and we make up take-out meals to deliver to the shut-ins."

"She makes the best, moistest turkey," Sally agreed. "She won't tell us her secret, but that's okay. If we knew it, we'd cook turkeys all year and Thanksgiving wouldn't be as special."

"The four of us cook all day. I make the cranberry salad, and Minilee does the hot rolls. Ilene makes the pumpkin pies and sweet potatoes," Opal said.

Ilene glanced over at Libby. "I'd be glad to turn over the pies to you if you are still here."

There's that if *word again,* she thought. "Be glad to do that," she agreed. "My six-month contract isn't up until after then. And I make a mean pumpkin pie."

"You'll need to make about six," Ilene said. "It helps if you make them in a sheet pan and cut them in squares instead of in pie pans. They fit in the take-out containers better that way."

"Maybe I'll make a pecan pie just for the five of us," Libby offered.

"Absolutely!" Opal said without hesitation. "I never can get them to set up. The inside is always weepy, and that makes the crust soggy.

And talking about food, it's time for us to think about the next book club meal. Ilene, it's your turn to bring the supper."

"Fried chicken it is," Ilene said with a grin.

"From that place in Hugo?" Opal asked.

"Yep, and I'll bring all the trimmings, too," Ilene answered. "For your information, Libby, I love to eat and hate to cook. When it's my turn to bring supper, we have store-bought fried chicken or barbecue ribs."

"Nobody complains, as long as she's on time," Minilee quipped.

"What's your favorite food, Libby?" Opal asked.

"That would be like choosing a favorite child in a family of twelve kids," Libby said with half a chuckle.

"Okay, then what did you like best when you were a little girl?" Ilene asked.

They are trying to get to know you. This time she was sure the voice came from her grandmother.

Libby answered honestly. "Fish sticks were a big treat. Victoria had a cigarette and coffee for breakfast, and I had cold cereal. Lunch was a bologna sandwich at the shop. Supper was usually canned soup. Sometimes on Sundays we went out to a burger joint for lunch."

"After church?" Sally asked.

"We didn't go to church. I didn't attend until I was in college, but if my grandmother won at the poker tables on Saturday night, we celebrated with a burger and fries. On the days she didn't win, I made myself a peanut butter and jelly sandwich," Libby said. "As you can see, not eating my vegetables didn't stunt my growth one bit."

"Mine either," Ilene said with a serious nod. "Green beans, broccoli, and brussels sprouts should be thrown out in the backyard for the raccoons and possums to eat."

"Of course, I acquired a taste for all that in the college cafeteria," Libby said. "The other students fussed about the food, but I thought I'd plumb died and gone to heaven. Instead of the freshman fifteen, I gained twenty pounds that first year."

"Well, after that dessert I see in the cooler, I expect I'll be up another three to five pounds in the morning," Sally declared as she pushed back her chair and headed across the room. "I'll get it out, and we can have it with our coffee as we discuss the book. All y'all take your positions at the other end of the table while I serve it up."

Minilee stood, gathered up the dirty plates, and put them in the trash can behind the counter. "Libby, why don't you sit beside Opal since I'm the club moderator tonight. Our book deals with facing our fears. It's women's fiction—the story of a young woman who was date-raped twenty years before. It's set down in South Texas, and it had a terrible effect on her life until her friend helped her get control of things."

Libby drew a quick intake of breath and covered it with a cough. She had never been raped, but she sure had a lot of fears she could confront. Still, from what she had read and learned from the internet, getting over her own personal nightmares would require talking about them. She wasn't ready to do that—not yet, and quite possibly, not ever.

Libby moved to the other end of the table to sit beside Opal. Sally cut the pie into five pieces and served it on disposable lavender plates. While she did that, Minilee brought the coffeepot and five mugs to the table on a tray.

"The table looks pretty tonight, and I love the jar of wildflowers," Sally said.

"I hope they don't have chiggers crawling out of them and down my bra," Ilene practically groaned. "I hate those bugs. When I was pregnant with my last child, me and my husband went out in his uncle's pasture to pick blackberries." She glanced over at Libby. "Back then, we wore maternity smocks to hide our big bellies. We didn't flaunt them by wearing skintight things like girls do today. Anyway, I got tired and sat down on the ground. The next day, I had a circle of red marks all the way around my waist where those things had burrowed into my skin."

"Maybe that's the reason why girls today wear something tight," Opal said. "You just provided a nice shady tent for the chiggers to crawl up under."

"Enough about anything that resembles a bug," Sally said. "Just so you know, Libby, no matter who brings dessert, it's my job to serve it. I would very much like for you to make a pecan pie for me to serve at the next club meeting. I don't want to wait until Thanksgiving to test your skill at making one."

"Yes, ma'am, I will be glad to do that," Libby agreed and wondered if Tatum could boil water without the smoke alarm going off.

"Maybe you can just be in charge of desserts each time, and we'll take care of the main dish and sides," Opal suggested.

"But I make a really good bologna sandwich," Libby teased. "I even use cheese, mustard or mayo—your choice—and lettuce and tomatoes. Pickles are optional."

"Maybe you can fix up those for lunch at the shop one day next week." Minilee took out a notebook from her huge black purse and sat down at the head of the table. "Okay, ladies, the meeting is in order. Who finished the book all the way to the end?"

Everyone raised their hand except Libby.

"This here is the book we read." Minilee held up a book with a colorful cover. "It will be on the bookshelf if you want to read it, Libby. Who would recommend it to her?"

Four hands went up.

"The author had me at the first line," Ilene said. "When she said, 'Something was stolen from me, and I thought I would never get it back . . .' From that point on, I was engrossed. The poor girl lost her dignity, her trust in people—basically, she was afraid of everything."

Minilee shook her head as if to commiserate. "I was up until midnight finishing the book because I couldn't put it down."

"So was I," Opal said. "I never did believe in all that stuff about not being able to put a book down until I started this one. I cried with the heroine in the story and hoped that she learned to face her fears. Before the end she realized that love is a precious thing."

"Whatever our fears are," said Sally, "we should face them so that they don't hang around and ruin our lives. So, Miz Libby, if you have any fears about anything, I recommend that you read this book. It will help you put things in perspective, for sure."

"I would definitely recommend it to you. It was pure therapy for me," Sally said and then took a bite of her dessert. "This is delicious. I need your recipe. Maybe you could write it down for me before the next club meeting?"

"Sure thing," Libby agreed, and planned to start reading the book that very evening.

"Opal and I already decided that we would put a five-star review on the internet for this one. Libby, we go around the table and answer one book club question at a time. The first one is, Did you feel sorry for the main character, Deidre? Why or why not?"

Ilene swallowed the bite in her mouth and then nodded. "Yes, but I can't imagine any woman letting her mother control her life like Deidre did. She should have stood up to the woman years ago."

Libby thought of the control her experiences had on her own life. Being left alone several nights a week at ten years old had made its mark on her. Even though she wouldn't call what her grandmother had done a control issue, it had affected her all the same.

Sally took a sip of her coffee. "I agree. No one—not even Opal, who always bossed me around—could control me like that, so it was hard to sympathize with her. But then, she had a different background than I did, so who am I to judge her?"

Opal pursed her lips. "I didn't feel sorry for her, but I understood her. I'm terrified of spiders, but even at my age, I'm not so sure I can face my fears. I'll go to my grave praying that there are no such evil critters in heaven."

"Me too, when it comes to mice," Minilee said.

Libby looked across the table at Ilene and Sally. "What are you afraid of?"

"That my pistol won't fire or that I'll miss the shot if someone tries to hurt me or my family," Ilene answered. "I have nightmares about that. I've got my gun in my hand, and some evil person has broken into my house, and the danged Smith & Wesson won't shoot."

Libby could sure relate to that fear. She'd never thought of using a gun, just always tried to outrun whatever was chasing her in her dreams.

"For years it was that someone would catch me cultivating a few little plants of marijuana in the cellar," Sally said with a giggle. "But I faced my fear. I grew it for medicinal purposes and only for my personal use." She lowered her voice to a whisper. "And just between us five people, I grew some of the best kush in the state."

Opal chuckled. "She said it was so she could lose weight, but she would smoke some of it and then devour half a bag of chips and two candy bars. She wanted me to try it for my arthritis, but I just couldn't do it."

"But she could take a little nip of peach moonshine for her aches and pains," Sally said and shook her finger at her sister. "When I was smoking, my reality was that I wore a size six and was movie-star beautiful. I stopped using it a few years ago because I got tired of Opal fussing at me."

"Apple pie moonshine was my favorite, but I also made peach and blackberry in those days." Opal giggled. "But I figured out pretty quick that it was eating holes in my stomach, so I quit drinking it. Now, back to the book. We might be too old to face our fears, but the good Lord has promised that we won't have any sorrows or fears when we get to heaven."

Face your fears.

The three words kept playing over and over in Libby's mind as if they were on a constant loop. How could she have a standoff with what scared and scarred her when it was mostly emotional and not physical?

She thought about Ilene quoting that first line of the book. Libby felt like her entire childhood—maybe even her life and soul—had been stolen from her. She wondered if she would ever get it back.

Chapter Seven

Libby read a couple of chapters of the book after the club meeting that evening and fell asleep with it still in her hands. She awoke sometime in the wee hours, sitting straight up in bed with clammy palms. In the nightmare, burglars and child molesters hid behind all kinds of furniture and waited until a little girl went to sleep to grab her.

"This is what I get for watching reruns of cop shows. Sure, they always catch the bad person, but not until after someone is hurt."

She went to the refrigerator, poured herself a glass of milk, and drank it slowly. Afraid to close her eyes, she picked up the novel and started reading again. Sometime just after dawn, lightning lit up the room through the one window in the apartment, and thunder sounded like it was stomping on the roof of the old service station.

She laid the book aside and slept for another three hours without even a hint of a dream. When she awoke later that morning, she was fully rested—just like always. As a little girl, she had convinced herself that she was safe in a storm. Evil people didn't go out when it was lightning for fear that they would be the first one to get struck. It was a silly notion, but it had worked.

Libby made herself a toaster pastry and a pot of coffee, had breakfast, and got dressed in a pair of old jeans and a T-shirt. No one would be at the store today, and she would be working in the office, so she didn't need to dress up.

"I could get used to this," she said as she poured herself a cup of coffee. "Heck, I could go to work in my sweats or pajamas, for that matter—and here I am, talking to myself again."

That little bad habit, as Victoria had called it, had started way back before she could even remember—probably when she had been left alone in the back of Victoria's old station wagon the first time. She'd never been able to get past it. She did try to curtail it when she wasn't alone, for fear—there was that word again—that folks would think she had lost her mind.

A few minutes later, she went outside and half expected to see Elvis lying under the shade of the table. Then she remembered that he had gone with Benny and most likely wouldn't be home until Thursday. "That is the reason why I had the bad dreams again," she whispered. "I slept better when I knew Elvis was here to act as a guard dog."

She felt an empty sadness without Benny and Elvis there to keep her company that morning. "That's silly," she scolded herself. "I haven't even known Benny for a week, and I'm missing him." She had known people at her previous workplace for months, and when they left, retired, or were fired, she hadn't missed them at all.

She opened the door to the store and found Opal and Minilee sitting at a scarred-up wooden table with a pot of tea and a platter of cookies in the middle. Opal waved and Minilee nodded, and then they both motioned her over to join them.

"It's break time, so come have some mint tea and chocolate cookies with us," Opal said.

"Did the storm keep you up? We are too far out to hear the tornado sirens go off, but on bad nights, we keep the police scanner on so we know if we need to take shelter," Minilee told her. "We've got a storm cellar out behind my house. If we hear that there's a tornado coming toward us, we'll call you, and you can hightail it over to shelter."

Libby pulled out a third chair and sat down. "Thank you. A cup of tea sounds great."

Opal poured a cup for her and then pushed the platter across the table. "Have one of Minilee's double chocolate chip cookies to go with it. They're really good."

Libby picked up a cookie and bit into it. "This is delicious. What time did—"

A loud clap of thunder rattled the few windows in the store.

Minilee shivered. "I hate storms. Good thing you got here when you did, or you might have had to run between the raindrops."

"How long have you been here?" Libby asked.

"Only an hour or so," Opal answered. "We got an early start."

As if on cue, hard rain hit the store's metal roof, sounding like a wave of BBs.

Libby reached for another cookie. The mint tea and chocolate were a good combination. She'd have to remember to buy tea and a package of Oreos next time she went to the store. Might not be as good as homemade, but they would do in a pinch.

She remembered her grandmother saying those words—*do in a pinch*—lots of times and wasn't even sure what it meant.

Opal raised her voice above the noise of the rain. "Did you enjoy the club meeting?"

"Yes, very much. And I read a chunk of that book last night. Y'all are right about it being very good. I'm afraid of the dark," Libby blurted out, and immediately wished she could put the words back in her mouth. *But in for a penny . . .* "I'm thirty years old, and I still sleep with a light on somewhere in my apartment. I didn't even care that my college roommate teased me about having one on in our dorm room. Evil things come out in the dark."

"When did this fear of the dark start?" Opal asked. "My fear of spiders came about when I was about five years old and woke up to find a tarantula on my pillow. It was just sitting there, staring at me. I woke up the whole house screaming. I wanted Daddy to kill it, but he took it outside and turned it loose in the barn. I wouldn't go back in that place and was glad when a tornado blew it away a couple of years later."

Libby had never thought about the time frame before, but now it made sense. "Up until I was ten years old, I had a babysitter when my grandmother went to the casino. Mary Lou was her name, and that year she graduated from high school and went to college. She was a short girl, and I was almost as tall as she was. Victoria decided that I was big enough to stay by myself on the evenings when she and her friends gambled. Looking back, that's probably when I became afraid of the dark."

"Whew!" Opal gasped. "That's awful young to be left alone. I'm surprised that the authorities didn't take you away from her."

Libby didn't tell them about spending hours in the back of a station wagon, with no one to talk to but herself and her Barbie doll. "There were strict rules. I wasn't to call my friends on the phone or tell anyone I was by myself. I was told to lock the doors, stay inside, and go to bed at ten o'clock, just like if she was home. The only reason I was to open a door was if the house was on fire, and then only after I had called 911. I was told to only watch kid shows on television, but I disobeyed and binge-watched old reruns of cop shows and scary movies that played late at night." Libby had never told anyone that bit of news—not even Amanda—but admitting it to these two elderly ladies wasn't embarrassing.

She took a sip of her tea. "I don't want anyone's pity. I'm sure there are lots of kids who lived in much worse conditions than I did."

"Did you ever break any other rules?" Minilee asked.

"No, ma'am," Libby replied. "Victoria was a handful when she lost at the poker table. I didn't want to tempt fate by making her mad at me."

"Smart girl." Opal's face was deadpan serious.

"What about storms?" Minilee asked. "When you were left all alone, did thunder bother you?"

Libby shook her head. "No, I liked those nights. I don't know if I read a book that had a line or two in it or where I got the idea, but I was and still am convinced that evil stayed in at night when it was storming. Those were the times I slept the best." She pushed back her chair, finished off the last sip of her tea, and took a step toward the office. She had walked down memory lane enough for one day. "I should be getting busy with filing the hard copies of last week's sales and trying to make a dent in organizing that messy office."

"Our break time is over, too," Opal said. "We're only going to work until a little after noon today and then come back tomorrow to finish dusting and arranging things. What's on your agenda for the rest of the day and tomorrow?"

"From the looks of the desk, it's going to take me a few hours each day to get all that filing caught up. Benny meant it when he said he didn't like to do the office work. There must be a month's worth of filing in there."

"Oh, honey!" Minilee's mouth turned up in a smile. "That is an understatement if there ever was one, and it's what made us fuss at him to hire someone. He's a crackerjack antique dealer, but even just a few hours in the office makes him cranky."

"You can expect him to spend more time on the floor as soon as you get settled in, and you'll be the only one doing the computer work, even on days when the store is open," Opal told her. "This week is so you'll get used to the system."

"Work is work," Libby said. "If he tells me to sweep the floors and clean the bathrooms, that's what I'll do. If he wants me to file and print out receipts, then I'll do that." She thought again of Tatum and wondered where her next job would take her if she had to move after the six-month contract was finished.

Minilee stood up and put the leftover cookies into a plastic bag. "Now, that is a wonderful attitude. You want to come over to my house for supper tonight? We're just having beans, summer goulash, and corn bread, but you are welcome to join us."

"I'd love to," Libby answered. "What time—and what is summer goulash?"

"That's potatoes, crookneck squash, and okra all fried up together," Minilee told her.

"And we eat about five o'clock." Opal picked up a dust rag. "We'll just have frozen peaches and the rest of the cookies for dessert, so don't go asking if you can bring anything."

"Thank you," Libby said. "I'll see y'all then."

When she reached the office, she stood in the middle of the chaos and sighed. She had visions of trashing everything in the room and starting all over with a clean slate. But that would never work, especially if the IRS came snooping around, wanting to see the books. She had lived through the nightmare of an audit at her old job. She opened the top drawer in the first cabinet to see how Benny liked his hard copies arranged.

"Sweet Lord!" she gasped.

Two huge spiders crawled up over the top of the disarray and dropped to the floor on long, spindly webs. She quickly killed both of them, cleaned up the mess with a napkin, and tossed them in the trash. Those kinds of critters weren't new to her. Being around antiques all her life had toughened her up when it came to spiders, crickets, roaches, and even mice. But not once in all her past had she ever seen such a mess. She groaned when she slid open a second drawer and found papers crammed between files and a few that had slid under the faded green folders. Even *beginning* to make a dent would take days and days.

"How did you find anything?" she muttered.

The old landline phone—gold, with the receiver on the cord—rang right beside her hip and startled her so bad that she came close to jumping right out of her skin. That was another thing she'd heard her grandmother say whenever she won a large amount at the casino.

Every time the bells and whistles went off, telling the whole place that someone had won a bundle at the slots, I almost jumped right out of my skin. But that was my lucky sign. When someone else won big money, then I nearly always raked in the chips next.

Libby picked up the receiver and hoped that when she checked the other file cabinets, they would be in perfect order. "Sawmill Antiques,

Libby speaking," she said, but her voice sounded a little breathless in her own ears.

"Hey, this is Benny. I'm just calling to see how things are going. I figured you might be in the store this morning," he said.

"These file cabinets are a mess," she crabbed.

"Yep, but you're going to put them to rights, aren't you?" he asked with a chuckle.

"If I'm going to work in this office, it's got to be in order. To get it in shape is going to take some serious overtime," she answered.

"Just keep track of your time. There are some sheets in the left-hand drawer of the desk. Use one of them to write down your hours," he said. "Organize the cabinets any way you want since you'll be taking care of all that from now on."

From now on? her inner voice screamed.

"I'm looking at six four-drawer file cabinets. Do you really want to keep everything in them?"

"They date back to when my grandpa first started the business, and everything was done on paper. I got the computer program up and running when I took over, so the last four or five drawers are mainly backup hard copies for tax purposes. But to answer your question, yes, I do want to keep everything. It's all like a big old history book to me."

"Do you want me to enter any of it into the program?"

"Just the last five years' worth," he answered. "What if you ignore the old files right now and start organizing the ones for the past five years? Those are the ones we definitely need to keep in order. But look, Libby, I don't care about the hours or the money—and with your experience, I'm sure you don't need me to bird-dog you."

"'Bird-dog'?" she asked.

"It's my grandpa's old saying and means that I'd have to tell you every little thing—or in the case of a huntin' dog, point him in the right direction," Benny replied with another chuckle. "And one other thing: I'll be home tomorrow evening. I've got a whole trailer full of merchandise for us to catalog, price, and put into the computer files, so

Thursday will be a full day for both of us. I've got another call coming in. See you soon."

The line went dead. She put the receiver back on the base and walked over to the last cabinet in the row. The papers in the bottom drawer were dated four years before, so she closed that one and tried the next one.

"Yep, here we go," she whispered. "First drawer from the top of this one is where it all started five years ago." Fifty-two file folders, each one representing a week in that year, with hard copies of each sale, plus one file folder marked Taxes. The hanging green folders looked as if a tornado had snatched them out at random and then put them back in the wrong places.

Libby sat down on the floor and removed every one of the file folders, lined them up on the floor, and then cleaned the dead spiders and cobwebs from the drawer. Her plan was to go through each file folder and organize it before replacing it. She liked things filed front to back.

"He said it's *my* office," she declared, "so I'm doing it *my* way."

Chapter Eight

*L*ibby left the store and went straight to Minilee's house, grumbling the whole way. She had hoped to have a lot more done before suppertime, but she'd spent the whole day getting only one drawer into shape.

"But that one is a beautiful thing," she muttered as she walked up on the porch and knocked on the door.

"Come on in," Minilee yelled. "You can wash up in the kitchen sink while me and Opal put the food on the table. How did your day go?"

Libby's stomach growled when she got a whiff of bacon. "I smell bacon and onions. I thought we were having beans and summer goulash."

"Got to fry up some bacon for the drippings to flavor the beans and make the goulash. I used fresh green onions in it this time," Minilee told her as she brought a cast-iron skillet full of sizzling vegetables to the table and then another one of corn bread. Steam rose from the crock of beans already in the middle of the table.

"I can get the glasses ready for tea," Libby offered.

"That would be nice," Minilee said with a nod. "You'll find them in the cabinet to the right of the sink, and the ice cubes are in a bowl in the freezer. This time of year, I empty them fast as they freeze so that we've always got some ready. Tell me what you did all afternoon up there at the store. Opal and I were going to come up, but we got all involved with freezing a bushel of okra."

"Those filing cabinets are a nightmare!" Libby answered. "I only got one drawer cleaned and organized. There's four more to go, and that will just cover the last five years of receipts we're required to keep for tax purposes. It will take forever to get them all in shape."

"I'm here with the peaches," Opal yelled as she came through the back door. "What are y'all talking about?"

"Drawers," Libby answered.

"Wearable or dresser type?" Opal asked as she set the bowl of peaches on the cabinet.

"File cabinet–style," Libby said.

Opal took the glasses filled with ice to the table and poured the sweet tea. "Benny asked me to work on those files a year ago. I told him that I would retire permanently before I'd open one of those drawers. As long as it had been since anyone cleaned them out, there would be spiders in them."

"Yep," Libby said. "So far only a couple have been alive."

"Dead or alive or anywhere in between is all the same to me." Opal sat down and pointed to a chair on the other side of the small table. "You can sit there."

Libby pulled out the chair and eased down into it with a sigh. Minilee brought a divided plate with carrots and pickled beets to the table and then took her place. "I cooked, so Opal will say grace."

Libby bowed her head and was grateful they didn't ask her to bless the food. She could talk out loud to herself with no problem, and she had prayed many times in her life—not for food, but for Victoria to win at the casino so she would be in a good mood. Back then, she didn't pray out loud, but her prayers were earnest. Maybe she should practice saying a few lines, she thought, just in case, sometime in the future, she was ever asked to thank God for the summer goulash. She realized that Opal had finished talking, and she raised her head to see both elderly women staring at her.

"Amen!" Minilee said and passed the corn bread over to Libby.

"Y'all really should think about putting in a food wagon on week-ends. You could make a fortune," Libby said before taking the first bite of warm corn bread.

"Like I said before, we're too old to get into a new venture," Minilee said. "We like to garden and cook and make a little money a few hours a week at the store—but other than that, we want to be free to garden and watch our shows in the afternoons."

"Changing the subject here . . ." Opal said with a broad smile. "Tatum called and said that she and Benny talked again today, and she's excited about their date." She held up her hand and crossed her fingers. "Here's hoping that this is just the beginning. It's time for Benny to get married and start a family."

"Why would he need to be married?" Libby asked.

Opal nodded and reached for a piece of corn bread. "If he don't get on the ball soon, we won't be around to rock the babies."

"Walter had his fingers in lots of pies, and Benny is very rich, but what good will all that do him if he doesn't have a child to inherit when he's gone? The clock is ticking," Minilee answered.

Libby drew her dark brows down in a frown. "Haven't y'all heard? Thirty is the new twenty. Folks are getting married later in life these days."

"Maybe so, but I want him to get married so me and Minilee can enjoy the babies," Opal said.

"I'm surprised that every gold digger in the state of Texas and half of Oklahoma isn't pounding on his trailer door," Libby said.

"Are you thinking that my great-niece is a gold digger?" Opal's tone was as cold as a mother-in-law's kiss in a Siberian winter.

Libby was surprised that her next bite of summer goulash was even still hot. As a child, she had learned to read people, especially her grand-mother. How the woman ever won a single dime at the poker table was a mystery. Maybe folks just couldn't read her the way Libby could. If she was angry, her eyes showed it. Those were the days that Libby stayed far away from Victoria. If she was happy, the crow's-feet around her eyes deepened, and her lower lip looked like it turned to stone. The change in the aura of this kitchen brought her right back to those moments.

"No, ma'am," Libby answered after a pause. "I don't know her well enough to know what her intentions are."

"I would imagine that she'd be willing for one of them prenup things that rich people insist on." Minilee's tone was only a little warmer than Opal's had been.

"If Benny loves her, he won't insist on making her sign such a thing," Opal fussed. "Neither one of us were ever asked to put our names on a prenup."

"Look around you, woman," Minilee said after a long sigh. "We don't own anything other than some outdated furniture and a cellar full of canned goods. We've had a good life, but neither Floyd nor Ernest left us anything but the rights to their pensions."

Libby's thoughts went to what she had been left with when her grandmother died—a box with her name on it that still had duct tape wrapped around it. Everything else had been sold.

"Tell me again, what's in this goulash stuff?" Libby asked, as much to distract herself as the older women. "It's really good. What's your secret?"

"In addition to the green onions, it's got new potatoes, yellow squash, and okra in it, all fried up in bacon drippings," Minilee answered, and finally smiled.

"You met Tatum. What was your first impression?" Evidently, Opal wasn't finished defending her great-niece.

"That she is independent and maybe just a little bullheaded." Libby glanced over at the bowl of peaches and wished she hadn't been so honest until after dessert.

In an instant, Opal's expression changed, and she giggled. "You called that one right. She's just the kind of woman that Benny needs in his life."

Libby inhaled deeply, let it out silently and very slowly, and made a mental note to never, ever mention Tatum in the future.

Face your fears.

Those three words looped around in Libby's mind that evening as she took a shower and got ready for bed. She made up her mind as she pulled a faded nightshirt over her head: she would sleep in the dark that night.

Tatum wasn't afraid of the dark—no doubt about that. That woman would probably face down a Texas wildfire with nothing more than a cup of water. If asked what her greatest fear was, she would likely say, "Not one thing scares me."

You do not need to compare yourself to anyone, the voice in her head whispered.

"If you can convince me of that, you are one damn good therapist." She crawled into bed and was just about to switch off the bedside lamp when her phone rang.

She saw Benny's name on the screen and answered it on the third ring. "Hello, is everything all right?"

"Yes." He hesitated. "Not really, but . . ."

"What's the problem?" she asked.

"I like an independent woman," he blurted out.

"Do I hear a *but* in there?" Libby asked.

"Have Opal and Minilee told you about Tatum?" he asked.

"They did," she answered, "and I met her when we went grocery shopping."

Benny chuckled.

"She tried to grill me for personal information about you," Libby told him. "I told her that you were a hardworking man, but that's all I knew."

"Thank you for that," he said after a sigh. "I realize we've only known each other a few days, but pretty often, someone looking in from the outside can see things clearer than those of us on the inside."

So Libby *was* on the outside looking in, was she? She had certainly gotten that feeling when Tatum's name had come up at supper that evening. "How long does it take to go from outside in the cold to inside, where your opinion matters?" she asked.

"You'll have to ask someone else for that answer. From the time my grandpa died, I've been half-afraid of getting into a relationship with anyone for fear a woman would just be liking me for the money," he admitted.

"So that's *your* fear?" she asked.

"What?"

"Minilee is afraid of mice. That's kind of funny when you think about it—Minilee Mouse. Opal is afraid of spiders. I'm afraid to go to sleep without a night-light. Your fear is a woman won't fall in love with you for yourself," she said. "A therapist would tell all of us to face our fears."

He laughed. "I can't even imagine Minilee emptying a mouse trap or Opal getting near a spider. I'm not sure about you and the night-light issue. Want to talk about it?"

"Not right now," she answered, his sense of humor dispelling some of her tension.

"Okay, then, what would you do with so much money that it boggles the brain? Would you have trust issues?"

"My bank account is starving, so I don't have that kind of problem, but I can truthfully say that if trust issues were dollars, I would probably have more money than you do," she told him.

"How would you really know if the person was"—he paused—"marrying you and having a family with you for love or just for the money?"

"I guess you would also keep your eyes open to see the signs. And you should probably ask for a prenup." Libby shifted her focus over to the window, where millions of stars peppered the sky, almost as if they'd been thrown against the glass. But there was only a tiny sliver of the moon sitting in among them. She wished for the natural light of a big full moon to help her through the darkness.

"Are you still there?" Benny asked.

"I am," she answered. "I just noticed that there's very little moon in the sky tonight."

"There's none where I'm staying. Elvis and I are listening to rain falling outside our motel room. Do you believe in signs?"

"You don't?"

"Never did, but looking back at the way things have happened, maybe I should rethink that," he said. "Thanks for talking to me. I guess we both need to get some rest. Oh, I got word today that there's three estate sales going on in Jefferson next week. I plan on driving down there on Monday. Want to go with me?"

"I don't know . . . Are you in a hurry to get the file cabinets in order?" She hadn't been back to that area in years. Maybe a return trip would help her face her own fears. Or would seeing the old store—and maybe even the house—give her even worse nightmares? She figured she wouldn't ever know if she didn't go.

"Those files have waited this long." He yawned loudly. "A few more days isn't going to matter. Sorry, didn't mean to yawn in your ear."

She let loose with a big yawn of her own. "I'll excuse you if you do the same for me. Looks like we've both had a long day." Suddenly, Libby felt a need to overcome all her fears: darkness, trust, the inability to forgive. Maybe when she did, she could find closure and look toward putting down roots somewhere. Maybe if she got away for a whole day, she could squelch the visions of that miserable box.

"I would love to go," she said.

Chapter Nine

$\mathscr{L}$ibby discovered that the second drawer of the file cabinet made the first one look like a room in a five-star hotel. A whole commune full of granddaddy longlegs had taken up residence. Opal would have dropped from acute cardiac arrest if she had even peeked inside that drawer. Victoria had always said the only good spider, mouse, or snake was a dead one. She didn't care if any of them helped with the environment. According to her, if one got too close, it would soon head off to wherever varmints go after this life.

Libby thought about asking Opal for a can of bug spray—surely she had one in the shop or maybe even a small one in her purse—but then she thought better of that idea. Spraying the drawer would possibly destroy some of the documents. There was nothing left to do but carefully remove one file at a time, take off one of her sandals to use as a weapon, and go to work.

She eased out a file folder, laid it on the floor, and took care of a dozen spiders that went in all directions. She felt like she was playing Whac-A-Mole when several more ran over the sides of the drawer.

"Feels like a military invasion," she said.

"Did I hear the word *military*?" Tatum poked her head into the room.

"I was talking to myself about all these spiders being like an invasion of troops." Libby swatted half a dozen scaling the wall. Evidently,

Madam Universe had turned off her hearing aid when Libby hoped that Tatum wouldn't come around the store.

"I'm not afraid of bombs, shells, or the desert heat, but I'm not stepping foot in a room with spiders." Tatum shivered and slammed the door shut.

"Must be an inherited thing," Libby whispered and kept playing Whac-A-Spider until she didn't see another one anywhere. Then she pulled a second file folder out and started all over again.

She was still killing spiders and putting their carcasses into the trash when Opal yelled from outside the door a few minutes later. "We're done for the day."

Minilee peeked in the door, rolled her eyes, and said, "We're going to have lunch with Tatum."

"Where are y'all going to eat?" Libby thought she might hand Minilee a few dollars and ask them to bring her back a burger or maybe even a Subway sandwich.

"At my house," Opal answered. "I made Tatum's favorite soup this morning, and it's been simmering all day."

Libby had quickly formed a polite *no* answer in case one of the three on the other side of the door asked if she would like to join them, but no one did. Then she decided a bowl of warm soup would sure hit the spot if Opal offered to bring some to the store for her. Again, no one did.

Apparently, family trumped friends. Maybe Minilee's little eye roll was a sign that she wasn't too keen on spending time with Tatum, either.

But then, if Libby was truly honest with herself, she couldn't even call Opal and Minilee her friends. She had had meals with them, worked with them for a few hours, and gone grocery shopping with them once. Even though she'd shared some of her past with them, she still wasn't sure she could call them anything but acquaintances.

"I am not kin to the people in Sawmill. There hasn't been enough time to build anything like a bond between any of them. This is a job. Period."

"We're home," Benny told Elvis when he could see the SAWMILL ANTIQUES sign up ahead of the truck. "Seems like this trip took longer than any of the past ones, and yet it was a day shorter." He pulled the trailer around to the rear of the store and opened the truck door.

Elvis bounded across him, ran to the nearest bush and hiked a leg, and then ran inside.

"I figured you'd be ready to chase a squirrel or maybe flop down under a shade tree. I guess you want to check the place before we go home and fix us some supper. Well, there you go—have at it, old boy." Benny unlocked the overhead door and swung it open.

Elvis sniffed the air, ran through the store, and lay down in front of the settee where Opal and Minilee often sat. He'd done the same thing a few other times when they had stopped at a roadside park on their trips. Usually, Benny would find the stub of a joint not far from Elvis when it happened, but he had never found drugs in the store.

"Not again, Opal! I thought Sally had stopped smoking pot." Benny growled and narrowed his eyes. "Did a customer drop something, or is Libby using drugs?"

Elvis stood up, put his nose on the floor, and like a bloodhound on the scent of a raccoon, he went to a red velvet settee beside the table and chairs where Opal and Minilee usually sat for their break times. He barked and flopped down again. Benny checked the sofa and found a joint between the cushions.

"Good boy," he said after a long sigh. "Now, what do we do about it? I can't deal with Opal today—especially with Tatum. You were in the store on Sunday, and you didn't detect anything then. The only people who've been here since then have been Opal, Minilee, and Libby. Maybe it's Libby."

Elvis went to the front door, looked back over his shoulder, and barked.

"You've done your job, and it's up to me to decide what I have to do." Benny fumed all the way across the parking lot.

Elvis flopped down under the shade of the table on the front porch of the station. The dog could stay there if he wanted, but Benny intended to walk all the way to the river and toss the joint into the current. The red water would carry it away, destroying it bit by bit until it was completely gone. He hadn't gone a hundred yards before Elvis ran past him. How the animal could rest for five minutes and then act like a puppy for the next hour or two was a complete mystery to Benny.

He rounded a curve, and Elvis shot ahead of him. Running full blast on three legs and trying to wiggle with happiness at the same time made for quite a sight. Then the dog came to a halt so fast that, had he been a truck on the highway, there would have definitely been the screeching of tires. He flopped down beside Libby and laid his head in her lap.

Benny had run out of time to plan what to say to her, so he just sucked in a lungful of air and slowly made his way down the path to the edge of the river. He walked right past her, tossed the joint into the water, and then stooped down and washed his hands, hopefully taking all the scent off.

"Welcome home," she said. "I didn't know you smoked."

He straightened up and dried his hands on the legs of his jeans. "I didn't know that *you* used drugs."

"What makes you think I do?" she asked.

He let out a long sigh. "Come on, Libby. You might as well own up to it. Elvis detected drugs at the door to my office, and then he went straight to the settee beside Opal and Minilee's break table. Your joint must've fallen out of your pocket and landed between the cushions on the settee. If the authorities found drugs in my place of business, it could cause all kinds of problems."

"Is that what you threw away in the river?" she asked. "Maybe it was yours and you don't want to take responsibility for your actions."

She seemed to be awfully mild about protesting the accusation. Benny couldn't make sense of her calm attitude. If she was guilty, she should be shrugging and saying that everyone smoked a little pot. If she wasn't, she would be throwing a fit over the fact that he'd accused her of using drugs in the store. Still, his two elderly neighbors . . . He drew his brows down. What if one of them was growing pot behind the warehouse beside the wild blackberries? Opal could be doing that for Sally.

"It was not mine," he snapped, vowing to confront Opal and Minilee about the issue tomorrow. "Are you sure—"

"I want you to think about something." Libby's eyes narrowed, and she spoke through clenched teeth. "But first, let me tell you about my day. I killed at least a million granddaddy longleg spiders that had hatched in and then crawled out of the file cabinet. I worked right through lunch, and now we can lay our hands on an invoice in a matter of seconds in two whole drawers."

What does all that have to do with marijuana? Benny wondered, but he didn't say anything.

"I finished at four o'clock," Libby went on after taking a breath, "and my legs were aching from sitting on the floor for hours, so I decided to take a walk to stretch them out. I like it here by the river. It's quiet, and it's a good place to think about a lot of things. I haven't even been in my apartment, much less taken a shower to get the smell of dust and sweat—or what you are accusing me of, marijuana—from my clothes and body. Elvis bounded down the path and laid his head in my lap." She locked eyes with Benny in a daring stare-down and continued to pet Elvis at the same time. "Consider that for a minute."

"What does Elvis have to do with . . ." He stopped and slapped his thigh. "Because if you had even touched that joint, Elvis would have given me the sign that you had been handling drugs, right? I can't believe I missed that."

She nodded. "I'm not addicted to anything, Benny. I lived with a gambling addict and swore I would never have a problem with drugs, alcohol, gambling, or even chocolate. The only thing that comes close to being an obsession—if I can even use that word—is that I talk to myself. Out loud."

"Chocolate?" He raised an eyebrow.

"Yep, even that. I refuse to eat it every day in case it could get to be a habit."

"I'm sorry I accused you," he apologized and felt so guilty, he couldn't look her in the eye.

And then Libby giggled.

He looked up. "What's so funny?" he asked.

"I just got a vision of Opal and Minilee smoking a little pot. Maybe that's why they don't complain of backaches after bending over and working in their garden all day." She giggled again.

Benny chuckled and then laughed out loud. "I never thought of that—and I'm sorry I accused you."

"I can't blame you for accusing me instead of asking me or not trusting me yet. I don't trust anyone I haven't known for a long time. This is the first time you didn't just ask me nicely, so you get a pass. The next time you do that, I'll pack my things and be gone within a couple of hours. I respect the people I work for, and I expect a little of that in return."

Benny frowned again. "Was anyone else in the store other than Opal and Minilee?"

"You'll have to ask them about that," Libby answered. "I was in the office all day. Opal's afraid of spiders, remember? Now, I'm going back to my apartment and making myself a sandwich. Do you want one?"

Benny couldn't imagine Opal or Minilee having marijuana—maybe a glass of homemade wine occasionally. He'd heard that Sally liked to dabble in a little kush when she was younger, but not Opal.

Chapter Ten

*L*ibby laid the sealed envelope with her paycheck aside, grabbed a bottle of water from the refrigerator, and flopped down on the sofa in her apartment on Thursday evening. Before she even twisted the lid off the water, she rolled the icy-cold plastic bottle over her sweaty forehead. Every inch of her T-shirt was soaked with sweat, and her underpants were stuck to her body. Cleaning out file drawers for three days in the office was nothing compared to unloading and getting a trailer load of heavy oak furniture positioned in a steamy, hot warehouse.

"Benny should bill the place as the Sawmill Spa Steam Room and charge admission to come inside." She shivered in the cool air flowing from the overhead vent right above her.

She could take a nice, cool bath and read a few chapters of the next club book, but poor Benny had to rush to his trailer, take a shower, and then go on a date with Miss Tatum, who had to have been the one who'd left a joint in the store. Libby sat up, opened her bottle of water, and gulped down several long drinks.

Why didn't you tell him that Tatum had been in the store? the pesky voice in her head asked.

Libby stood up, set her water bottle on the coffee table, and peeled her shirt off her sticky body. "I am not a snitch. Like Victoria always told me, finding out things for myself is better than being told by someone else."

She finished undressing on the way to the bathroom, leaving a trail of her clothing on the floor behind her. She adjusted the bathwater to barely lukewarm and crawled in when the bottom of the tub was covered with only a couple of inches. She propped her neck on the rounded edge of its sloped back and closed her eyes.

She didn't mean to fall asleep, but within seconds she was off in a dream world, transported back to the day that one of Victoria's best friends brought her the unopened box that plagued her thoughts at least once a day and had now slipped into her dreams.

In her dream, she took the box, used a bottle of vodka for accelerant, and set it on fire. Then her grandmother literally flew in from the clouds and blew the blaze away like she was blowing out candles on a birthday cake. She shook her finger at Libby and set her mouth in the firm line that meant she was really angry, and said, "You have to open this someday to understand."

"Understand what?" Libby muttered, and opened her eyes to see that the bathwater was about to overflow. She glanced around to be sure that the box hadn't transported itself to her bathroom. Unfortunately, she remembered it was still sitting in the living area, where she had put it when it arrived earlier that day.

There are several steps to grieving for a loved one, she reminded herself. "I skipped the first one about denial and went straight to anger," she said. She couldn't even put a finger on why she was upset. The money that Victoria had squandered away was hers to handle however she wanted. All she'd promised Libby was that she had enough put back to pay for her college, and part of that was what Libby had saved from working in the antique shop.

She quickly stood up, turned off the faucet, and stepped out onto the bathroom rug. The sun had set, leaving the apartment in darkness. She wrapped a towel around her body, left the bathroom, and felt along the wall for a light switch. Then she remembered that she had to use the wooden thread spool and pull the cord. She groped around in the dark for a full minute before she gave the spool a jerk, and the light from the bare bulb illuminated the room, and she could breathe.

She glared at the box with the words *For Libby* written on the end in Victoria's fancy handwriting. She blinked several times and looked away. If she left it alone, whatever was inside couldn't hurt her. But if she ripped the tape off and saw what was inside, it could very easily be like Pandora's box and cause her nothing but heartache. Better to ignore the thing and not know.

She took it off the shelf, turned it around so the other end was showing, and shoved it back in the same spot. Now it was only a box with a faded label that declared it was full of reams of paper.

Benny was splashing on aftershave when his phone rang. He hit the accept button and then the one for the speaker. "Hello, Opal," he said.

"I just wanted to tell you to have a good time on your date tonight," Opal said. "Tatum is really looking forward to it, and she even bought a brand-new outfit especially for you. We appreciate you picking her up from Sally's."

Benny covered a yawn with his hand and nodded. "Thank you."

"Tell him about tomorrow," Minilee yelled in the background.

"We're going to drive up to Hugo, too, and go to a craft fair with Sally, and then we're going to play dominoes with her and Ilene. We should be home before dark," Opal told him.

"Have fun," Benny said, wishing he could curl up on his sofa and watch reruns of *Longmire* on television—maybe even with a cold beer in his hand. He had brought home a trailer full of merchandise, and even with Libby's help, unloading it had just about used up every drop of his energy. A visual of the four old women sitting around in Sally's living room, passing a joint back and forth, put a grin on his face.

"You too," Opal said in a cheerful voice.

He hit the end button on the phone's screen, got dressed, and took time to stop and pet Elvis. "Hold down the fort until I get back, and maybe we'll have time for one Walt Longmire episode before bedtime. There might even be a wolf or an owl on the show for you to growl at."

He'd been to Sally's house only once before but had no trouble finding the place since it sat right off the highway. It was still painted bright blue, with white shutters and trim, like it had been back when Opal took him with her to Hugo and they'd stopped by Sally's to pick her up. He got out of the truck and shook the legs of his jeans down over his boots.

"That's where the marijuana came from," he whispered as he got a faint whiff of skunk before he even reached the porch. Sally must still be sneaking a little pot every so often, and she had dropped one of her joints when she came by the store. Opal would throw a pure old southern hissy fit—as his grandfather used to say—if she knew what her younger sister was doing. But Benny wasn't about to tattle on a seventy-year-old woman.

He raised a hand to knock on the door, only to have it swing open before his knuckles contacted the wood frame.

"Well, hello," Tatum said. "Don't you look handsome."

"I pale in comparison to you," Benny said and hoped that the line wasn't too mushy. "Are you ready?"

She took a step out onto the porch and nodded. "Yes, I am, and I'm starving. Aunt Sally wanted to be here and take a picture of us before we left on our first date, but she's got a meeting with the ladies from her Sunday school class. Something about a wedding shower they're throwing for one of the local girls. I'm kind of glad. It's not like this is a high school prom."

"Small towns have a different set of rules," Benny said as he escorted her to his truck and opened the passenger door for her. Maybe the smell that the breeze had brought to his nose was really a skunk and not marijuana. He reminded himself to check out all the plants around the blackberry patch.

She slid into the seat and immediately sneezed. "Something must be pollinating." She barely got the words out before another sneeze came, sounding like a full-fledged tornado. "Sorry about that." She smiled and grabbed a McDonald's napkin from the console.

"I guess allergy season—"

"Has a dog been in this vehicle?" she gasped, just before another round of uncontrollable sneezing started as she buckled her seat belt.

"I have a dog, and he goes with me on trips," Benny admitted. "I was petting him before I left Sawmill." A wave of relief at the idea that the date might have an early end washed over him.

Tatum unfastened the seat belt and jumped out of the truck so fast that she was barely a blur. "We'll have to take my car. I'm allergic to dogs. Let me take a shower and an allergy pill before my eyes swell shut."

"I'm really sorry," Benny said and felt guilty for lying to her. "I had no idea you couldn't be around animals."

She stopped when she was on the porch and turned around. "Just dogs. Cats don't bother me, but I hate them anyway, and now you know. I thought I was allergic to the old furniture when I had a minor attack at the antique store yesterday. I bet your dog had been in there."

An attack at the store? Benny closed the passenger door, rounded the front of the vehicle, and opened the driver's-side door. "He comes and goes wherever he pleases."

Tatum kissed him on the cheek. The smell that her perfume couldn't cover up left no doubt that a little black-and-white-striped animal was not the source of the pungent scent that evening.

"We can reschedule, darlin'," she said and sneezed again. "Maybe we'll just meet at the restaurant, and you can borrow Aunt Opal's car. I'll take an extra allergy pill, and you can be sure to stay away from the dog before you leave." She hurried inside the house.

"We'll talk about that later." Benny closed the door and waved as he drove away. "I don't think there will be another date," he muttered. "Even if we got serious, I would not give up Elvis, and I sure don't want to find joints stuck all over the place."

Texas sunsets were always beautiful, but that night, the sky was painted in a bright array of pinks, purples, oranges, and even a streak of minty green. Down to the southwest, a bank of dark clouds rolled in slowly and blotted out the beauty of the sunset. Grandpa Walter would have called it an omen—a sign to let Benny know he had been saved from taking steps down the wrong path. He had never been keen on dating Tatum, but there weren't a lot of choices or even chances for dates in a community with a population of three—no, make that four now, and five if he counted Elvis. Plus, he didn't want to disappoint Opal.

He couldn't believe that no one, not even Opal, had mentioned Tatum's allergy to dogs. But to be fair, he'd been around her only a few times when they were young, and back then, there'd been no pets in their community.

The sky was split when he reached Sawmill. Half of it had a lovely sunset on the western horizon. The other part looked like a tornado funnel could drop down out of the clouds any minute. A bolt of lightning zig-zagged through the sky and lit up the dark part. It reminded him of the two different paths he could take in his life. He could be married to his job like his father—a businessman who didn't want anything to do with antiques and had little time for his own dad or for Benny—or he could make a different choice and enjoy a family of his own. The latter appealed to him more, but he would choose the first option if Tatum was involved. A few seconds later, thunder rolled. He parked the truck and was on his way to let Elvis into the trailer when Opal yelled at him from across the street.

"You back already?" she asked.

"Had a little problem," he answered.

"What kind? Is she sick, or are you?" Minilee asked.

He walked across the street with Elvis at his side. "No one told me that Tatum is allergic to dogs."

"I forgot all about that," Opal gasped. "And to tell the truth, I thought she'd outgrown that when she was in the service. What happened?"

Benny sat down on the top porch step. "She got into my truck and had a sneezing fit. She went inside to take a shower and get some medicine. I came home."

"Does that mean we're back to square one in looking for a wife for you?" Minilee asked.

"Unless you want to rehome Elvis," Opal suggested.

"Not a chance," Benny said, shaking his head. "I promised my friend that I would take care of Elvis. I won't go back on my word."

Minilee sighed. "Well, there goes that dream of you really being kin to us. That's probably why she sneezed in the store yesterday. She was only there for a few minutes before we came home for lunch. Opal made her favorite soup, and she showed us the dress she'd bought for your date."

"Aha," he said under his breath as his earlier suspicion was confirmed.

"We thought it was the pollen or maybe something in the old settee where she was sitting," Opal said. "It was almost time to leave, anyway, so I yelled through the office door and told Libby we were leaving."

"She stood up and dropped her purse when she sneezed. Everything spilled out on the settee, and she found an old buffalo nickel when she was gathering up her things." Minilee took a step toward the door. "I'll get it for you."

"Keep it," Benny said with a smile. *It all makes sense.* "Put it in your coin collection."

"Well, thank you very much," Minilee said with a wide smile.

"I'm so disappointed that I'm going to go inside and have a big piece of chocolate cake. You want some?" Opal asked Benny.

"No, thank you," he answered. "I'm going over to my trailer and popping a frozen pizza in the oven, and then Elvis and I are going to watch some television if the storm doesn't knock out the electricity." Benny refrained from slapping his forehead over his earlier misjudgment.

The voice in his head didn't share the same restraint: *You jumped to conclusions and blamed Libby.*

Libby was reading the novel for book club when she heard the crunch of gravel heralding a vehicle coming down Sawmill Road. Then headlights flashed through the window above her sofa, and she laid the book aside and went to the front room and looked out the window. Benny got out of his truck. Opal yelled something across the road, and then Benny walked over that way.

"Good Lord!" she gasped. "Have I been reading that long, or did I fall asleep for a couple of hours?" She pulled her phone from her hip pocket and checked the time. He had been gone only thirty minutes.

Even though bits and pieces of their conversation floated across the road, she didn't understand what they were talking about. She went back to her book, and a streak of lightning zigzagged through the sky with a clap of thunder right behind it. She put the book aside and lit the candle that had been left on the cabinet. Even that tiny bit of light would keep her from going into a panic if the electricity went out.

Benny's deep voice was clear as he crossed over to his trailer. "Come on, Elvis. Let's get inside before the rain starts."

Libby settled down on the sofa and was in the middle of an emotional scene in the book when it sounded like a load of rocks had been dropped on the roof. Then poof! The electricity went out. The air conditioner and the refrigerator stopped humming, but the three wicks on the jar candle provided enough light to keep it from being completely dark.

She traipsed through the book club room, opened the front door, and stepped out onto the porch. She sat down in one of the chairs and watched the lightning as thunder crashed around her. The sweet smell of rain surrounded her. A dim light flowed through the window in Opal's house, and a couple of times, the lace curtains were pulled back, but no one came out to enjoy the sheer beauty of the storm.

It passed over Sawmill within half an hour, leaving behind a clean scent and a sky full of stars that looked like diamonds had been strewn over dark blue velvet. She heard the trailer door open, and in a few seconds, Benny came around the corner of the station. Elvis beat him up onto the porch and laid his head in Libby's lap.

"Is he afraid of storms?" she asked.

"No," Benny replied as he went to the cooler and opened it. "Want a beer?"

"Love one," she answered.

He took out two longneck bottles, twisted the caps off both and handed one to her, and then sat down across from her at the table. "What about you? Do storms frighten you?"

Libby shook her head and then took a long drink of the cold beer. "I think they are beautiful and a powerful source of protection."

"What does that mean?" he asked.

"I was left alone a lot when I was young. I figured that evil people weren't so stupid that they would come out in bad weather, so during that time, I was safe," she explained. "The way storms fascinate me, maybe I should have been a tornado chaser. Did the weather knock out the electricity in the restaurant where you and Tatum were going?"

"Nope," Benny answered. "I came home early."

The only sound that Libby heard for the next two or three awkward moments was a few crickets, who seemed to be glad for the cool front that the storm had left behind, and some tree frogs out in the distance.

"She's allergic to dogs," Benny finally said. "Why didn't you tell me that she was in the store yesterday?"

"It wasn't my place to tattle—and for your information, I did have the door closed most of the day. She poked her head inside one time when I was muttering about the spiders being like a military force," Libby admitted. "It didn't take her long to retreat when she saw all those granddaddy longlegs. If I remember right, I told you to talk to Minilee and Opal. Was it her marijuana?"

"Most likely," Benny answered. "I'm sorry that I accused you."

"Apology accepted." A surge of gladness filled Libby's heart, not only because she had been right about Tatum, but because Benny was man enough to apologize. "Lots of folks smoke a little. You can't hold that against her. Did you reschedule the date?"

"No, and I do not intend to do so," Benny said. "We might as well nip this in the bud—no pun intended. She can't be around dogs. I won't give Elvis up. So it's over."

Libby laid her hand on Elvis's head and rubbed the spot between his ears.

"Elvis lost a leg defending my best friend. When they were taking my best friend, Grady, into surgery, I promised him if he didn't wake up, I would take care of Elvis. I don't go back on my word." Benny took a sip of his beer and shook his head.

"Does Opal know?"

"Yes, she does."

"She may be pissy for the next few days. She had her heart set on you marrying Tatum," Libby said.

"Yep, but that probably wasn't ever going to happen anyway. Tatum has always been too . . ." He paused.

"Too what?" Libby asked.

"Too everything for me," Benny answered, stood up, and tossed his empty bottle into a nearby trash can.

She stood up and took a step toward the door. "Then why did you ask her out?"

"I didn't want Opal to be all pissy," he said with a grin. "And besides, she did the asking, not me."

"She'll call again."

Benny frowned. "What makes you think that?"

"You are rich, and even if you weren't, just look in the mirror. You'd be quite the catch, Benny Taylor. I'm surprised that you haven't installed one of those number machines on the front of the store so women can peel off a piece of paper that says when their turn will be," she said with half a giggle as she stepped inside.

"Yeah, right," he chuckled.

"Good night, Benny. See you in the morning." The rattle of the air conditioner turning back on stopped her. "Would you look at that? The lights are back on, too. Think that's a sign?"

"Yep, that the storm is over and the beer isn't going to get warm." He nodded before he disappeared into the night with Elvis at his side.

Chapter Eleven

Libby stepped out of the old station on Friday morning to a sweet-smelling breeze and met Benny just coming out of his trailer. She took a deep breath, and the faint aroma of bacon and coffee mixed together wafted across the road to her. A vision of a full plate, complete with eggs and hot biscuits, zipped through her mind. Tomorrow, she promised herself, she would get up fifteen minutes earlier so she could make herself a hot breakfast. She would not use those minutes to do anything about her grandmother's box. Of course, it would turn up like a bad penny. She should have tried harder to talk Amanda out of sending it.

"Hey, you two!" Opal yelled and waved from her porch. "We had leftovers, so I made up a few breakfast biscuits for y'all to have at break time."

"Thank you!" Benny jogged across the street and took the covered dish from her hands.

Libby raised her voice. "Thank you. From the looks of the parking lot, we'll have to eat them on the run."

"This is the first weekend of the month. I knew it would be really busy," Opal said. "I saw the UPS truck over at your place yesterday. He put several boxes on your porch."

"Yep, my friend sent the rest of my things to me," Libby told her.

Minilee poked her head out the wooden screen door. "If y'all need help, call us, but we have to be home at two o'clock for our shows."

"We'll keep that in mind—and thanks again," Benny said on his way across the road.

Vehicle doors began to slam shut as Benny and Libby crossed the parking lot, and by the time he opened the door, a whole line of customers had formed behind them.

"Do you feel like we're playing follow-the-leader?" she whispered.

"Little bit," he answered and flipped on the overhead lights that also set the ceiling fans in motion.

The big building was almost cool that morning, but as the day wore on, it would get warmer and then downright hot before closing. Four huge ceiling fans circulated the air, but there was no way to air-condition an enormous place like this. The store wouldn't hold the cool air, and the electric bill would eat up all the profits. Swamp coolers weren't even a possibility because they would cause everything in the place to mold.

Some folks greeted Libby with a *good morning* and a smile. Others barely nodded and went right to the business of looking around. When she was a little girl, she had been mesmerized by an anthill out behind the antique store. The people milling about in the store reminded her of that experience. Some of them were there with friends and discussed every piece they came across—like the little ants stopping to touch another's feelers on their way to and from the nest. Libby thought of Dolly and her cronies, and a feeling of nostalgia swept over her. She made a mental promise to call her elderly friend soon for a long visit.

"Could you help me, please?" a young lady asked and then cocked her head to one side. "Are you Libby O'Dell?"

"Yes, to both questions." She tried to place the woman. Her voice sounded vaguely familiar, but Libby couldn't put a name or a face to it.

"I'm Raisa Clapton. From the puzzled expression on your face, I don't think you remember me."

Things finally clicked. "You went to Jefferson High School at the same time I did, right?"

"Yes, and now I work for my aunt in her antique store," Raisa said.

"Now I'm putting it together. You sat behind me in history class when we were seniors," Libby said. "It's good to see you again. What do you need help with?"

"Right over here." Raisa led the way, and kept talking. "I would have flunked that class if it weren't for you. I needed every credit I could get, so I cheated off your papers during test days. If you hadn't slid down in your seat so far, I wouldn't have been able to see over your shoulder."

"I was self-conscious about my height," Libby admitted.

Good job facing one of your fears, her inner voice said.

Raisa pointed up to a pink deviled egg plate and a divided relish dish. "Those two right there, and if you've got any more of any pattern in pink, I'd like to see it. And it's a little late in coming, but thank you for helping me get through school. I couldn't make myself taller, but I could learn to change my lifestyle, which I did because of you."

And I would have gladly traded those positions for a stable family like you had, Libby thought.

"That's my ego trip for the day. You are so welcome—but I've got to admit, I always envied you more than a little bit. You were the class president and secretary of the student council." Libby set the two glass pieces on a nearby buffet. "I believe we've got some more pink crystal in the kitchen area, if you want to look at them."

"Definitely, and I'll take both of these," Raina said.

Libby showed Raisa where to go, filled out a Sold tag for each piece, and then turned to wait on a new customer.

"I was in here last weekend—I'm a cousin of your old neighbor, Dolly. I should have bought a set of Martha Washington lamps, and I've regretted not buying them all week. Now I can't remember where they are. Could you point me in the right direction?" the lady asked.

"Yes, ma'am, glad to have you back. We have two sets of those back in the living room part of the store. Over there on the buffet," Libby answered.

"Thank you. I'm Teresa Wilmington. Dolly said to tell you hello," the woman said. "She loved the little handmade cards you sent to her."

"Take her a hug from me. I sure miss her," Libby said.

"I'll sure do that," Teresa said. "She misses you, too."

"I would love that." Libby had figured out how to make cards on the computer, and Benny had given her permission to print them at the office. Dolly had sent back a long letter for each one received, and Libby loved reading them over and over.

"When you get done, I'll take all of these," Raisa called out. "Just tag them, and I'll keep looking around."

Libby gave her a thumbs-up and focused on Teresa. "Where do you live?"

"Over in Clarksville, and I'm so glad that my friends and I decided to come over here today. My mama had a set of lamps like these, and I can't believe they are still here. Today is my lucky day."

"Tell Dolly I'll be looking for her to come visit someday," Libby said and hurried back to tag the pieces Raisa wanted.

At one o'clock, there was a slight lull in business, and Benny motioned for Libby to join him in the office. He opened the covered dish to find half a dozen biscuits stuffed with scrambled eggs and bacon, and he slid it across the desk to her. "I made a fresh pot of coffee, but there's bottles of sweet tea in the fridge."

"Coffee sounds great. Can I pour you a cup?" she asked on her way across the room.

He held up a half-empty bottle of tea. "This is good. Been a hectic several hours, hasn't it? This could be a record-breaking day for sales."

Libby nodded as she filled a cup and carried it back to the table. "I need to replenish my Sold tags before I leave. You're going to need to visit several sales next week to build the stock back up." She picked up a biscuit. "Give me one of these over a quick protein bar any day of the week."

"You might as well sit while you can," he said. Hiring Libby was the best thing he had done since he'd decided to quit the law firm and manage his grandfather's antique business. She fit right into Sawmill.

She was a hard worker—and more than that, she liked Elvis. Plus, she was personable when she dealt with customers, knew antiques, and was a wonderful bookkeeper.

And she's a blue-eyed brunette, and even tall. Just your type. His grandfather's whisper was so real that it put a smile on Benny's face.

She eased down into a chair, polished off the biscuit, and reached for another one. "The customer that bought all that pink glassware this morning was an old classmate of mine from Jefferson . . . Why are you smiling like that?"

"My grandfather's voice popped into my head. That always makes me happy," Benny answered. "And your friend sang your praises the whole time I was invoicing her items. You should have put her down for a personal reference."

"To tell the truth, I have forgotten most of my classmates. She had to tell me who she was," Libby said. "And there's the doorbell ringing . . . and ringing . . . and ringing again. I'd better eat the last of this one on the run."

"We are going to trade places this afternoon. You can invoice the purchases, and I'll wait on customers," he said as he downed the rest of his tea and stood up. "See you in a few hours."

Benny was more than glad to get back out on the floor and stretch his legs. He had checked the progress Libby had made in the two drawers and was amazed at the organization. If she kept up the good work, the office would be in tip-top shape in the next six months. He hoped that if everything kept going the way it was, she would agree to sign a year's contract when the current one played out. There was no way he could ever find another person—male or female—who would fit the bill for what he needed like Libby did.

The afternoon went by as fast as lightning, and then there was another lull at about four o'clock. Only half a dozen people were in the place when Opal and Minilee arrived.

"You missed the party," he teased as he sat down at the break table with them.

"We've been keeping an eye on the parking lot and figured that this was a bumper crop of a day," Minilee said. "I see that pretty oak secretary is gone, and lots of glassware."

"Yes, and two of the four-poster beds, a couple of chifforobes, and that old pie safe that's been in the store since before Grandpa passed away. I'm going to get a bottle of water. Y'all want something?"

"I'm good," Opal answered.

"Me too," Minilee said.

"Okay, then," Benny said with a nod. "Libby and I were sure thankful for the food you sent, and I'm grateful that you talked me into hiring her. I'm not sure I could have handled everything today without her."

On the way from the front of the store to the office, he stopped and told a couple of dealers where the rolltop desks were located. When the cool air in the office hit him, he almost told Libby that he would trade places with her for a while, but then he realized she was working on files in between customers.

"I just came to get a bottle of water. Opal and Minilee are here. Want to come out for a few minutes' break?" he asked.

"Thanks, but if I keep at it, I can get today's work all in a folder and be that much more ahead when it's time to do that drawer," she answered without looking up. "If I don't get some of these off the desk, the stack is going to fall onto the floor."

"Remember to stop and get something to drink every now and then," he suggested.

She pointed at a bottle of root beer on the desk. "Tell Opal and Minilee that the biscuits were wonderful. I had another one a while ago, but there's still one left if you want it."

He picked up the dish and headed back out into the shop, leaving the coolness behind. When he got back to the table, Opal was waiting on an elderly lady. The woman bought a set of six china salt dips with tiny gold spoons. She was telling Opal that she had a thousand in her collection, but most of them were crystal. Opal stuck a Sold sticker on the box, and the lady went off toward the office.

"That sale should get Tatum another date," Opal said when she returned to the table.

"She's made it clear that she's allergic to dogs, and I'm not willing to put up with all that entails." Benny didn't usually argue with his pseudo grannies, but he hoped his tone didn't leave room for debate.

"You're going to regret that decision," Minilee whispered. "Choosing a dog over a lifetime mate don't make a lot of sense."

"Do you believe in signs?" Benny asked.

"Always have," Minilee answered. "But not in this case. I think you're being stubborn."

Benny's phone rang. He held up one finger and whispered, "We'll get back to that later," before he answered the call.

"Hello, darlin'," the sugary-sweet voice on the other end said.

"Who is this?" he asked.

"I'm hurt even more than I was when my eyes swelled up last night," Tatum said with a sexy giggle.

"Sorry about that." Benny held the phone to his side and glanced over at Minilee and Opal. "Excuse me. I'll be back in a minute."

Opal motioned toward the door and said, "We've got to get back to the house. See you later."

"I've decided to forgive you for not mentioning that you have a dog," Tatum said. "I really, really like you, Bennington . . ."

He heard *blah, blah, blah* for a few seconds. He hated to be called *Bennington*. It sounded so stiff and formal, and he wasn't that guy. When he tuned back in to what she was saying, he bristled even more. "I've found a wonderful home for your dog."

"Oh, really? Does your potential adoptive friend or his acquaintances ever use drugs of any kind?" Benny asked.

"A little pot now and then, but nothing hard," Tatum said.

"Would she or he be happy with a former police dog that has a front leg missing? Elvis lost it in a battle with a drug dealer at the same time his owner and my best friend was shot and killed," Benny said.

Tatum laughed. "Probably not."

"It's not funny," Benny spat. "And I wouldn't give him away if the president of the United States asked to adopt him."

"Oh, come on, Bennington." She lowered her voice back to a sexy tone. "I know you feel something for me. I can see it in your eyes, and God only knows how much I'm attracted to you. Let's give *us* another try. I believe I can change your mind if you give me a chance. I'm worth more than even a pedigreed show dog with all its legs."

Bennie gritted his teeth. "I'm at work, and more customers just came into the store—but, Tatum, there can't be another try for us. I wish you all the best. Goodbye, now."

He took several deep breaths to clear the anger from his mind and was glad that Minilee and Opal had left. He needed time before he talked to them. At seven o'clock, when the last customer left without buying a single item, he quickly locked the doors and turned to find Libby coming out of the office.

"Been a day, hasn't it?" he said.

"Yep, but I'd rather be super busy than bored," she answered. "That said, I don't expect a case of *bored* to happen until I get all the files organized."

"You are doing a fantastic job, Libby—both in the store and in the office. Let's go home and prop up our feet for the evening. Want to share a frozen pizza with me? We could have a front porch picnic."

"Love to," she said. "I've got a couple of pieces of the leftover book club dessert in the fridge. There's no mold on it, so I guess it's still good enough to eat."

"If there's a speck of green, we can scrape it off," he suggested.

Elvis met them on the far side of the lot, and Libby squatted down to hug him. "You are such a good watchdog. I just know that you've kept all the varmints like possums and skunks away from the station all day, haven't you?"

He wagged his tail so fast that it stirred up a breeze.

"You really like him, don't you?" Benny asked. He shouldn't compare Tatum and Libby, but it was hard not to do so. Tatum was trying to rehome Elvis, and Libby would probably take him and love him if Benny wanted to give him away—which he did not!

Libby straightened up and resumed walking. "I always wanted a dog, but Victoria said no, and there was no use in arguing with her."

"Have you always liked antiques?" Benny blurted out, and then wondered why he would even ask such a misplaced question when they had been talking about dogs.

"I thought I didn't, but maybe it was working with my grandmother that I didn't like. I don't seem to mind this place."

"Why didn't you like your grandmother?" Benny asked, then winced inwardly. "I'm sorry. Don't answer that. It's way too personal."

"Not really. On a scale of one to ten, with one being the worst and ten being the best, Victoria was probably a minus two," Libby said. "But I'm told that with time, I will find closure for the way she treated me."

"How much time?"

She held up a finger and shook her head. "I'm kind of personal and don't share a lot, but something about this place is making me open up."

"Sawmill seems to have that effect on folks," he said after a long sigh.

"You too?" she asked. "Want to talk about it? I'm a good listener."

"Not tonight. I just want to sit on the porch, eat pizza, drink beer, and watch the sun set. Meet you there in thirty minutes?"

"I'll be the one with wet hair because I'm going to take a quick bath," she told him.

"I may jump in the shower while the pizza bakes," he said with a nod. "That store can get downright hot in the afternoons. I don't know how those poor men could do hard manual labor in there when it was a sawmill."

"They were tougher than us," she said and went on inside the station.

Chapter Twelve

"You can count today as overtime," Benny said as he opened the truck door for Libby that Monday morning.

"Are we friends?" Libby asked and added *gentleman* to the long list of Benny's attributes.

"I like to think so," he answered. "Why are you asking?"

"Because today I want a friend, not a boss." Libby fastened her seat belt and watched him round the front end of the truck and slide in behind the steering wheel. "I'm seeing files in my dreams, so I need some time away from the store. I have never charged a friend to spend time with them, but a boss might be a different story."

"Then I am your friend, but not just today, Libby. What's going on?" he asked.

"I miss Amanda—my best friend. We talk on the phone and FaceTime pretty often, but it seems like our lives are going in two different ways. She's moving in with her boyfriend that she's been dating for about a year, and I'm seven hours away, working at a new job. I also miss Dolly, my neighbor who was responsible for me being here in the first place. I want to be free to talk about anything that pops up, not just business," she told him. "You don't often leave Elvis at home. Will he be all right?"

"Like I said, I'm your friend," Benny said. "Don't worry about Elvis. He told me that he was looking forward to a day of resting under the table on your porch. His food and water bowls are both full, and he'll keep one eye open to protect them from pesky birds and squirrels."

The words *your porch* stuck in Libby's mind. She kept it swept and cleaned the road dust off the table and chairs, but was it really hers? Or was it just another temporary—six months, in this case—situation?

"How many sales are we going to today?" she asked.

"Two in Marshall, and then we'll have lunch, hit one this afternoon between there and Jefferson, and one in town. It'll probably be dark before we get back home," he answered. "Are you sure you don't want to keep track of the hours?"

"Absolutely," she answered. "I haven't been back to Jefferson since my grandmother died. It'll be interesting to see if the town has changed. Do you really expect to fill up the trailer?"

"Grandpa said the best lesson he learned when he decided to turn the sawmill into an antique shop was to always be prepared. The first time he went out to an estate sale, he bought too much to get into his truck and had to have it all shipped. He bought the trailer when he got back home and never left Sawmill without it. Once, he came home with only two punch bowls and a couple of vases and figured he had saved money. Then he passed a garage sale on the way through Tyler, and he bought so much that he had a full load."

"Yep," Libby said with a nod. "I cut my teeth on garage sales. Victoria said that the best buys were at those places because folks just wanted to get rid of stuff. That's where the people our age usually sell off their grandparents' crystal and furniture pretty often. Or they give it to thrift stores, and we would buy it from those places. Victoria's favorite one was in New Boston."

"Oh, really? We're going right through there. Show me where it is, and we'll stop for half an hour. We could still get to Marshall in plenty of time before the first auction begins," Benny said.

Libby had always dreaded going with her grandmother, especially when Victoria was in one of her losing—or maybe only breaking even— gambling sprees. But today she actually looked forward to stopping at the thrift store. Maybe she would find a few more pink pieces that Raisa would be interested in buying.

"How long does it take a stranger to become a friend?" Libby asked, and then wondered if that might be the stupidest question that had ever come out of her mouth.

"Why are you asking?" Benny slowed down to go through the little town of Blossom.

"I feel like Opal and Minilee are my friends, but less than two weeks ago, they were strangers."

"I guess it depends on the people involved," Benny answered. "Some of my coworkers at the law firm were barely acquaintances."

"The *good morning* or *how are you* type, right?" Libby had had several of those people in her life at the insurance agency.

"Yep, but maybe my grandfather can answer the question better than I can. He told me once that working beside a person was the way to really get to know someone." Benny sped up as they reached the highway after the town.

"That makes sense." Libby had worked with Benny for two weekends now, and she liked his work ethic, his kindness toward the customers—and even toward Opal and Minilee when they disagreed with him about Tatum.

"Are you trying to figure out if we are really friends?" he asked.

Her brows drew down in a deep frown. "I guess I am."

"Are you trying to determine if we are friends enough that you can open up to me?"

She whipped around to look at his profile—chiseled cheekbones, a perfect nose, and full lips. Were they really friends, or were they just working acquaintances?

"Yes . . . No . . . Maybe," she stammered. "I probably shouldn't be asking someone that I've only known a little while to help me face my fears."

"I'm willing to help you out, unless it's got something to do with snakes." One side of Benny's mouth turned up in half a smile. "I'm not going to handle one of those for you. Our friendship isn't that strong."

Libby laughed. "Same here, but I don't want to talk—not yet."

"Anytime you are ready, I'll listen. Look! Did you see that bright orange sign?" His forefinger shot so close to her nose that she jerked back.

She gasped. "No, I was trying to keep you from knocking my nose off my face."

"There's a garage sale one mile ahead," Benny said. "And sorry about startling you."

Throwing his hand across the console had stirred the air and filled the truck cab with the scent of whatever shaving lotion he had applied that morning. Something that reminded Libby of a crisp morning run with a little leather and sawdust. She turned to look out the side window, took several deep breaths, and exhaled slowly.

"Second sign says turn right on Fallen Oak Road." He chuckled.

"What's so funny about that?" she asked.

"Haven't you ever heard about the directions older folks used to give? 'Go about two miles down this here road.'" He changed his voice to mimic an elderly man. "'Turn right at the old schoolhouse that's falling down and then watch for the big oak tree on the left that got hit by lightning back in 1942. The house you are looking for is about a hundred yards from that tree on the right. It'll have a blue porch swing, and most likely, Grandpa Hester will be sittin' on the porch, sellin' turnip greens.'" He slowed down and chuckled again. "The sign says a hundred yards ahead on the right."

Libby giggled. "It's been years since I've heard those kinds of directions. GPS kind of made all that obsolete. There's the sale!" She pointed to a yard covered with full tables and a garage packed with furniture. "I'll bet you that we're going to find some good bargains."

"I'm going straight for that four-poster bed up there on the porch," Benny said as he parked out on the side of the road. "I wonder why we're the only ones here."

"It's Monday," Libby answered as she opened the door and unfastened her seat belt.

"That's right," he said with a nod. "Most garage sales are held on the weekends so folks who work can go to them, and this is pretty far out of town. Most likely, whoever is holding it depended solely on those orange signs out on the road for advertising and didn't even put an ad in the local newspaper."

"Good for us," she said, "but not so much for the folks trying to sell all this stuff. Do we stay together, or do you want me to look for something in particular?"

"Let's stay close to each other," Benny answered. "We'll need to make sure what we buy is authentic and not knockoffs."

She slid out of the seat and planted her feet on the ground. A tiny black blur came from around the back of the truck, stopped dead at her feet, and put one paw up like it wanted to shake hands with her.

"Her name is Fancy, and she's free if you want her," a lady yelled from the porch. "She's housebroke, been fixed, and isn't good for anything but yapping at wild animals that come up in the yard."

Libby bent down and picked up the little critter. "What breed is she?"

"Teacup chihuahua and mini-poodle mix," the woman answered. "My great-aunt had her mother and thought the little chihuahua was too old to get pregnant. The dog went visiting the neighbor's little dog, and when Fancy was born, Aunt Molly kept the puppy. She's about three years old now, and I can't have dogs in my apartment in Boston. I'm just here for a few days to get rid of all her things. She had lived in this place her whole life."

Benny headed over toward the porch and nodded at Libby. Did that mean the bed was authentic? Did he like the price on it, or was he nodding to tell her that she could take the dog home with her?

"Why is her name Fancy?" she asked.

"Aunt Molly's favorite Reba McEntire song was 'Fancy.' My name is Gina Woodland, and if you think anything is overpriced, just make me an offer," she said.

"Glad to meet you. I'm Benny and this is Libby," he said with a smile. "How long are you going to have this sale?"

"Today only," Gina replied. "What doesn't sell will be donated to a place that helps take care of an animal shelter. I thought Aunt Molly would like that."

Benny picked up a punch bowl, ran his finger around the edges, and set it back down. "How much are you hoping to make on this sale?"

"I didn't have a goal in mind. Where I come from, you can't give this old stuff away," Gina said with a shrug.

"What if I offered you five thousand dollars for everything here and took what I wanted?" he asked.

Libby whipped around to stare at him so fast that she almost dropped Fancy. "We can't get all of this in the trailer," she whispered.

"No, but we can pick and choose what we want and still have a bargain," he said, lowering his voice. "That bedroom outfit alone will sell for three thousand, not to mention the glassware, and folks are always looking for crocheted tablecloths and handmade quilts."

"I'd say sold, but only if you take Fancy. I can tell that Libby will be good to her by the way she's holding her," Gina said. "I hate to put her in a shelter, but I will if I have to."

"I've got Elvis, so if we take her home, she's your dog, Libby," Benny said. "You sure you want a pet?"

"I'm very sure. I've wanted a dog since I was a little girl, and Fancy is perfect for apartment living." She hugged the dog closer to her chest and got a faint whiff of something that reminded her of her grandmother. "What kind of perfume did your aunt wear?"

"Dew Drops," Gina answered. "I used to send her a bottle for Christmas every year. All of her clothing still smelled like that when I donated it to a homeless shelter. Why do you ask?"

"There's still remnants of that scent on her," Libby replied and then turned to face Benny. "You think she could get along with Elvis?"

Benny pulled a tape measure from his pocket and measured an oak washstand. "Don't know until we take the critter home and see."

"If you were serious about buying it all and leaving what you don't want, we've got a deal," Gina said. "I could call the folks at the shelter and tell them to come on and take what you don't want and be done with this whole thing today."

"Libby, do you want to take Fancy home?" Benny asked.

She glanced down to find the dog looking up at her with big brown eyes. Of course she wanted to take her home. "Can I take her to the office?"

"Yep," Benny said and measured a magazine rack. "Miz Gina, why don't you go ahead and make that call. I'll get your cash from the truck and have what I want loaded before the other folks get here."

"This is fantastic!" Gina's voice went all high and squeaky. "The new owners wanted the house cleaned out by the weekend. The guys I paid to haul all of this are sitting around back in the shade. I'll get them to come and help you. I can't believe that I've been this lucky. While y'all go through things, I'll get Fancy's collars, leashes, and what food she has left." She almost sprinted across the yard and into the house.

"I can't believe that either of us just did that. Do you often buy out a sale like this?" Libby asked.

"I've only done it one time before, but this stuff is mostly gold, Libby—and you get a pet for free." Benny smiled, and his eyes twinkled. "You'll be amazed at how much I can pack into that trailer."

Fancy squirmed, so Libby set her down on the lawn. "Does this mean we're going back home after we've loaded up? There won't be room for anything more after that."

Benny headed for the truck in long strides. "No, let's go on down to Marshall and Jefferson. We've still got a little room in the back seat of the truck—and maybe the bed, if we don't need it to pack stuff."

Fancy ran along beside him and hopped up on the running board, but that's as far as she could go. Libby picked up the little dog and put her in the cab of the vehicle. She jumped onto the console and sat there like a queen.

Benny pulled a bank bag from under the seat, counted out several one-hundred-dollar bills, and put a rubber band around the stack. "Looks like she's eager to take a road trip with us."

"Are we doing the right thing?" Libby whispered. "What if Fancy doesn't like Sawmill? What if Elvis hates her? She's so little, and he's a big old boy. Or what if—"

"What-ifs are just worrying about tomorrow," Benny butted in before she could finish the sentence, "and we don't have control over that. It robs us of our joy today. Be as happy as that little ugly mutt is right now. I am over the moon at the deal I just made."

Libby reached across the seat and covered the dog's ears. "She's not ugly!"

"Honey, that mutt would come in last in a doggy beauty pageant," Benny teased as he headed back across the yard to tell the two big, burly men who had come around the house what he wanted loaded.

"Leashes, collars, and food," Gina said and handed off a tote bag to Libby. "Evidently, Aunt Molly bought birthday and Christmas presents for Fancy."

Benny gave her the stack of bills. "I counted it, but you should do the same."

Gina let out a long sigh. "Thank you for everything. If there's really holes in the floor of heaven, Aunt Molly is peeking down through them and smiling."

Libby attached one of the leashes to Fancy's collar and set her back on the ground so she could get a little exercise before they hit the road again. "Come on, baby girl. Stretch your little legs because you're going to do a lot of riding today."

Two hours later the trailer was packed solid from front to back, and as Benny drove away, a large moving van pulled up to take the rest of the stuff. Fancy must have been used to traveling, because she sat up on the console and seemed to enjoy the air from the air-conditioning vent blowing back the fur on the top of her head.

"Do you ever think about selling out and returning to a law firm or maybe starting your own business?" Libby asked.

Benny shook his head. "Nope. I made my decision to leave that behind, and I have no intentions of going back. Especially not after all the fun we just had. Do you realize that we will triple—or maybe even quadruple—the money on what we've got in the trailer?"

"And yet Gina felt like she got a great deal," Libby added.

Did you get a good deal? her inner voice asked. *What happens when you leave Sawmill and your next stop says you can't have pets?*

"I'll sleep in my SUV," she said.

"What was that about an SUV?"

"I was talking to myself," she told him. "My grandmother warned me more than once that people would think I was hearing voices if I didn't quit."

"Sometimes it's a good thing." Benny made a right turn back onto the paved highway. "My grandpa often said that he had to talk to himself because he needed an intelligent person to converse with."

"Smart man," Libby said with a giggle.

Fancy added a yip of agreement.

Chapter Thirteen

"Well, well, well, we haven't seen each other for over a decade, Libby, and now I run into you twice in less than a week," Raisa said as she came out of the bedroom of one of the estates. "Have you got your bidding ticket?"

"Benny has one," Libby answered and gave Raisa a quick sideways hug. "It's great to see you again. Are you still looking for pink crystal?"

"Yes, I am," Raisa answered and shifted her focus over to Benny.

He held up his paddle with the number 13 written on it. "Have we met?"

"I bought some pink glassware at your store," Raisa explained. "I went to school up in Jefferson with Libby—and I was actually talking to her about bidding."

"I remember you now," Benny said. "We chatted about that."

"Yes, we did!" Raisa said and looked over at Libby. "Now, who's this cute little doggy? Did you have it at the store last time I was there?"

Libby glanced down to see Fancy peeking out the top of her big purse. "This is Fancy—I just got her this morning, and of course now it's too hot to leave her in the truck. The folks at the door said I could bring her inside as long as I didn't let her out of my purse."

Raisa reached out and petted Fancy. "My beagle wouldn't fit inside one, but I bet one of the cats would. I have six of them. Three inside the house and three beggars that I feed on the back porch. For the most part, I like my animals more than I like people."

Libby knew how she felt. "I hear you. So, what else have you ear-marked to bid on when the auction starts?"

"Those pink pieces I picked up at your store have already sold, so my aunt has me out scouring all the sales for more," Raisa said. "How about y'all?"

"Whatever strikes Benny's fancy," Libby answered.

"We picked up several more pieces of that pink glassware this morning at a yard sale, if you want to come back up to Sawmill and look at it," Benny told her. "I'll be glad to hold them for you. Even give you the dealer ten percent discount."

"If you'll set them back for me, I'll be there Friday morning," Raisa said. "I'll bring lunch with me if you can take a break at noon, Libby."

"That will depend on how busy we are, but I'd love to give it a try," Libby said.

Raisa's hand shot up in a wave, and then she disappeared into another room of the massive two-story home.

"Was she your best friend?" Benny asked.

Libby readjusted the tote bag after a slight shrug. "I'm not sure I had one of those in high school. She was more of an acquaintance. Amanda was the only person I would ever consider a best friend—and maybe Dolly, but she was more like a grandmother figure as a neighbor."

"I see," Benny said. "I'm going downstairs to look at a matched set of ladder-back chairs. Holler if you spot something you think we could take home."

He left, and within a minute, Raisa was back. She scanned the whole room and then looked out in the hallway.

"Are you and Benny dating?" she asked in a low voice.

"No, he's my boss." Libby thought of the main character in the book she was reading for the club the following week. Another character had asked her the same question, and her answer had been identical to Libby's.

"You do know that he's rich, don't you?" Raisa whispered.

"I've heard rumors."

"He used to be a lawyer, and he gave up a salary like that to run an antique store. I heard that his grandfather left him a huge inheritance," Raisa whispered. "If you are smart, you'll latch on to him—and besides, he's taller than you. That has to be a plus."

Her grandmother had left the poker table to come back and haunt her. *You don't need a man to complete you,* she grumbled.

"Don't you think marriage should involve love?" Libby started across the room toward the door and Raisa followed.

"Sure, but you can love a rich man just as quick as a poor one." Raisa shot a wink at her. "If you're not interested in him, I'll ask him out when I come up to look at all that pink crystal next week."

"Knock yourself out," Libby told her, but a little streak of jealousy shot through her body.

She was halfway down the stairs when she saw Benny smiling up from the bottom. "I turned in my paddle. Nothing here for us. Let's go get some lunch."

"There's not a café in town, or anywhere else for that reason, that is going to let us take Fancy inside. How about we hit that food wagon I saw parked in the Walmart lot? We can have a picnic in the truck."

"Sounds good to me," he agreed.

She worried all the way from the auction site to the back side of the Walmart parking area about whether she should warn him that Raisa was going to ask him out. That was what friends did for each other, wasn't it? She finally convinced herself that Benny was a grown man—and even as a new friend, telling him about Raisa's comments could be meddling. Besides, she might damage her equally new friendship with Opal and Minilee if she got in the middle of Benny's love life. They seemed to be taking care of that side of things for him.

He pulled his truck and trailer into one of the spots that semis used, not far from the food truck. He rolled down both the driver and the passenger windows. The air-conditioning rushed out, and the aroma of smoked meat wafted into the vehicle. Fancy had been sleeping on

Libby's lap, but she perked right up. Her tail thumped against Libby's leg, and she stretched her neck to catch whiffs of the barbecue.

"Are you hungry, sweet girl?" Libby's tone jacked up a couple of octaves. "You shouldn't have what we're about to eat, but I'll get out a handful of your food." She reached behind the seat and shook some dog food into a small bowl that Gina had tucked into the tote bag. Fancy jumped out of her lap, scarfed down several bites, flopped down on the floor, and closed her eyes.

Libby turned her attention to the vendor wagon, where Benny was the third in line to order. Suddenly, as if out of nowhere, Tatum's face was right there in front of her, so close that Libby had to blink several times to get it in focus.

"You startled me," she gasped.

"What are you doing here?" Tatum asked.

"Buying antiques, having some barbecue." Libby could hear the chill in her own voice. "What are you doing in Marshall?"

"That isn't really any of your business," Tatum said with a snarky smile.

"I guess it isn't," Libby said. "The barbecue smells great, doesn't it?"

Tatum's nose turned up in a snarl. "Not to me. Never liked it all that much."

How could a Texan not like barbecue? Libby wondered.

"I hear you don't like dogs, either?" Libby's tone was a question, not a statement.

"Yes. That's right. I'm glad Bennington's dog stays away from Aunt Opal's house."

Libby raised a dark eyebrow. "You might want to steer clear of that big old shade tree out in the yard. Elvis does like to lay up under it."

"I'll remember that. Where is Bennington?" Tatum asked.

Libby pointed in his direction. "He's in line at the barbecue wagon."

Tatum leaned into the window and whispered, "Watch and learn, honey. I always get what I want."

"What is it that you want?" Libby asked, surprised that the woman hadn't already started sneezing.

"What does any woman want?" Tatum snapped.

"Love, happiness, a family."

"That depends on who you are, I guess." Tatum flashed a grin.

Libby heard a deep growl behind her and turned to see that every hair on Fancy's back was standing straight up. She remembered the first time she had met Elvis and how friendly he had been. Evidently, her grandmother's old saying to beware of anyone dogs or kids didn't like was more than just words.

For the first time in years, Libby agreed with Victoria.

Tatum took a step back. "Why didn't you tell me you had a dog in the truck?" Her tone had gone from low and sexy to a high squeak in seconds.

"You didn't ask, *darlin'.*" Libby dragged out the last word. "Do you really want to make a play for Benny with snot running out of your nose and your eyes swelling up? And before you get close to him today, you should know that Fancy"—she nodded toward the dog—"has been right up next to him for the past few hours."

"You are a—" Tatum sneezed.

"Be careful what you call me," Libby said with a sweet smile. "I can always get out of this truck and hug you like a sister. Like you said, 'Watch and learn.'"

Tatum gave her a look meant to melt her into nothing but a greasy spot on Benny's leather pickup seat, then whipped around and headed across the parking lot at a fast trot.

Spoken like a true smart-ass. Victoria's giggles were so real that Libby could have sworn she was right behind her. *I'm proud of you.*

Benny stepped up to the window and ordered two chopped-brisket sandwiches, two large sweet teas, and a couple of bags of potato chips.

He had a brown bag in one hand and two drinks in a cup carrier in the other when he noticed Tatum jogging across the lot.

He passed the food through the window to Libby and rounded the front of the truck. "Was that Tatum?" he asked when he slid in behind the steering wheel.

"Yep." Libby removed the two tall cups of sweet tea from the flimsy cardboard and put them in the cup holders in front of the console. "Did you order the same thing for both of us?"

"Yes, I did," he answered. "What did she want?"

"She said that it wasn't any of my business what she was doing in this area, but I reckon it was to stalk you."

Benny's brows drew down into a deep frown. "That's aggravating, but we are not going to let it spoil our day."

Fancy sniffed the air and yipped.

Libby pinched off a tiny bite of the bun and handed it to her. The dog turned up her nose and went back to her dog food. "Well, darlin' girl, that's what we've got today."

"I'm not giving up Elvis for anyone," Benny declared and took a bite of his sandwich.

"Evidently, Tatum is used to getting what she wants."

"Did she tell you exactly what that was?" he asked.

Libby nodded. "Not that I can't guess—she's pretty obvious—but I told her that most women want love and a family."

Benny swallowed and took a drink of his tea. "Oh, really?"

"Yep, and she calls you *Bennington*," she told him.

"I don't know why she does that. I wasn't even Bennington at the law firm. The people there called me Ben."

"This is great barbecue. If we're ever back in this area, we should drop by here again."

"Are you trying to change the subject?" Benny asked with half a chuckle.

"Not trying," she answered. "Whatever relationship—or lack of one—that y'all have is for the two of you to figure out. I don't need to be the middleman."

"Fair enough, but I'd like to know how Fancy reacted to her," he said. "And before you answer, remember how the dog came right up to you and didn't growl at me."

"Every hair on her back was standing up, and she acted like she might attack the woman," Libby replied.

"Just as I expected," Benny said. "I think Tatum would be much happier with someone other than an antique dealer, and that's all I've got to say about that."

"A fitting line from a great old movie."

"Yes, it is, and it fits the moment so well," he said with another one of his deep chuckles. "When we finish eating, we'll head on up to Jefferson. There's one major sale going on up there that I especially want to check out before we head home. One of those bed-and-breakfast places is being auctioned off. They're selling the contents, and then the house at the end. I don't expect us to stay for the final part, but I would like to see what's inside."

"What's the name of the place?"

"Five Oaks. If we find another trailer load, we might have to ask them to hold the items and come back once we unload what we've bought. If not, we can do whatever you want." He paused. "Maybe visit some folks or your grandmother's grave site?"

Libby shook her head. "I didn't leave anything behind that I need to see again. My grandmother left instructions with her gambling buddies. She was cremated, and her ashes were buried in Louisiana where a new casino stands right now. Back then, the only thing there was a sign on the property that said a casino was coming soon."

"Was that legal?" Another layer to the person that was Libby O'Dell peeled off, making Benny wonder how many more there were hiding under all that independence.

"Her friends went out there at midnight, dug a hole, and dumped her ashes into it, along with a poker chip, a tiny bottle of Jim Beam, and a fresh deck of cards." Libby's strained tone said that she didn't think it was a bit funny.

"You should write a book," he whispered.

Libby smiled, but her big blue eyes floated in tears. "The truth is stranger than fiction. No one would believe the stories if I told them."

Chapter Fourteen

*L*ibby could hardly believe her eyes when Benny stopped the truck in front of the house where she grew up. The sign swinging from two of the porch posts—Five Oaks—squeaked when the wind blew it back and forth. A wind chime over at the west end, and two kids making an old porch swing glide back and forth on rusty chains, added even more to the noise. Fancy stuck her head out the top of Libby's purse and growled.

"I know, baby girl," Libby whispered. "It's full of unfriendly ghosts to me, too."

"What was that?" Benny asked as he held the door open for her.

"Nothing," Libby answered. "Fancy was telling me that she doesn't like this place."

"Could be . . ." Benny's nose wrinkled.

"Lemon oil," Libby said, finishing the sentence for him. She frowned. So many memories rose to the top, like scum on a swamp, and no matter how hard she tried, she couldn't get rid of all of them.

With paddles hanging out their back pockets, people milled around with notebooks, making lists of what they might be interested in buying. The buzz of conversations filled the air, but Libby's pulse was jacked up so high that she couldn't make out a single word. She had not set foot in this house more than half a dozen times since she had left to go to college. Coming back wasn't bringing closure, but it sure was tightening her chest and making it hard to breathe—especially with that lemon-oil scent filling every breath she took.

"I'll get my bidding paddle and meet you on the porch when you're done looking around," Benny said.

Libby could see his lips moving and nodded when she made out the words *paddle* and *porch*. She started up the staircase to her old room and heard the familiar screech of the second step from the top. She smiled at the memory and looked up to see a gray-haired lady at the top of the stairs.

"I bet if there were teenagers in the house, they would avoid that step when they came home after curfew." She giggled and then stared at Libby for a full five seconds before she spoke again. "Libby, is that really you?"

"June?" Libby whispered.

The woman took one more step and wrapped Libby up in a fierce hug. "I can't believe it's been more than ten years since our precious Victoria left us. Are you thinking about buying the house back?"

Libby shook her head. "No, ma'am, but it's good to see you. How have you been?"

June wiped away a tear that had rolled down her cheek. "Lonely, for the most part. I'm the only one of the three of us that's left. Jeanie passed two years ago. I go to the casino on their birthdays once a year." She pulled a tissue from her big black purse and dabbed at her eyes. "Just so they'll know I haven't forgotten them. There's a lot of wonderful memories in this old place."

One woman's good memory is another woman's nightmare, Libby thought.

"That's sweet. It's so good to see you," Libby said and went up a couple more steps.

"Darlin', it's just made my day to lay eyes on you. Take care of yourself. I never did agree with some of the ways that Victoria treated you when you were a child, but no one crossed that woman. She was my friend, but . . ." June shrugged.

Libby forced a smile. "I understand."

"Did you ever open the box?" June asked. "When I gave it to you, I had the feeling you might just toss it in the trash."

"No, ma'am, I did not open it," Libby answered. "But I do still have it."

"When your daddy died, Victoria put that box together," June said, "and then Jeanie and I liked the idea so much that we each made one, too. Then Victoria and Jeanie both gave theirs to me to pass on, and I gave mine to Jeanie. I often wondered if they died first because I had those boxes."

"Who has yours now?" Libby asked.

"I gave it to my niece, with instructions not to pass it on to my granddaughter until I'm gone," June answered. "We never discussed what was in the boxes, but Jeanie's great-granddaughter said that there was a letter addressed to her among a lot of the keepsakes. Maybe Victoria wrote you a letter; I put one in my box. You should go ahead and open yours, honey."

"Maybe I will pretty soon," Libby said. "Do you know what's in it?"

June shook her head. "No, darlin', I do not. Victoria was great fun and, like I said, a good friend, but she didn't tell me. I imagine it's just stuff she thought you would like to hang on to. Strange, how a whole life can be reduced to what goes into an old box, ain't it? But then, on another note, those things that you don't know probably kept you from a lot of headache."

"How's that?"

June waved a hand around in a motion that encompassed the whole house. "You didn't have to deal with all this."

A stream of folks started up the stairs.

"Looks like we're holding up traffic," Libby said.

"It's been good to see you," June said. "If you are ever in this area again, give me a holler, and we'll have coffee."

"Will do," Libby agreed and headed on up to her old bedroom.

All the doors off the wide upstairs hallway were open. Other than the crowd of people who were interested in buying the antiques, she felt like she had been transported back in time. Nothing—not one blessed thing—had changed. The furniture was still the same, a little more worn than it had been the last time Libby was there, and the aura surrounding her was so eerie that it gave her goose bumps.

She laid a hand on one of the wingback chairs that sat on either side of her bedroom door for support and stared into her old bedroom, feeling like she was being pulled inside and yet dreading the very idea of taking another step forward. Her hands were clammy, and her heart pounded in her chest. She could almost see Victoria coming in late at night from the casino, either singing off-key or cussing a blue streak because she hadn't won a damned thing.

"'You gain strength, and courage, and confidence by every experience in which you really stop to look fear in the face . . . You must do the thing you think you cannot,'" she whispered. "Eleanor Roosevelt said that."

The saying came from an old book of famous quotes that had been in the drawer of a dresser her grandmother had bought for the store. Libby had kept the book for herself and read through it too many times to count. It had gone with her to college, and then to the bookcase in her Austin apartment, and was now stored in one of the boxes that Amanda had shipped to her.

Why, she wondered, did it come to her mind today? Then the Miranda Lambert song "The House That Built Me" floated across her thoughts. Did she need to come back to this very house—the one that built her—to this very room in front of her to really find closure? Did she need to grab the fear by the horns like it was a charging Angus bull, look it right in the eyes, and throw it over the barbed wire fence?

"Maybe so," she muttered.

"Are you all right, honey?" a woman with blue hair asked her. "You look like you could faint at any moment."

"I'm fine." Libby's voice sounded as if it were coming up out of a deep well. "Just a little too warm."

"Too many folks coming in and out of this place for the AC to keep up," the woman said and patted her on the shoulder. "You should sit down for a minute. Want me to stay with you until you feel better?"

"No, ma'am, but thank you," Libby answered. "I'll just go into this room and sit on the bed for a little while. I'm sure it will pass soon."

"If it don't, you go straight to the drugstore and get you one of them pregnancy tests, honey," she whispered. "It ain't natural for a young woman like you to be so pale."

"I'll do that," Libby agreed, knowing full well that she could not be pregnant.

Determined to face her fear once and for all, she had every intention of going into the room, but her feet still felt like they were glued to the floor. The step on the stairway creaked when the woman and several other folks left the second floor, and then there was silence. She could see most of her old room from the door. The old bedstead was the same one she had slept on for two years, but from the look of the mattress, it had been replaced. The gooseneck lamp—something she had bought at a garage sale for two dollars—had been replaced with a Martha Washington.

Why didn't I do this when Victoria died? June and Jeanie offered to come with me, and the people at the bank said I could come get any personal belongings if a representative came with me.

If you really want closure, open the box! her grandmother shot back, her tone edgy.

"What does that stupid box have to do with anything?" Libby asked, then braced herself and entered the room. No ghosts floated above the bed. It was just a room, nothing more.

She set her purse on the floor, and Fancy immediately hopped out and began to explore. Libby plopped down on the edge of the bed and ran her hand over the chenille bedspread—white, with a rose pattern in the middle.

Fancy whined at her feet, and Libby picked the dog up. "Want to see a secret?" she asked, and carried her over to the closet. She squatted down and ran her finger over her initials, EVO, on the doorjamb. She had carved them there with a fingernail file the first time her grandmother had left her to stay alone in the creaky, old house.

"I felt so guilty after I did this that I couldn't look Victoria in the eye for a week." Libby grabbed her purse and slipped the dog back down inside it when she heard the creaking step again. "You, darlin' baby, have to stay cooped up until we get out to the truck," she whispered. "I've seen enough of this place, and I'm ready to get out of here."

She was at the top of the staircase when her foot slipped, and she thought for a minute she would tumble down the steps headfirst. But she went backward instead of forward and sat down with a heavy thud. Fancy jumped out of her purse and ran into Victoria's old bedroom. Libby stood up and dusted the seat of her jeans off with her hand. Evidently, fate or the universe or God wasn't ready for her to leave the house just yet.

When she finally caught her breath and hurried into her grandmother's old room, Fancy whined and poked her little nose out from under the purple satin bedspread. Poor thing was probably thanking her lucky stars that Libby hadn't fallen on her and squished her as flat as a skunk on the highway.

Libby sank down onto the floor beside the bed and coaxed the dog out. When Fancy was in her lap, she glanced around. No mysterious aura filled the room. Apparently, Victoria's spirit had gone back to hovering over a poker table at the casino down south, because she didn't have a thing to say even though Libby was in her bedroom, and that had been a big no-no when Libby was a child.

"My bedroom is my personal space, and other than cleaning day, you stay out of it," Victoria had told her when she was barely old enough to remember. She had accented each word by poking her finger right at Libby's nose.

Libby tried to shake the past from her head, but it didn't work. Her mind went right back to cleaning day, which had been Sunday back then. The antique store hadn't opened until after lunch. As soon as Victoria was up and on her second cup of coffee, Libby went into her room and put fresh sheets on the bed. The floor always looked like an explosion at a thrift store, with shoes, clothing, and even magazines strewn everywhere. But within thirty minutes, Libby had it cleaned up and the sheets in the washing machine.

Now the only thing on the floor was one little leaf that someone had tracked in from the pecan tree at the end of the porch. Victoria's perfume didn't linger in the room, but Libby could swear she caught a whiff of it when she glanced over at the top of the dresser. Did that mean Victoria's soul was still lingering around the house?

June had advised Libby to open the box. Was that what Victoria was waiting for? If so, her grandmother was probably pretty angry.

"I'll open the box and then toss everything in it in the trash. I'm trying to move on, not live in the past," Libby muttered as she stood up with Fancy in her arms. "But not today."

Benny had been at far too many antique auctions and sales to remember, but something about this one was different. Nothing excited him—but then, he had just found the mother lode of all mother lodes when he lucked into the garage sale that morning.

"This old place has history," a woman said at his elbow. "I know it as well as my own house. Anything in particular you are looking for? The previous owner was one of my friends—I'm June."

"Thanks for the help," he said. "How long did she run the B and B?"

"She didn't. She died about ten years ago, and the folks that ran the house as a B and B bought the place at the sale. But they weren't very business savvy. They didn't do a bit of remodeling, so it didn't go over well. Folks insist on having a bathroom for every bedroom these days. They bought it as it was—furniture, dishes, and all—and just set up shop the next week. My friend Victoria owned it before those people bought it." June heaved a sigh. "I bet she turned over in her grave at the idea of strangers staying in her home."

"Did you say Victoria?" Benny asked. "Did she own an antique store here in Jefferson?"

"That's the one." June sighed again. "She's been gone for years now, but walking through this house and seeing her granddaughter, Libby, again sure brings back a lot of good memories."

Benny had only been listening with half an ear, but suddenly he was ready to pay close attention to what the woman was saying. Good Lord! What had he done by bringing Libby to this place? And why hadn't she told him that this was where she grew up?

"Where was Libby?" he asked.

"Going up the steps when I was coming down. I expect she'll be going to her old bedroom. Do you know her?"

"Yes, I do," he answered.

June patted him on the arm. "She's a good person, though she has had to be independent her whole life. Just like her grandmother. Now, we were talking about this old house, weren't we?"

Benny was torn between going to make sure Libby was all right and finding out more about the house. His gaze traveled from June's bright smile to the stairs, where he saw Libby waiting for a horde of people to pass by so that she could make her way down to the foyer. She caught his eye and nodded toward the door leading outside.

"Victoria's grandparents built the house, and her parents were born here," June was saying when he tuned back in to her story. "As each generation passed on, they left the place to the next one. Victoria inherited it and the store when her mother died. By then she had lost her husband, and she had a small son, Quinton, to raise alone. Her folks had always loved antiques, so she started her own business in the old grocery store she had inherited."

"What happened to it when she passed away?" Benny figured he already knew the answer, but he wanted to hear it anyway, and Libby was now weaving her way toward him through the throng.

"She owed a lot of money, so it and the store were sold to pay off her debts," June answered. "Has anything caught your eye?"

"Not yet, but my associate is taking a look upstairs," he replied.

June waved at another group of people coming into the house. "I've taken up enough of your time. Nice visitin' with you."

"You too."

She disappeared into the crowd, and he met Libby halfway across the living room.

"I don't see anything down here worth taking back to Sawmill. Did you see anything up there?" he asked.

"Nope," she answered. "Are we ready to go home?"

He reached out to pet Fancy. "I am if you are. Why didn't you tell me this was the house where you grew up?"

"How did you find that out?" she asked.

"A lady named June seemed quite talkative about the history of this place," he answered and escorted her through the crowd with his hand on the small of her back.

"It's complicated. I haven't been here since my grandmother died," Libby said after a long sigh. "June and Jeanie, her two friends, drove over the border to Louisiana and scattered her ashes—but then, I told you that story."

Benny heard anxiety in her tone, and the expression on her face said she was fighting tears. "Let's get out of here and go get some ice cream."

"Thank you," she whispered. "That sounds good."

Chapter Fifteen

Libby was on the last leg of her early-morning run Tuesday morning when she heard the rumble of a vehicle rolling down the gravel road. Then the wind blew a fine mist of gray dust toward her. She stopped at the porch in time to see the tail end of the trailer in the distance. Benny had said the day before that he was heading to northern Oklahoma to check out two huge estate auctions and wouldn't be home until Thursday.

Back at the service station, she grabbed a bottle of water, let Fancy out of the apartment, and sat down in one of the chairs. "Your job is to guard the store and keep all the snakes, spiders, and mice at bay today while I work on the computer."

Fancy's tail wagged so fast that it was a blur.

"I'll take that as a promise to protect me," she said and then realized that she had slept through the night without nightmares.

"Hmm," she mused. "You must be my good luck charm. Maybe tonight we'll try to do without a night-light. Think we can handle such a big thing?"

Fancy sniffed the air and stared at the house across the street.

"It's bacon and coffee," Libby told her. "I'll introduce you to them later, when they pop into the shop. Just between me and you, I think they're checkin' up on me and reporting back to Benny. Not that I would throw blame at either of them. They don't really know me—yet."

Opal stepped out on the porch in a red-and-white-checked ging-ham robe over a pair of blue silk pajamas and waved. "You had breakfast yet? We've got leftovers we can bring over, if you don't mind us coming before we get dressed."

"No, I haven't, and come as you are," Libby yelled across the road.

"Be there in five minutes. Put on a pot of coffee, and we'll have a visit," Opal hollered and then went back into the house.

The coffeepot had just begun to gurgle when Opal and Minilee came inside the station and set a plate covered with plastic wrap on the table.

"Good Lord!" Libby gasped. "That's enough food for three meals."

"We figured you could use the leftover eggs and bacon to stuff inside the biscuits for your breakfast tomorrow. Now, sit down and eat before it all gets cold. We'll get the coffee when it's done. We want to know how the day went yesterday," Minilee said.

Opal pulled out a chair, sat down, and glanced down at Fancy. "Just tell us about it between bites."

"You aren't going to ask about the new dog?" Libby took the first bite of eggs.

"Tatum called and said you had gotten one," Opal answered. "You do know that dogs of any size can't come into my house, don't you?"

Fancy tucked her head down and went over to where Minilee was standing beside the cabinet.

"That was hateful," Minilee scolded. "But then, Tatum had to get her attitude somewhere."

"I'm just stating facts." Opal shook her finger at Minilee. "Tatum is my great-niece, and she comes before a dog."

Minilee reached down, picked Fancy up, and hugged her. "You can come to my house anytime you want. Tatum is just shirttail kin to me, and I already like you better than I do her."

"Minilee Stephens!" Opal gasped. "What has gotten into you?"

"I really thought that Tatum would be a good match for our Benny, but I've changed my mind. From the way she's acting, she's only interested in his money so she can be one of them social butterflies like the people on those reality shows I don't like. She would never be happy here in Sawmill or helping Benny in the store. And he wouldn't be happy anywhere else. They just ain't a match. She won't even call him *Benny!*" She put Fancy on the floor and poured three mugs full of coffee.

The tension jacked up so high that Libby felt it sucking the oxygen right out of the room, and she wondered if the two elderly ladies might start slinging fists. Fancy escaped through the open door into the apartment, and Libby wished she could follow her. As wonderful as the breakfast tasted, she would rather eat a toaster pastry than listen to Opal and Minilee stand off like a couple of banty roosters.

"Okay, okay. You're right, but it pains me to admit it," Opal finally said. "And the dog still can't come into my house."

Minilee brought the coffee to the table. "That's your right, but I like the little critter, and she can visit me anytime she pleases. I won't let Elvis in because he's too big, but . . ." Her focus went from Opal to Libby. "What's her name, anyway?"

"She was already named Fancy when I got her at the garage sale. An older lady had had her from the time she was a newborn puppy." Libby was glad the subject had gotten away from Tatum.

"Don't look at me like that, Minilee," Opal scolded. "I don't hate the dog. I just have to think of family first. Now, let's put all that aside and talk about something else."

"I agree," Minilee said with a nod. "We were at a church committee meeting for hiring a new preacher when y'all came in yesterday, so we want to hear all about the day."

"We found a great garage sale and bought out the whole place," Libby answered. "We picked out what we wanted for the store, and then the lady who was selling her aunt's things called a shelter to come get the rest of the merchandise to sell. But"—she paused and took a sip of coffee—"the only way that she would make a deal with us was if we took Fancy. She was going to send Fancy to the shelter if someone didn't adopt her that day. We got a trailer load of really good stuff."

"That was a good move, and now you've got a little critter to protect you," Minilee said.

"I think maybe you are right," Libby agreed. "I didn't have nightmares last night. I slept better than I have in years. I believe it's because Fancy protected me."

"That wee thing couldn't do anything but bark and maybe chew on someone's ankle." Opal giggled. "If she was a boy dog, she might take a whiz on their shoes."

Libby almost choked on a bite of bacon. "I can't believe you said that."

"Just speakin' the truth," Opal said, laughing harder.

"What about the estate sales? Did y'all come right back to Sawmill, or did you go ahead and hit them up?" Minilee asked.

"We went to one in Marshall and then drove back to Jefferson for another one. Didn't buy anything at either of them," Libby replied. "But . . ." She went on to tell them about the house where she had grown up.

"I thought I'd have some sense of closure if I ever faced off with that house again, but it didn't work so well," she admitted and blinked away a tear.

"How did you feel when you went back inside your old bedroom?" Minilee asked.

Libby finished off the last bite of the eggs and bit into a biscuit that had been slathered with butter. "*Strange* is the only word that comes close to describing the feeling. I could . . ." She paused.

Minilee leaned forward in her chair. "What happened there, other than you having to stay alone at night when you were only ten years old?"

"Nothing, other than a lot of fearful nights that I probably brought on myself by watching television shows that kids have no business seeing," she finally murmured. "The memories were even more vivid because I ran into June—one of my grandmother's old friends—in the house yesterday. Seeing her, even for a few minutes, and being in that house brought back a whole raft of feelings of abandonment and fear."

"Go on," Opal said.

"Did you ever confront Victoria about staying alone?" Minilee asked.

"Not ever. I was too afraid to even think about that. I did tell her about a dream I had one night that was so real that I thought some man had broken into the house. She was more concerned about whether he might have found her stash of cash than she was about my well-being or if it was even real. That taught me to not ever tell her about my night terrors again." Libby couldn't believe she had just bared her heart and soul to these two old gals, but she felt better than she had in years.

Opal got up from her chair, rounded the table, and hugged her. "I'm so sorry that you had to live in circumstances like that. A child should feel safe and protected."

"And loved," Minilee added. "Did you find a little bit of closure?"

Libby shook her head. "Not even when I went into Victoria's bedroom. I could swear that I got a whiff of her perfume when I was in there, but she's been gone too many years for that to even be possible."

"Most likely, someone walked through there wearing the same scent and left traces of it lingering in the room," Minilee said. "And, darlin', don't rush it. Sometimes it takes a lifetime to finally find closure. Before you can do that, you have to learn to trust your heart. The heart won't ever lead you wrong."

"Like in the book we are reading for our club meeting?" Libby asked.

"That's right. The lady in the book has had lots of past troubles with her own life and with the men she trusted, but she's working her way through it. If a fictional character can learn to trust people again, then you can, too," Opal told her.

"Thank you," Libby said, forcing a smile.

Minilee stood up, refilled their coffee mugs, and then sat back down. "Don't you worry about anyone breaking in here. Fancy might not be able to attack someone—but, honey, she can sure sound the warning bell, and you are a strong woman. Do you have a weapon? I've got a sawed-off shotgun I will loan you."

"I have pepper spray and a Taser," Libby told her, "but thank you for the offer."

"Me and Minilee learned to shoot when we were just married," Opal said. "There's snakes out in these parts, and some of them have two legs. I can knock the end out of a beer can at fifty yards, but Minilee is better than I am. And, honey, a bullet travels faster than pepper spray or a Taser."

"I always wanted to be a sniper in the army, but girls didn't get to do that back when me and Opal were young," Minilee said with a great deal of pride mixed with a touch of sadness.

"You ever shot a gun?" Opal asked.

Libby shook her head.

"Well, this evening, after you finish in the office, you come over to our house for supper. After we eat, we'll take our pistols out in the backyard and set up some targets. When you are comfortable shooting a handgun, we'll teach you how to load, shoot, and clean a sawed-off shotgun," Minilee said. "But for now, we should be getting back across the road to get dressed for work. And you need to do the same. Just remember, if anyone tries to break into this place, don't dial 911—just poke in my number. I'll get here faster than the police, and I'm a helluva lot meaner than they are. We'll take care of you, darlin' girl."

"Thank you, but—"

"No *maybe*s or *but*s." Opal frowned. "If you live out in the boonies, you got to know how to protect yourself. We'll see you at five for supper. Maybe we'll even see a snake or two, so we don't waste ammo."

"Yes, ma'am," Libby agreed, but she was already trying to think of excuses not to go. She hadn't even thought about getting a gun, and now she had a yappy little chihuahua to sound the warning if anyone was around.

Minilee took a step toward the door. "We'll let you get ready for work now. From what you said, you've got a lot of items to catalog in the computer today."

"We'll see you in a little while," Opal assured her. "I want to see all the new stuff, and it might need a thorough cleaning before folks look at it this weekend."

"Thank you for everything," Libby said. Opal and Minilee whirled in and out of the antique shop, seeming to have endless energy when it came to their gardening and cooking and the sweetness in their attitude toward her—it was all too much for Libby to take in, but she wanted to grow up and be just like them . . . and Dolly.

Minilee stopped, stooped down, and patted Fancy on the head. "You are very welcome. And, honey, scars like the ones on your heart and soul tell you where you have been, but they don't have to dictate where you are going. You have your whole life ahead of you. Shake off all those fears and enjoy the journey from here on out."

"I hope I can," Libby whispered as she walked the ladies to the front porch and watched them cross the road.

Libby had seen target practice on TV. Paper targets with a bull's-eye right in the middle. Putting a hole in that little thing was the ultimate goal. She was surprised to see a whole row of tin cans hanging on a clothesline with wooden pins, flapping in the wind like someone's underwear that had been put out to dry on wash day.

"I thought we'd be shooting at—" Libby said.

Minilee butted in. "Honey, if someone is coming at you, they ain't goin' to be standing still and waiting for you to take aim. They'll be in survival mode. You need to learn to shoot a moving target—and better yet, shoot six of them cans off the line before you stop to reload."

"It'll teach you to put some faith in yourself," Opal assured her with a pat on the back. "Until you do that, you won't ever have closure for any of those bad dreams. Now, lesson number one: make sure the first thing you do is take the safety off."

"And then you hold the gun like this, not like they do on those gangster shows you see on television. They're just showing off. When you have to use a gun for protection, you hold it with both hands," Minilee said. "I'll show you after we put our earplugs in. This can be noisy business."

Libby felt a little like the character from the movie she had watched with the kids at the women's shelter when she shoved the bright orange things in her ears. "I'm Shrek," she whispered.

"What was that?" Minilee already had the pistol aimed but dropped it to her side.

"Just talking to myself."

"Okay, then, here we go!" Minilee fired off three shots and knocked two of the cans off the line.

Opal wiped her hands on the tail of her faded apron and boom, boom, boom—two more cans hit the dirt. Then she handed the pistol to Libby.

Hold like this, Libby thought as she took the gun. *Aim and fire.*

Minilee raised her voice so Libby could hear her. "Don't be afraid of the gun. It's a tool to be used in time of need, like a hoe is used to chop off a snake's head. Never aim it at anyone unless you mean business, and don't be afraid to shoot if it's a matter of your own injury or death."

Libby's hands were shaking so badly that she lowered the weapon. "I'm not sure I can do this."

"Yes, you can," Opal encouraged her. "Remember when you were a kid and you used your forefinger and thumb like a gun? Think of it like that. Look down the barrel and fire!"

Libby raised the gun, pictured one of the cans as the faceless man in her dreams, and fired. She missed the target, but she set her mouth in a firm line, narrowed her eyes, and fired two more times. Two cans hit the ground and rattled against each other.

"Way to go, Libby!" Opal and Minilee threw up their hands to high-five her.

She dropped the pistol to her side and slapped both of their palms. "Beginner's luck."

"Nope," Minilee disagreed. "That was raw talent. It took me and Opal weeks to hit even one can."

"But just in case you are right," Opal declared, "I'm going to reload that pistol with six more bullets, and you are going to fire it two more times. If you hit four out of six cans, then we'll go inside, and I'll show you how to clean your firearm."

"Can you show me how to load it?" Libby asked.

"Yes, ma'am," Opal said with a nod. "Just push that little lever right there, and the side will pop out. Then you simply put six bullets in their spots and shove it back in place."

Libby was surprised that her hands were steady as a rock when she loaded the gun with more bullets, but even more so when she put a hole in five out of six cans.

"I'd say that she's a natural for sure," Minilee said as she pulled the orange plugs out of her ears.

Opal narrowed her eyes and cocked her head to one side. "Either that or she's been lying to us about never shooting before."

Libby handed the gun to Opal and removed her earplugs. "I'm not lying—but I have to admit, that was fun. I pictured the man in my dreams on each can. Now, can I learn how to clean that thing?"

"You sure can," Minilee said. "We'll pour up some sweet tea and have a visit about that man while we get these weapons ready to put back."

"All but the one you are holding. It goes home with you," Opal told her. "Remember—"

"To keep the safety on until I need it, right?" Libby said before she could finish.

"That's right," Opal said with a nod.

Chapter Sixteen

Libby glared at the box sitting across the one-room apartment, but it didn't melt into a pile of ashes. She planned to carry it over to a cubicle on the far wall and shove it in there until she was ready to deal with it, but instead, she carried it to the coffee table. She slipped her fingernail under a strip of brown packing tape, but she couldn't force herself to go any further. She sat down on the sofa and gave herself a stern talking to about not being such a wimp.

"If I can shoot all those moving targets, I can do this. Why is this so difficult?" she muttered.

Fancy jumped up on the sofa and cocked her head to one side, then leaned against Libby's leg.

"Thanks for the support—and to be honest, I only shot the pistol a total of nine times, but that was enough to show me that I wouldn't miss if I ever needed to use a gun." Her voice sounded nervous in her own ears.

You should have opened it years ago. Victoria's tone now was exactly the same as it had been in the evenings when June and Jeanie were late getting to the house to pick her up. If her grandmother had been addicted to drugs rather than gambling, she would have been pacing the floor, waiting for her dealers to bring her a fix.

"You don't know how many times I've almost thrown this whole box away, so get out of my head. I'll treat it like the Band-Aids that you ripped off my scrapes. Just grab it and yank," Libby said as she pulled the first strip of duct tape from the top.

She got the next length of tape started, but then her hands began to shake again. Did she really want to know what secrets were hiding inside? Did she even care? There was no doubt that it held mementos of the past—things that had inflicted pain on Libby. Minilee had said that the scars from the past didn't have to dictate her future. Would opening it cause her even more pain, or would it bring a modicum of closure?

Her phone rang, and it startled her so badly that she dropped the tape like it was a red-hot poker. She picked it up from the sofa's armrest, saw that the call was from Amanda, and hit the accept button.

"Hey, girl, how are things in Austin?" Libby asked.

"You sound out of breath," Amanda said. "Were you making out with that handsome boss of yours?"

"Lord no!" Libby gasped. "I'm making myself open *the box*!"

"What box? You mean that old one marked *For Libby* on the side?" Amanda asked. "Why didn't you open it before now? Hang up. I'll FaceTime you."

Libby ended the call, shot another dirty look at the thing, and wished she had left it behind in Austin with what she had tossed into the dumpster while she waited.

"You look like you're so mad, you could eat liver, and we both know you hate it. What's wrong?" Amanda asked when she appeared on Libby's screen.

"You remember how those last two years of college were for me? All those horrible calls and trips to the financial aid office? You picked up the phone more than once. I was—I *am*—angry with her for gambling away all my college money, my high school paychecks, and my father's insurance money on top of that." She stopped for a breath, then went on. "I either had to take out student loans or else quit and go to work. You know the rest."

"I know—but, girl, you should still have opened it years ago. We are best friends"—Amanda's finger was a blur as she shook it at Libby—"and I've told you my whole life story. You've cried with me more than once. You probably needed to go to therapy back then and likely could use a few sessions now. You are the strongest woman I know, but all of us need to talk things out with someone who isn't partial."

"Thank you, but I'm working through it, and the ladies across the street are helping me."

"So, what's in the box?" Amanda asked.

Libby closed her eyes so she wouldn't have to see the thing. "I haven't opened it, but I promise I will tell you all about it when I do. Now, let's talk about you."

"John's got most of his stuff moved in, and I can tell it's going to be an adjustment, but I'm so happy. And I've loved the homemade cards and notes you've sent. I can't wait to get to the mailbox every day to see if there's something there for me." Amanda's voice left no doubt that she was on cloud nine.

A small stab of jealousy shot through Libby, but she pushed it back so she could be excited for her friend. "I'm happy for you."

"This won't change our friendship. We might not talk every night like we've been doing, but we will make up for it at least once a week. You know how I hate watching sports, so on Sunday afternoons, while John has his friends over to see whatever games are on, we can have a girls' time out," Amanda promised.

"Yes, we will." Libby forced a smile. But something told her that in time, the phone calls or texts would get further and further apart, and she didn't mention that she would be working Sunday afternoons. Their lives had already started down different paths, and soon they would have little to talk about when they reconnected.

"Okay, then, call me when you get up the courage to see what your grandmother left for you," Amanda said. "Hugs to you from me."

"Hugs back at you," Libby said and ended the call.

A strip of tape dangled off the side of the box, but Libby didn't jump right up and finish the job she had started before she was interrupted by Amanda's call. Maybe the phone ringing at the exact time it did was an omen that she should forget about the contents, carry the whole thing out to the burning barrel behind Opal's house, and set it on fire.

Victoria's voice tormented her. *You've never been one to take risks. I'm surprised you even went for the interview in Sawmill. Open the damn box so I can rest in peace.*

"So, this is more about you than it is about me?" Libby muttered. "Why would that surprise me?"

She waited for a full minute, but Victoria didn't have anything more to say. She waited for a little longer, until Fancy awoke and jumped off her lap. Her little toenails made clicking sounds as she walked across the floor toward her food bowl. The noise reminded Libby of her grandmother's long, bright red fingernails hitting the keyboard as she entered data into the computer. It seemed like the only way Victoria would ever allow Libby to have peace of mind was for her to look in the box.

She leaned forward, grabbed the loose end of the tape, and gave it a hard tug. The top layer of paper came off with it, leaving a long white stripe on the dingy cardboard. She didn't give herself time to think about it—she threw the lid off with such force that it scooted across the floor. Fancy whipped around and growled when it came to rest beside her water bowl.

"Sorry about that," Libby said and peeked into the box.

No eerie music played in her head. All in all, it was more than a little bit anticlimactic.

The first item she pulled out was a little pink cotton gown that had tiny buttons down the front. She recognized her grandmother's flowery handwriting in the note attached with a safety pin. *This is the outfit you wore home from the hospital when you were born.*

How did you feel about that? Libby wondered. *Were you excited to have a new granddaughter? And how did my father react to being a dad at such a young age? Did he think his life was over?*

The next item was a pink blanket, and it also had a note: *June crocheted this, and we used it to wrap you in when we brought you home.*

She laid both aside and went through more items: her school report cards, a small box with her first tooth and a tiny baby ring, pictures of her and her father on the front porch of the house and one of Libby waving goodbye to him. She studied that photograph for several minutes.

Quinton was on the edge of it, and the expression on his face seemed to her to be one of relief. He had done his duty and come back to Jefferson for a holiday—most likely in the spring since the fancy little dress Libby was wearing looked like something Victoria would have bought her for Easter—and now he could escape back to the life he really liked.

"That was just months before he died. I wasn't even three years old, and he was leaving for his final year." She held the picture up to see it better. "I look nothing like him. He had blondish-red hair and brown eyes. I must have taken more after my mother."

She dug through what was left and found a couple of faded awards she had won in spelling bees, copies of her birth certificate, and her social security card. Her whole life up until she was eighteen was right there.

"But my future doesn't have to be so small," she muttered.

The last thing she picked up was an envelope with her name on the front: *To Elizabeth Victoria.* Why hadn't her grandmother used her last name as well? When she had been upset with Libby, she always raised her voice and yelled, "Elizabeth Victoria O'Dell!"

Libby ripped open the envelope and expected to pull out a sheaf of coloring pages she had done as a child, but she found a letter instead. She leaned back on the sofa and read:

> Dear Libby,
> If you are reading this, June will have given you these things, and I am dead. There are things you need to know, but I didn't want to tell you or even admit them. However, you are an adult now, and it's time you knew the truth. I'll go back to when I married Vance. Neither of us knew he had inherited a heart condition from his father. Everyone just thought that his dad died of a heart attack at a young age, but the knowledge and treatment of something called familial dilated cardiomyopathy changed a lot in the next few years. Too bad it didn't change fast enough for my

Vance. He died at age thirty, leaving me with Quinton
to raise by myself. I never forgave him for that.

Libby laid the letter aside for a few minutes before she picked it up again.

Quinton was ten that year, and immediately after
Vance's funeral, I took him to the doctor to see if he
had the condition, and he did. But there was medicine
and ways to treat the disease, so I wasn't too worried
about it after that. Then he went to college, stopped
taking his medicine, started smoking and drinking and
gained weight—all things that he shouldn't have done.
The crazy thing is that it was a car wreck that killed
him, not his heart condition. He and his best friend
from right here in Jefferson had been out drinking, and
Daniel lost control of the vehicle he was driving. They
were both dead by the time the police got to the scene.

It's unusual for a young child to show evidence of
that inherited heart condition, but I had you checked out
by experts and was assured that your heart was just fine.

Libby heaved a sigh of relief and kept reading.

That sounded some warning bells in my head that
I couldn't get past, so I got a DNA kit, took some hair
from Quinton's brush, and swabbed your cheek. A
couple of months later, I found out that you were not
his child. Both your parents were dead, and I was left
again with a kid to raise. This time, it wasn't even my
own blood. I was so angry that I had already spent
almost three years raising a granddaughter that I didn't
want, and that Quinton was supposed to take responsibility for when he finished school and had a good

job. You had upset my whole way of life, and I didn't
feel like I could do a damn thing about it. If I sent you
to an orphanage or gave you up for adoption, I would
be looked down on by the whole town, and certainly
June and Jeanie. Facing Vance's death would be easier
by far than losing my best friends.

Tears began to flow down Libby's cheeks and drip onto her shirt. No
wonder she had felt like a soul with no home all these years, and now
she could understand why Victoria wouldn't let her call her *Grandma* or
any other form of endearment. Libby wondered who her father was and
whether she could find him if she tried. She swiped the tears away, laid
the first page of the letter to the side, and went on to read the second one.

So I made the best of a bad situation. I gave you a
home, a roof over your head, and food, but I couldn't
make myself love you. Every time I looked at you, I
felt betrayed. Did Quinton know that you weren't his
and he lied to me? I asked myself that for a couple of
years, but the dead do not answer questions. Then, as
you grew older and taller, and your hair turned darker
and darker, I realized exactly who you belonged to—
his best friend, Daniel Griffin, and the boy was as dead
as my son and the girl who died giving birth to you.

"My biological name is Griffin!" Libby slapped a hand over her
mouth. Her eyes went back to the name on the letter: *Griffin*. She
frowned, but she couldn't remember anyone with that last name in
Jefferson—at least, no one that she knew.

I imagine that you are in shock by now and wondering about your biological family. Close that door
and look no further. Daniel was a foster child.

Libby wiped away tears flowing down her cheeks again. In essence, she had two families, and yet had none. One tear dropped onto the letter and left a smudge. She didn't even try to dry it, just kept reading.

But to be absolutely sure, I had your DNA run against a toothbrush that he always kept at our house. I was right. The test came back 99.9 percent positive. The only thing I can imagine is that your mother had no idea which boy you belonged to, and she named Quinton because he had a better homelife than Daniel did. Whatever the reason, I was stuck with the job of raising you, and I was not happy about it. I apologize for all the times when I left you alone. I hope that you will forgive me and find some form of closure in understanding my reasons for everything. Like why I used your money to gamble. You didn't belong to me, so the money shouldn't be yours anyway. I wish you all the best, though, Libby. I have to admit, I wish Quinton hadn't insisted on naming you after me and your maternal grandmother, whose name was also Elizabeth. Your mother's name was the same, but she went by Liza.

When you take risks, you *learn* that there will be times when you succeed and there will be times when you fail, and both are equally important, so don't be afraid to dive into the deep water. That's the best advice I can give you.

Maybe we'll meet again on the other side.

Victoria

Libby read through the whole letter two more times before she folded it carefully and laid it on top of the pink baby blanket. She felt as if she were in a vacuum where everything was gray and there were no emotions at all except an abundance of tears she couldn't control. Sobs came so fast and furious that she couldn't breathe. Then anger set in, and she picked up a throw pillow and slammed her fist into it, again and again, until she was exhausted.

So many emotions flooded through her that she couldn't control them. Her thoughts were a jumbled mess, jumping from wondering about her biological parents to whether she should change her name. She didn't even realize she was pacing from the sofa to the bed, to the front room, and back again until she had made the loop half a dozen times. Finally, she saw that she'd left a mess on the coffee table and stopped to put everything back into the box.

She tossed in the letter first and then noticed another piece of paper lying at the bottom. She picked it up and turned it over to see a picture of her father—no, that wasn't right . . . a picture of Quinton—with a young man and a pretty young lady with him. On the back, in faded pencil writing, were the words *Quinton, Daniel, and Liza on the way to the Christmas formal.* She hurriedly flipped it back over and studied it carefully. Daniel was several inches taller than Quinton, and he had dark hair and blue eyes. Liza was a short girl with black hair and clear blue eyes. Quinton's eyes were so dark that they were practically black.

Libby had gotten her hair color from both her biological parents and her eyes from her mother. She focused on the picture until her eyes went all blurry. She blinked several times and held it up to the light to stare at it some more. All three looked happy. So what had happened to make Liza sleep with both boys? Had she and Quinton had an argument? Had things gotten out of hand when she talked to Daniel about it?

There didn't seem to be any answers to the questions, until another quote she'd read once—maybe in the same book Eleanor Roosevelt's quotation had been in—came to her mind.

"'If you stare into the abyss long enough, it will stare back at you,'" she whispered. "Or something like that."

The phone startled her for the second time that evening. Expecting it to be Amanda, she picked it up without looking at the number. "I opened the box, but I'm not ready to talk about it."

"What box and why?" Benny asked.

"Nothing," she said quickly. "I thought you were my friend Amanda calling back."

"Okay, I'm turning onto the gravel road with a small load," Benny said. "Will you meet me at the store and help me empty the trailer? It won't take but an hour at the most."

Like she had done her whole life, she crammed all her feelings into an imaginary box and tucked them away deep inside her mind. "Sure, but I thought you were out until tomorrow evening."

"So did I, but I think I'm coming down with a cold, so don't give me a big welcome kiss," he teased.

"Only in your dreams." She couldn't believe that she could joke after what she had just read. "Shall I bring Fancy to the store and introduce her to Elvis?"

"Might as well," he answered. "Here's hoping they don't try to kill each other."

"My money is on Fancy if they do."

"Here's hoping it doesn't come to that," Benny said. "I'm passing the station now. I'll have the door open when you get there."

Libby shoved the letter in her hip pocket, along with her phone. She planned to file it away in one of the organized drawers. Tomorrow she would shred it and put the whole thing out of her mind.

"You want to go meet Elvis?" she asked Fancy. "Don't let him intimidate you. He's huge compared to you, but he's just a big teddy bear." She snapped a leash onto Fancy's collar, and the dog jumped off the sofa and pranced across the floor.

Stars had begun to show up around an almost-full moon hanging in the sky, and a soft breeze coming from the west blew her hair away from her face. She half expected Victoria to sneak into her thoughts with some caustic remarks, but apparently, the woman she had thought was her grandmother was finally resting in peace.

Chapter Seventeen

"Good grief!" Libby exclaimed when she saw Benny. His face was flushed and his eyes glassy. She rushed over and laid her hand on his forehead and found it hot and dry. "You've got more than a little cold, feller. You could have the flu. All this stuff can wait until morning. You need to take some medicine and go to bed."

"I won't argue."

In all the emotional upheaval that was going on when he called, she hadn't realized how hoarse his voice was. "You sound horrible. You need hot lemon tea, a couple of pills to bring that fever down, and maybe some chicken broth."

"I haven't got—"

She butted in before he could finish. "If you're about to say that you don't have any of those things, then rest assured. I've got everything we need at the station, so you can come home with me."

"Would you look at that?" Benny tried to smile, but it came out more like a grimace.

She glanced over her shoulder to see Elvis lying down in front of the break table and Fancy licking his face. Right then, she was far more concerned with Benny than seeing the two animals getting along. "That's great. You stay right here, and I'll jog back to the station and get my vehicle."

"I just drove for five hours," he said. "I think I can walk that far."

"Don't try to convince me you are all macho," she fussed. "You look like you are about to drop. I'm going to get my SUV."

"I need to stretch my legs—and besides, we can be there before you would drive back to pick me up," he argued and headed for the door with Elvis and Fancy right behind him.

"If you fall, I'll leave you in the gravel," she threatened.

"Elvis will drag me home by the shirt collar," he shot back at her.

"If that happens, I'll have the hot tea ready when he gets you there." She forgot all about the letter in her hip pocket and handed him Fancy's leash. "See you there."

She jogged all the way to the station and put the teakettle on the stove. She wondered how she could be so lighthearted when she'd just found out that her family—such as it was—wasn't even related to her.

"The truth will set you free. I think that's in the Bible," she said as she cut up a lemon. She dropped a few slices in a huge mug and added a little bit of grated ginger and a tablespoon of honey. The kettle had just put out the first whistle when she heard the door open. "Come on in and sit down," she yelled. "Elvis is welcome if he wants to come in."

Benny had already sunk down onto the sofa when she turned around. "Elvis is tired of being cooped up. He's out exploring. Fancy flopped down on the cool tile under the table, and I looped her leash around a chair leg. I almost joined her."

"Why didn't you stop at a hotel and call me?" She poured hot water into the mug and covered it with a saucer. "I would have come up to wherever you were and taken care of you."

"You'd do that for me after we've only known each other a few weeks?" he asked.

She ladled out the soup into an oversize mug and put a spoon in it. "You are my boss and my friend—and yes, I would."

"Thank you," he muttered. "Whatever you are making smells good."

"What I make from scratch is better, but this will do for tonight. Crackers or not?"

"Just the soup," Benny answered. "I'm too tired to chew. I haven't been this sick since I was in college."

"Me either, but then I don't work three twelve-hour days and then drive all over the country the other four," she fussed. "Your body is telling you to slow down and take a day off every so often." She took his soup to the sofa, swept all the items that were scattered on the coffee table right back into the box. "You can eat right here, and when you finish, I'll get you a pillow and a thin sheet."

"Why not a blanket?"

She handed the mug to him and went back to make the tea. "Because we need to break that fever, not make you hotter."

"So, you think I'm hot?"

Libby almost choked on a suppressed giggle. She strained the tea into a cup, took a bottle of pain pills from the cabinet, and carried both across the room. She set them on the coffee table; then she dragged a kitchen chair over and sat down across from him. "I don't *think*, Benny Taylor. I *know* you are hot. Didn't I feel your forehead in the store? You probably have a temp of over a hundred."

"Are you afraid to sit beside me?" he asked as he ate the noodles out of the soup.

"Nope, but when you get through eating, you are going to stretch out on that sofa and go to sleep," she replied.

He raised both eyebrows over his bleary eyes. "I'm going home to my trailer and my bed when I get done."

She shook her forefinger at him. "You are going to stay right here until that fever breaks, or I will call an ambulance and have them take you to the hospital."

"Why are you doing this?"

"You are my boss. I like my job, thank you very much. If you die, I won't have a boss *or* a job, so I intend to get you well. Tomorrow, you will rest." She pointed at the bottle of pills. "Take two of those. They are generic, but they work as well as the name brand."

"I trust you not to poison me," he said after a long sigh and shook a couple of pills out into his hand.

Fancy yipped, and Libby hurried out to the porch to bring her inside. "So, you've had enough exercise for the night, have you?" she asked the dog when they were in the apartment and she had removed the leash. The dog went to her water bowl for a long drink; then she hopped up on the sofa with Benny.

"See there?" Libby said. "She's going to keep you company tonight, and I will be right across the room."

Benny pointed to the box sitting on the floor. "Were you unpacking when I called?" He finished off the soup and swallowed the pills with a sip of the tea.

"Yes, I was." She fought against the feelings that were slowly creeping back out of the imaginary box she had put them in.

"Opal called and said y'all did some target practice last night," Benny said.

"We did, and I slept all night without nightmares or a light," she said. "But right now, you need to stretch out and rest."

"That box looks really old. Is that a baby blanket? Was that yours?" he asked. "I'm sorry. None of that is my business."

"Those are just some keepsakes from my life—and yes, it was mine," she answered.

"Fair enough. And again, I shouldn't have pried. This is good tea. Where do you get it?"

"I make it from scratch from lemons, fresh ginger, and local honey if I can find it. You need to rest, so . . ." She stood up and went over to the bed, picked up a pillow, and tossed it over to him to distract him from any more conversation about that box. Then she got a clean sheet from a cubicle, shook it out, and covered him with it when he had stretched out. "Sweet dreams."

"You are bossy," he muttered as his eyes fluttered shut.

"Yep, I am," she whispered. *I guess I do have a little Victoria in me!* she thought.

He was asleep before she finished refilling Fancy's water bowl. She tiptoed across the room, just like she always did when Victoria had a headache—that's what she'd called a hangover when Libby lived at home. Fancy looked up but didn't stir from her spot at Benny's feet when Libby slipped out the door and through the front room with food and water for Elvis in her hands. The dog's tail beat out a rhythm on the wooden porch when Libby opened the door.

"It's not what you are used to eating for supper, but it's what I've got. Fancy seems to like it." She sat down in a chair and thought about what she had read earlier. The words seemed to be burned on her brain as if they had been branded there. She pulled the letter and her phone from her pocket and started to call Amanda, but then she changed her mind and laid them both on the table.

She tried to control the tears and force herself not to think about the words in the letter, but it didn't work. They flooded down her cheeks and left spots on her shirt as they dripped off her chin. She didn't even try to wipe them away, just let them flow freely. If her mother had acknowledged Daniel as the father of her unborn child, and the two of them had made a home and a family, Libby wondered how her life would have turned out.

You are looking into the abyss, a voice she didn't recognize whispered softly. *The past is gone. It made you who you are, but it doesn't determine who you will be.*

"I know that, but it doesn't help with the pain right now," Libby whispered back.

Benny awoke to the smell of coffee filling the small apartment. His fever had broken sometime in the night, and now his shirt was stuck to him from all the sweating. He had stayed in lots of hotel rooms, so it wasn't unusual for him to be disoriented for the first few seconds after he opened his eyes—or to get a faint whiff of coffee since, when possible, he chose places that offered free breakfast. But he couldn't ever remember a woman being in the room with him. He rubbed his eyes and focused on the lady, who was humming as she cooked. She wore jogging shorts and a gray tank top, and her dark hair was held up with a big clasp on top of her head.

What had happened the night before shot through his mind. "Libby!"

She turned around and flashed a brilliant smile. "Good morning. Are you ready for breakfast and a run?"

"Maybe breakfast." He sat up, and the room took a couple of spins in slow motion. "If you want a jogging partner, you better talk to Elvis or Fancy."

"Think you can make it to the table, or do you want me to bring it to you?" she asked.

"I can walk," he declared, but when he stood up, he wasn't as sure about it. "I haven't felt this wobbly in years. The last time that it happened, alcohol was involved."

Libby carried a plate of biscuits to the table. "Been there. Done that. Got the memories to keep me from doing it again."

He made it across the room and sat down. "So, do you make breakfast for all the men who spend the night with you?"

"Only the ones who let Fancy sleep on the sofa with them," she answered as she sat down across from him. "Help yourself. Food might help that weak feeling."

"I said *wobbly*, not *weak*." He slipped three fried eggs onto his plate.

She smiled again. "The sickness didn't kill your machismo."

He ignored the comment and added bacon, biscuits, and hash browns to his plate. "Thank you for taking care of me and for cooking."

"You are welcome," she said. "What's on your agenda for today?"

"When I finish eating, I'm going to my trailer and taking a long shower; then I plan to unload the trailer, and . . ."

She shot a look across the table that was so hot, it would have made a weaker man crawl under his chair and whimper.

"What was that all about?" he asked.

"You should rest," she said.

"I don't know how," he admitted. "I worked eighty hours a week when I was a lawyer, and even though it's a different job, I've kept up the pace since I took over the store."

"Then I will teach you. After you finish breakfast, you can go to your trailer and get cleaned up. Then we're going to the river for the day. I'll pack a picnic and take the book I need to finish for the book club next week. If you don't have something to read, I'll grab a few from the shelves out in the front. You can choose whichever one you want. Your body needs to unwind."

"And if I don't?"

"Then you are on your own. I feel like I need a day of downtime, so I'm taking it," she replied. "No phones go with us, either."

He polished off the food on his plate and slathered butter on a second biscuit. "What if I'm too old to learn new tricks?"

She raised one shoulder in half a shrug. "Never know until you try."

Was that a dare? Did she expect him to back down?

"I'll be ready in thirty minutes," he agreed as he pushed back his chair and headed toward the door with the biscuit in his hands. "What if—"

"If you are worried about Opal and Minilee, you can let them know what we will be doing so they don't panic when they see our vehicles at home and can't reach us," she suggested.

He agreed with a nod and planned to call one of them after he had taken a shower. But then he noticed that they were both in the garden, so he walked across the street. Elvis followed him, stopped at the edge of the yard, and flopped down under the shade tree.

Opal straightened up from a bent position and touched Minilee on the shoulder. "We're picking green beans. Want to help us?"

"Not this morning." He covered the last few feet, and even that little distance made him realize how much energy the fever had taken from him. He told them about getting sick and how Libby had insisted he needed a day of rest.

Minilee wiped sweat from her brow with the tail of a faded apron. "That's one smart lady. We've been trying to get you to slow down for a long time. Your body can't hold up forever, the way you abuse it. You kids have a good time."

Kids!

Benny chuckled under his breath at the idea of being called that when he was looking thirty-two right in the eyes. "I'll try, but I'm not used to doing nothing."

"A little nothing always helps clear the mind and soothe the soul," Opal said and went back to picking beans.

Chapter Eighteen

On the weekends and even some evenings after work when she was in Austin, Libby often took a book to the park near her apartment and spent a few hours with her back propped against a live oak tree. After the emotional roller coaster she had been on the night before, she needed a day of rest as much as—or maybe even more than—Benny did. They had both been sick. His illness had been physical, so a day of rest in the fresh air and sunshine would help heal him. Hers might never fully heal because it was mental, but escaping in a good book might help with the symptoms.

Talk to someone. Benny. Opal and Minilee. You need to get this out of you, or it will eat you alive. The voices were back, but thankfully, this one didn't belong to Victoria. Libby didn't want to talk to her again for a long time, if ever.

"Not today. I need to get away from everything today." Libby packed a tote bag full of sandwiches and snacks.

She finished that job and crammed a quilt and a small throw pillow into another bag, along with three books. She stared at the letter lying on the cabinet for several seconds before she finally picked it up and stuck it between the pages of the book she planned to read. Maybe she would look at it once again before she took it to work with her and shredded it.

Fancy danced around her feet the whole time she was putting things together.

"Yes, you can go with us," Libby said, "but only if you promise me you won't get in the water, and if you won't follow Elvis off on one of his adventures. A hawk could carry you off as quickly as he could a rabbit."

She snapped a leash to Fancy's collar and picked up a tote bag in each hand. The little dog yipped once, jumped up and down several times like a windup toy, and stretched the leash out to the end when she ran to the door.

"Silly girl. If you trip me, neither of us will be going anywhere," Libby said with a giggle.

The sky was that lovely shade of summer blue, and there wasn't a single cloud anywhere in sight when she and Fancy met Benny coming out of his trailer. Sunrays glistened in the water droplets still hanging on to his hair. A nice little breeze sent the scent of his shaving lotion over to her and stirred up feelings she hadn't had in a long time.

"I'll carry one of those bags for you," he offered.

She handed him the lighter one, and together they headed down the path toward the river.

"I have to warn you that I may die of boredom before we ever get to have a picnic lunch. I can't remember the last time I had a whole morning to do nothing. If I wasn't out looking for merchandise, then I was spending my time trying to bring some order to the office—which, as you know, I failed miserably at. By the way, thank you again for taking care of me. I'm at ninety percent this morning. Still a little fatigued but feeling much better. I'll be ready to unload the trailer after we have our picnic."

"We'll see about that when we've made it to the river," she told him.

"Yes, we will," he declared in a determined tone, then changed the subject. "Look at Elvis hanging back to protect Fancy. Did I tell you that my friend also had a Jack Russell terrier when he got Elvis? The two dogs were great friends until Rusty died about a month before my friend's accident."

"Nope, you never mentioned it. I guess there's a lot we haven't discussed." Libby shifted the bag over to her other shoulder so she could keep a better grip on Fancy's leash.

"We've got lots of time," he said, huffing with effort.

Libby slowed her pace a little, and then a little more a couple of minutes later. "Almost six months, anyway."

"Yep, and then we'll write up a new contract that has no end date."

Benny's breath was coming even harder now, and Libby deliberately slowed down more. The muddy, swampy scent of the river had replaced the sexy smell of his shaving lotion, so she knew they were nearing the water. They rounded one more curve, and she went straight for a willow tree growing back against a bank that had been carved out by time and lots of floods. She took the tote bag from Benny and spread the quilt out under its shade, laid the pillow at the top edge, and sat down.

Benny joined her, removed his sandals, and set them off to one side. "So, this is the spot?"

"Yes, it is," Libby answered. "You can't tell me that you've never been down here before. You run the path every morning that you are home."

"I've been down here, but not to this exact spot. I usually only run to the end of the path; then I turn around and go back home. That gets my three miles. Grandpa enjoyed fishing when I was a kid, but he didn't have much time for it later in life. I came with him a couple of times, but I was way too hyper to sit still—and still am," Benny said. "What do we do now? Watch the river flow or the sun make its way to the top of the sky?"

Libby handed him two books. "We read until noon. Choose one, and either lean on one of the trees or lay back on a pillow. You'll be surprised what a whole day away from your normal duties will do for your body and soul when you get lost in a story."

"Are you sure you weren't studying to be a therapist?" He looked over both books and set one aside.

"Not me," she replied. "I can't even analyze my own problems."

"What's this?" He pulled the letter from the book in his hands. "Please don't tell me it's your two-week notice."

She plucked the letter from his hand. "I gave you the wrong book. That's the one I need to finish for the club meeting on Monday. This is your other choice." She offered him the third book she had brought.

"Do you want the pillow?"

"No, that's for you. I intend to use the trunk of the tree for a back rest. I used to go to the park near my apartment on Sunday afternoons and take a good book with me."

"What did you do on Saturdays?" he asked.

"I volunteered to watch kids at a local women's shelter," she answered as she scooted back on the blanket and opened up to the last page she'd read. She reached the end of the chapter and realized that if she were to take a test on what she'd been reading, she would fail miserably. The words had gone through her mind, but her thoughts were on that letter at her side.

"Okay, I need to talk," she said.

Benny put his book aside and sat up. "What about?"

She picked up the letter and tossed it over in his lap. "That thing."

He glanced down at it. "What is it?"

"Read the letter, and then we'll talk," she snapped, and she caught the edge in her voice. "Wait . . . Benny, I'm sorry I came off like that. I don't want to *tell* you what's written in that thing. I want you to read it and tell me how it would affect you if your name was on the outside instead of mine."

Benny held it for a few seconds. "Are you sure about this? Seems to me like whatever is in this has caused you a lot of pain."

"A lot of pain, and even more anger and enough tears to flood this river, and I need a friend to talk to about it," she answered. "I'm not asking for sympathy, just for your opinion. Victoria left it for me, and I've had the box it was in since she died. But I only got up enough courage to unpack it last night. I found that letter among some keepsakes from my childhood and a couple of photographs of my parents."

"If you are sure . . ." He pulled the letter out of the envelope and read through both pages, then flipped back to the front page and read it again. Then he folded it, put it back into the envelope, and handed it to her. His brow furrowed and his mouth set in a firm line. "You have every right to be angry and feel betrayed. I'm surprised that you are as calm as you are. Do you think you'll ever trust anyone again?"

"I don't know about trust, but you hit the nail on the head when you said *betrayed* and *angry*. And yet I feel sorry for Victoria for being saddled with a child that wasn't even hers. Does that make sense to you?" Tears filled her eyes, but she refused to let them fall. She had cried enough for a lifetime.

Benny slid across the quilt, wrapped his arms around her, and drew her to his side. "I can see tears about to run down your cheeks. Grandpa used to say that tears on the outside wash the pain away, but tears on the inside stick to the soul and stay. So go ahead and cry. Get it all out."

"I've cried enough. I'm a big girl. I'm strong and independent; I can be grateful to Victoria for teaching me that much. Thank you for understanding." Libby couldn't remember a time when anyone had held her like Benny was doing. Unlike a couple of previous relationships, when the guy holding her had wanted something in return, Benny was simply being a friend. A good friend.

She finally moved away from him and said, "How do I live with this, Benny? I don't know who I am."

"Are you the same person you were before you read it?" he asked.

"I guess so—except for bouts of anger, usually followed by tears," she replied.

"Those are normal. It doesn't matter who your parents were or who raised you. You've learned from your past how not to be, and you moved away from all that years ago. I'm here if you ever need to vent. After all, we're more than just friends. You took care of me when I was physically ill. I'll take care of you when your heart and soul hurt."

She managed a weak smile. "You are getting the short end of the stick."

"No, I'm not," he disagreed. "This is just a bump in the road on the journey of life. Someday, you'll look back on it and . . ." He frowned. "Do you remember that old song about broken roads?"

"Yes, I do."

"Well, someday you'll bless the broken road that led you to Sawmill, where you found friends that love and appreciate you."

"I hope so," she whispered.

Benny opened his eyes to bright sunlight and wondered how he had slept so long. A small dog, not two inches from his nose, stared at him without blinking. The pillows must have gotten shifted, because they were shoved up against his back. And were . . . solid? He jerked himself fully awake and sat straight up.

The dog yipped, and Elvis came running. Benny rubbed his eyes and realized where he was. He wasn't in a hotel. The little dog was Fancy, and those had not been pillows against his back—that was Libby.

"Mmmm," Libby murmured as she stretched out her long body, flipped over to face him, and smiled. "Did you have a good nap?"

"Yes, I did," he answered. "Are you going to tell Opal and Minilee that we slept together?"

"What happens at the river, stays at the river," she said and then sat up, pulled her knees up under her chin, and wrapped her arms around them. "Are you hungry?"

"Starving," he replied with a nod.

She looked up at the sky. "Me too. It's past time for lunch. The sun has already gone past straight up and is starting to sink toward the west."

Benny reached for his phone, then remembered it was back at the trailer. "So, we are going to determine time by the sun?"

Libby pulled hero sandwiches wrapped in cellophane, a bag of chips, a container of guacamole dip, and two bottles of sweet tea from her tote bag. "We've got homemade cookies for dessert."

"It all looks great."

"If you don't like any of the vegetables on the sandwich, just toss them into the river for the fish." She brought out a baggie full of dog food for Fancy and one for Elvis. "I thought they might be hungry, too. I've seen them lapping up water from the river, so they'll be fine with that."

He picked up a sandwich, unwrapped it, and waited until she had dumped the dog food into a couple of disposable bowls before he handed it to her.

"Thank you," she said and bit into it before she opened the bag of chips. "Being near water always makes me hungry."

"What else is in the bag?" he asked.

"Supper," she answered between bites.

"We're staying all day?"

He had read a couple of chapters in the book before his long nap. His energy was restored, and he seemed to be over whatever twenty-four-hour bug had gotten hold of him the day before. He was ready to unload the trailer and get ready for business as usual the next morning.

"Of course we are. After we eat, we'll take the dogs for a nice long walk down the riverbank and come back here to talk about what we've read and then read some more until suppertime," she answered.

"How do you know when it's time to eat again?"

"Here's our afternoon agenda." She pointed to the west. "When the sun begins to dip down below those trees, we'll have supper, and then we'll gather up all our stuff and head home. Do you think you can handle that much time unplugged from the world?"

"I'll give it my best shot," he said, "but know that I wouldn't do this for anyone else. Not even Opal and Minilee."

"Well, now." She smiled. "That makes me feel special."

"You are," he said. "You're my friend."

"Yes, I am, and I appreciate your friendship."

"So, after our walk, we come back here and read some more?" he asked.

"We do." She nudged him on the shoulder. "Are you liking the book?"

"I am," he said. "I can't remember the last time I read a book for pleasure. I'm escaping into another world."

"What has been your favorite line so far?"

"There's this old fellow in it that reminds me of my grandfather. In one place, he's arguing with his grandson and says . . ." He paused, trying to remember word for word but couldn't. "'Forgive, forget, learn the lesson, and move on.' As I read that part, I added another line: 'With no regrets.'"

"Good words but hard to do." She brought out a container of cookies and opened it.

He recognized the crisscross pattern on the top of each one. "Minilee makes peanut butter for me on my birthday. They're my all-time favorite. What's yours?"

"Probably sand tarts. June used to bring some to me at Christmas," she answered. "The book I'm reading is set over the holidays. I can almost smell the cookies that the author talks about. There's a line in it that I really like. It went something like this: 'A heart that is hurt is like a broken bone. It takes time and a lot of tender loving care to make it whole again. If you don't apply those two things the way you would a cast or medication, then it never heals properly.' It made a lot of sense to me. I never thought of a heart being like that, or that it would need just as much help to get well as a broken bone."

"Me neither." Benny laid a hand on hers.

Chapter Nineteen

*L*ibby unlocked the door, turned on lights and ceiling fans, and went straight to the office to begin another day of sorting through files. Her goal that week was to have the place in spick-and-span order by the time Benny came home with another load of merchandise. Then it would take only a day at the most to catch up on each week's work.

As usual, Fancy sniffed every nook and cranny of the office, then flopped down on her fluffy blanket under the desk for her morning nap. Libby's thoughts went to the book that the club members would be discussing that evening. She had made her pecan pie that morning, and it was cooling on the kitchen table. Since her recipe had called for two tablespoons of bourbon, she hoped that none of the ladies were ultra-religious and refused to eat anything that had a single drop of booze in it.

What they don't know won't hurt them—and besides, the liquor evaporates during the cooking process. Dolly's voice inside her head put a smile on her face.

Fancy woke up, glared at the door, and wagged her tail.

"Opal and Minilee must be here," Libby said. "They would get along so well with Dolly. I should send her an invitation to come see me—a funny one that will make her giggle." Her thoughts went to the business of making a card.

Minilee poked her head in the door without knocking. "Hey. Just letting you know that we're here to do some cleaning until noon. After that, it's just too blasted hot in this place for us old gals. We'll have a little break around ten. See you then."

Fancy ran over to the door, and Minilee picked her up. "All right if I take her with me?"

"Want her leash?" Libby asked. "Last time we let her have the run of the store, she found a hidey-hole under a desk out there."

"She does like to snoop," Minilee said. "But I brought treats to lure her out of wherever she hides."

"See you in a couple of hours," Libby said with a nod and opened another file drawer.

She had barely gotten all the file folders lined up on the floor when her phone rang. She pulled it out of her hip pocket, saw that it was Benny, and answered on the second ring.

"Good morning," she said in a cheerful voice. "What's going on? Is everything all right?"

"Same to you. Everything is just fine, but I wanted you to know I've changed the itinerary. I just got a dealers-only invitation to the closeout of an antique store in McAlester, Oklahoma. Tomorrow is the only day that I can get an early look at what's there, and the sale will be open to the public on Friday. Elvis and I are going to skip the trip to Joplin, Missouri; check out an auction in Tulsa this afternoon; and come back to the dealer sale tomorrow. If we have a trailer load, we'll be home by suppertime tomorrow."

She hit the speaker button and continued to work. "And then you'll go to Joplin on Wednesday?"

"No, on Wednesday, the two of us are going to take stock of the warehouse, and then I want to do some measuring to put in shelving like you mentioned the first day you were in Sawmill. So I'll be staying home more in the next few weeks," he answered.

"And taking Thursdays off to rest?" she asked.

"Maybe," he replied with a chuckle. "I got to admit, I did enjoy being away from everything for a whole day. See you tomorrow evening."

"Be safe," she said and ended the call.

"Well, this is going to be a different experience," she muttered.

She tried to shift her thoughts over to the book she would be discussing that evening, but they kept coming back to the changes that were about to happen. On the days the store was open, she and Benny were both so busy with customers that they barely had time to nod in passing. Sometimes they watched the sunset together from the station's front porch, and they'd spent that one day together at the river. Other than that, she was on her own to get the office in order. She wasn't quite sure how she would adapt to working with him one-on-one, all the time.

When Opal rapped on the door by midmorning, Libby was down to just two more drawers, and then she could tackle the huge stack of file folders still on the desk. She could easily do that job the next morning—and maybe by the time Benny got back, she would be finished and could show him a nice, clean office.

"We're having tea," Opal called out from the other side of the closed door.

"Why don't y'all bring it in here where it's cool?" Libby asked.

"No, ma'am, not until you can swear on the Bible and sign your name in blood on an affidavit that there's not a single spider or mouse in there. It's not unbearably hot yet, so we'll just have our tea out here."

"Be out in a minute," Libby said.

"We'll have everything ready."

Libby stood up and did a couple of stretches before she opened the door. A blast of hot air hit her in the face, but at least it didn't smell like lemon oil. Three tall glasses of tea were on the table, along with a platter of brownies. Fancy was sound asleep in a little doggy bed beside the sofa.

"Where did that come from?" Libby asked.

"I found it tucked inside a dresser drawer over in the bedroom section. When I brought it up here, Fancy claimed it," Minilee answered.

Opal picked up a brownie and took a bite. "It can be her very own bed when she's in the store."

Minilee tilted her head up and looked down her nose at Opal. "I thought you weren't going to have a thing to do with Fancy."

"A woman can change her mind—and besides, I'm mad at Tatum."

Libby sat down at the table and took a sip of her tea. "What did she do to hurt your feelings?"

"I didn't say that she hurt my feelings," Opal argued. "I said that I'm mad at her. That's a whole different thing."

"She smarted off to her grandmother right out in public and made her cry," Minilee said.

"And then she packed her things and stormed out of the house. Sally said she's gone to Dallas to live with a friend and hopefully find a rich husband there." Opal sighed. "I feel so sorry for my sister. She's always doted on Tatum—but then, we both did. Lots of times, Sally did without things she wanted or needed so that that girl could have what she didn't even need."

"And you are surprised?" Minilee asked. "Tatum has always been a handful. Even when she came to visit in the summer, she *demanded* whatever she wanted rather than asking for it. I really thought that being in the service would help her, and I was so hoping that she would fall in love with Benny."

"Me too." Opal sighed again. "I'm just glad that we've got club tonight. Sally and I both need it."

Libby reached over and patted Opal on the shoulder. "I'm so sorry. It's tough when anyone makes you sad, but it's doubled when it comes from a loved one."

"Thanks, darlin'," Opal said, then abruptly changed the subject. "Did you get that pecan pie made for tonight? If not, you better go home early enough to make it because Sally is sure looking forward to a slice."

Libby picked up a brownie and bit into it. "Yes, ma'am, I did. This sure didn't come from a boxed mix, did it?"

"Nope," Minilee answered. "It's from my grandma's recipe that's been passed down in my family for several generations."

Libby didn't have a single recipe for anything that had been passed down for generations in her family. June had shared her sand-tart recipe, and Libby still made them at Christmas, but June wasn't a relative. But then, she didn't have any living blood relatives, so why would she have recipes?

"I opened the box," Libby blurted out, and then felt a blush crawling up her neck to her face.

"What box? Was there something in the office you weren't supposed to look at?" Opal asked.

"No, it was personal." The words were out, and she couldn't cram them back into her mouth. "My grandmother left a box to be given to me when she passed away. I almost tossed it in the trash, but I figured there might be important papers in it, so I kept it. But I didn't open the thing until . . ." She took a deep breath, let it out slowly, and went on to tell them about the letter.

"Oh. My. Goodness," Minilee gasped.

"How are you holding up after such a shock?" Opal asked.

"I'm still a little numb, I suppose," Libby answered.

"You have to talk to someone," Minilee said.

"I'm talking to you and Opal, and I let Benny read the letter. I never believed much in all that therapy stuff." She felt as if there were two people in her body: one who stood off to the side and watched things happen and another who drank tea with her two new friends.

Opal squared her shoulders and lifted her chin a few inches. "Who needs a therapist when you have us two wise old heads to use as a sounding board? We can listen anytime you want to talk. Bless your heart, darlin'—and I mean that in a good way, not a sarcastic one."

"Thank you," Libby whispered. She inhaled deeply. "From all the movies I've seen, a therapist would ask me how reading that news made me feel. I can truthfully say that I was in shock, and then Benny called right afterwards, so I just laid it aside, both mentally and physically. I understand now why Victoria didn't want me to call her *Grandma* and why she treated me the way she did, but I'm angry. I should have known there were reasons why I never felt like I belonged anywhere—but how do I get past it and move on? I'm so mad that I'm having trouble even thinking about forgiving her."

"That is understandable," Opal said, "but we don't forgive to relieve the person who hurt us. We forgive so that we don't have hate and anger in our hearts. Those two things are worse than cancer. They can rob us of love and happiness."

"You learn to trust your heart," Minilee advised. "It was telling you all those years that you were different from Victoria, and it's what led you here to Sawmill to make new friends."

"Kind of like the heroine in the book we're going to talk about tonight?" Libby asked.

"Absolutely," Opal said with a nod.

Libby's stomach growled loudly, and when she looked at the clock sitting precariously on the desk, she was amazed that it was after two o'clock. She closed the last drawer to the file cabinet and shot a dirty look over at the stacks of paper on the desk. "You are next," she said. "And then, as long as I'm working here, this place is going to be cleaned up every day before I leave."

Fancy must have heard her talking, because she left her new bed.

"Are you ready to go home, too? I think we might have time for a walk to the river before book club starts, but wait . . . Is that thunder?" She and Fancy both cocked their heads to the side. Another clap verified that a storm was on the way, so she picked up the dog and jogged through the aisles to the front door. She switched off the lights and the fans. A hard, hot wind blasted her in the face when she opened the door, and big drops of rain splattered in huge circles on the porch floor.

"Okay, Fancy, if we don't hustle, we are going to get wet," she said as she stepped outside, slammed the door, and locked it. Then she took off in a fast run toward the station. The downpour started when she was halfway there. She was wet to the skin and out of breath when she finally made it.

The front door swung open and Minilee reached out, grabbed her arm, and pulled her inside. Opal slammed the door shut, handed her a towel, and took Fancy from her arms. She wrapped a second towel around the dog and rubbed her fur dry. "We came over to get things ready for supper. That storm came out of nowhere about the time we got here. It's supposed to move on through the area in the next couple of hours, so Ilene and Sally should be able to get here."

"You should go on into your apartment and get some dry clothes on," Minilee said. "This poor little baby looks like a half-drowned rat, but we'll get her all fixed up while you get out of your wet things."

Libby went into her apartment and peeled out of her soaked jeans, underpants, shirt, and bra. She hung them all on the backs of the kitchen chairs to dry and then went to work on her hair with a blow-dryer. The fury and noise of the storm made Libby think of her own anger. Were the lightning and thunder a sign, telling her that it would blow through the area in a couple of hours? When it was gone, there would be a fresh, clean smell outside and the sky would be blue again.

"I just keep thinking back to how Victoria must have felt every day after she found out that I wasn't her blood kin. Did she cuss and feel like the bottom had fallen out of her world? Did she wonder if Quinton knew I wasn't his child and claimed me anyway? If so, was she angry at him even though he was dead?" she muttered.

The voice in her head sounded like Dolly. *Stop worrying about the past, trust your heart, and be grateful for these two elderly ladies that fate has brought into your life to help you.*

The weatherman had been right. The storm hovered overhead for the better part of two hours, and then it moved on to the southeast of Sawmill. The sun came out, and the skies were blue again, with only a few marshmallow clouds floating above the small community. Then Opal and Minilee dashed across the street to get the rest of what they wanted to bring over for supper and to get dressed for the book club meeting.

Sally and Ilene showed up at six o'clock. Sally carried in the chicken, and Ilene brought in a paper bag full of sides to go with it. Opal met her sister at the door, took the food from her, and then gave her a fierce hug. Then Minilee stepped in to wrap her up in another embrace.

"We're here for you," Opal said. "We can talk about Tatum while we eat."

"I'm finished talking about her," Sally said. "She can go on and do whatever she wants, but she needn't expect to come running back to my house to live when things don't go her way. She's always been bullheaded, but the service made her worse instead of better. Now, let's have our supper and talk about something else. I see Fancy peeking out around the leg of the table. I bet she smells chicken."

"How did you know about Fancy?" Libby asked.

"Minilee's been bragging about how the little thing loves her more than Opal," Ilene answered.

"Maybe so in the past, but not anymore," Opal declared. "She sat on my lap today at the store and even licked my hand."

Karma has surfaced, Libby thought as she went to her apartment and brought out the pecan pie. "Here it is, as promised."

"It's a good thing you left that hidden away. Opal would have eaten half of it before our supper even got started," Minilee teased.

"And you would have downed the other half," Opal snapped.

"Well, thank goodness neither of you opened up the box before I got here," Sally said. "Can I hold Fancy while the rest of you get the supper on the table?"

Minilee picked up the little dog and handed her to Sally. "She was raised by a woman who was probably about our age, and she's got a really sweet disposition. I've never heard her growl at anyone."

Except Tatum, Libby thought, but she didn't say anything out loud.

"Libby, do you mind if we share what you told us today with Sally and Ilene?" Opal asked when Ilene had said grace and they had begun to pass the food around the table.

"No," Libby said. "Maybe they've got some words of wisdom to help me get through these feelings that keep coming back even though I thought I had faced and gotten over them."

For someone who couldn't even tell her best friend about her past, she was in awe that she was able to open up so much to relative strangers. All that road dust she had sucked in must have turned her from an introvert into someone who could discuss her feelings.

Opal told the first part of the story, and then Minilee picked up the final part. Both Sally and Ilene listened intently while they ate supper. When the two ladies had finished, Sally's eyes were as big as saucers.

"You should write your story—turn it into a novel," she said. "This story would make a stellar movie. I would go see it at least three times."

"I'm good with numbers, not words." Libby still felt like she was on the outside looking in instead of being in the center of the conversation.

"This goes so well with our book for tonight." Ilene polished off the last bite of her chicken thigh and reached for a leg. "The woman in the story was able to learn to trust her heart after a failed marriage and a low-down sucker of a boyfriend who treated her like dirt. Her two girlfriends helped her get through the tough times. We're here to help you, Libby. If you need to talk during the day, call Opal or Minilee, but if you wake up at three in the morning, call me. I'm the night owl of the bunch, and I'm up until the wee hours."

"And if you get antsy and need to work off some energy, come up to my house, and we'll bake cupcakes and cookies until you feel better," Sally offered. "And then we'll take them to the nursing home."

"Y'all are amazing," Libby said. "Thank you, thank you . . . And I may take you up on your offers if I get down in the dumps. It's still hard to believe that I'm an O'Dell on all my legal papers—even my birth certificate—and I'm a Griffin by blood. How do I live with that?"

"Simple," Minilee said. "You get married and take your husband's last name. That will fix all of it. You will have learned to trust your heart, and your maiden name won't even matter."

"Two problems solved at one time," Ilene agreed.

"That might take some time," Libby said.

"Of course it will. This whole situation didn't happen in one day or even one week. You can't expect to get over all the hurt, the pain, and the emotions overnight," Opal told her. "But I do know one thing that will help. Bring out that pie, and I'll get the ice cream. Desserts help heal all kinds of problems."

Libby remembered crying with Amanda when she had broken up with more than one boyfriend during their first two years of college, and Opal was right: ice cream helped. But Amanda's situation had caused Libby to consider building walls around her own heart. Then, when she did have a couple of relationships that she thought could be serious, she got disappointed.

"Thank you all, again," she said with a smile she hoped they thought was genuine. Trusting her heart was going to take a little more than a pecan pie and half a gallon of ice cream.

Chapter Twenty

Benny loved going home with a good haul, but that afternoon, it seemed like it took an hour to pass every mile marker of the two-hour trip from McAlester. He started to call Libby, but he knew if he did, he wouldn't be able to be quiet about all the antique dishes he'd bought that morning, and he wanted it to be a surprise.

"Libby is going to be so excited when she sees what we've found," he told Elvis, who was sitting on the passenger seat beside him.

Elvis moved to the floor and stuck his nose against the air conditioner vent.

"Some company you are," Benny fussed at him. "I can always leave you at home."

The dog wagged his tail.

"Do you *want* to stay home?" Benny asked with a chuckle.

That word *home* caused him to realize how much *he* wanted to stay home more. In the same moment, he recognized that the feelings he had for Libby went beyond employee and employer, or even simple friendship.

He passed a WELCOME sign on the outskirts of Blanco, and then three different church signs. A few minutes later, he was on the other side of the town and traveling through ranching country again. Most folks would consider a town of fewer than two thousand people to be a small place, but it was all relative. To someone who lived in Dallas,

Blanco would be a dot on the map. To the four people in Sawmill, it would be a big city.

"The squirrels are having a race," he whispered.

His grandpa often told him that he needed to be still and focus on one thing at a time. "Your thoughts are like a bunch of baby squirrels just out of the nest, running from place to place," Walter had said.

And he had been right—back then and right up until this very day. Benny's thoughts jumped from his own realization that he was falling in love with Libby, to what he should do about it, to her possible excitement when she saw the dozens of pink dishes he was bringing to the store, to the letter she had let him read—the latter of which had very little to do with his feelings. From there, they wiggled around to the way she was getting the office in order and then back to the way she made him feel when she looked at him with those light blue eyes.

"I really do like Libby for more than a friend," he admitted.

His phone rang. He put the phone on speaker and laid it on the console.

"Hello?" He could hear the anxiety in his own voice. "What's going on?"

"I just wanted you to know that I've moved to Dallas." Tatum's words were slurred.

"Are Opal and Sally all right?" he asked bluntly.

"I have no idea about that old lady or my aunt Sally." She giggled. "I have a job interview tomorrow doing security work for a big firm. I need two personal references. Can I put you down as one of them?"

"Are you drunk?" he asked and checked the time—four o'clock.

"It's five o'clock in New York City." She giggled again. "Will you give me a good reference or not?"

"I don't really know you, Tatum, and I'd have to be honest if someone called me. I wish you all the best, but I'd rather that you not use me as a reference."

"We have known each other since we were kids." Her tone raised an octave with each word.

"We knew each other a little as children, but we haven't spent very little time together since we've been adults. Get someone else, please," he said. "Maybe one of the people you worked with in the service. They know you a lot better than I do. All I could tell them is to be careful about putting you in a job where a dog was involved."

The call ended so abruptly that Benny checked to see if he'd lost service. "I guess she didn't like my answer . . . but I would have to tell the truth."

Elvis sat up in the seat and scratched his ear.

"Does that mean you heard every word?" Benny asked.

His tail thumping against the leather seat sounded like drumbeats. Benny nodded and passed a sign that said Hugo was twenty miles ahead. That meant he would be home in half an hour—in time for supper. He had stopped at a supermarket in McAlester and bought up supplies to last for several days. Tonight, he planned on making spaghetti for supper and seeing if Libby wanted to join him for a front porch picnic.

The winds were with him, as his grandfather used to say, and he made it to Sawmill in twenty-five minutes. He stopped at the trailer long enough to unload the groceries and let Elvis out of the truck. Then he drove on to the store and parked out back in the usual spot. He started to go through the back door but figured Libby had already left. When he rounded the last corner, he saw her just leaving the building with Fancy running as far ahead as her leash would allow.

"Hey, are you just now calling it a day?" he yelled.

She turned around and waved. "You are home earlier than I thought you would be. How are you feeling?"

That she was interested in him made him feel like a king. He lengthened his stride, and the two of them walked across the parking lot together. "I'm fine. Evidently, whatever got ahold of me was a twenty-four-hour bug—or it didn't like me and went on to pester someone else."

"How did the trip go? Did you find anything interesting, or was it a disappointment?" she asked.

"I've got a trailer loaded with glassware," he answered. "We're going to build shelves in the next two days and get it on display by the weekend, I hope. There's still some lumber out in one of the warehouses that was left over from when this place was a real sawmill."

"What warehouses?" she asked.

"Grandpa let a stand of trees grow up between the store and the two warehouses back behind it, so they're not visible to most folks. It's where the lumber that was planed to the right thickness is kept, and where we still have some stock ready to bring into the store when we have room," he answered. "We'll go out there in the morning and measure the boards. If we don't like them, I can always have some delivered from the lumberyard in Paris."

"You are still buying stock when you've got a store full, a back room full, and some in storage?" she asked. "Summer is coming on strong, and it's shaping up to be a hot one."

"I was here through several summers back when I was younger, so I know how the heat affects sales," he said.

"I made a couple of graphs while I was cleaning out the files. Business always fell off considerably in July and August, then picked up in the fall," she said.

"I'd like to see those graphs. They might make a difference in the amount of time I spend away from home this summer."

Libby stepped up onto the porch, secured Fancy's leash to the back of a chair, and went straight for the cooler. "That's because folks won't stay long in a hot building. They'll come in and shop around a little while, but then they leave pretty quick. Victoria used to fuss about whether we could keep the lights on in those two months because there were so little sales. September wasn't much better because folks were more concerned with getting their kids or grandkids ready for school." She opened the old cooler and turned back to him. "Water or tea, or a beer from inside?"

"Tea is good," he answered as he sat down at the table. "Got any ideas about how to keep the customers in the store longer?"

"Victoria had an old refrigerator at the front of the store. She kept it filled with water bottles and gave them away free in those two months. You might consider moving this old soda pop cooler to the store and doing the same thing—free water made a difference at her store," she suggested. "We can keep the water and tea that we normally put in the cooler here with the beer inside the station."

"That's a great idea. We'll do that before we open on Friday." He took a bottle of tea from her. "I thought you'd be more excited about the glassware I brought home."

"Is it the pink and green patterns that sell as fast as we put it out?" she asked.

He nodded and twisted the lid off the bottle. "Yes, and a lot of carnival glass—some even in the purple color that is really hard to find."

"Are you serious?" Libby opened a bottle of water and poured a little of it in Fancy's bowl, then took a long drink before she sat down. "I can't wait to see it. How long do you think it will take to get the shelves up so we can unpack it?"

That was the excitement he had waited all day to see. "Half a day, at the most. I couldn't believe my eyes when I walked into that house. Two elderly sisters had lived there together until they passed on last year. They were both collectors of antique glassware. No one else seemed interested, so I bought the whole collection. The executors even helped me wrap and box it up."

"There's still a lot of daylight left," Libby said. "We could go do some measuring and check out the warehouses right now."

"You've worked all day," he said.

"And the office is clean and ready to go. The desk is even cleared off. If we get started tonight, I can put the data into the computer as we unpack, and it will all be out on the shelves this weekend."

"We can do that, but first we need to have some supper. I'm starving," he said. "I was planning on making spaghetti, but it will take less time to heat up a frozen pizza. We could share it before we go back to the store."

"That sounds great. I'll make a salad while it's heating, and we can eat in the apartment, where it's cool. It's a shame to pay for all that air-conditioning and not use it. There's a couple of small slices of pecan pie left over from book club last night, too." She hopped up, grabbed her bottle of water from the table, and headed inside. "See you in a few minutes."

Benny whistled all the way to his trailer, went inside, and turned on the AC. He pulled the pizza out of the grocery bags first, started it cooking in the toaster oven, and unloaded the rest of his supplies.

His grandfather's voice was clear in his head. *I always told you that working with someone was the best way to get to know them.*

"Where did that come from?" he asked.

His question got no answer, so he forced himself to focus on his grandfather's words. He had worked with a lot of people at the firm, but he still considered most of them acquaintances rather than friends.

"But it does when it comes to Libby," he admitted after he thought about it for a few seconds. "If she left and asked me for either a personal or a business reference, I could give her a glowing one in either instance."

A blast of stale, musty air rushed out of the first big building when Benny unlocked the door and slid it open. He flipped a switch by the door, and about half of the fluorescent bulbs hanging from the ceiling lit up. Long pieces of lumber were stacked on shelves against the wall to Libby's left, and to her right were several things covered with thick canvas.

"Those are huge pieces of furniture that would only fit into a mansion," Benny explained and pointed toward the racks of wood across the room. "There's some oak and a few pieces of pecan wood from back in the days when this was a sawmill, but most of it will be pine, and it warps pretty badly."

"How do you know so much about wood?" she asked.

"Grandpa taught me," he answered. "Think we should hang three or four long shelves, or make them shorter and stagger them?"

"Shorter," she answered without hesitation. "That way, if someone bumps one accidentally, we'll lose fewer pieces to breakage. And it'll be more appealing to the eye and give the customers a better view of each one."

"Smart thinking," he agreed. "And as an added bonus, we can use some of the shorter pieces that wouldn't be useful in building a house."

"Is that in your future plans?"

"Maybe . . ." He hesitated. "The idea popped into my head when the pizza was cooking. I found myself whistling that old Miranda Lambert song 'The House That Built Me' and got to thinking about the home that I loved the most. That was the time I spent with Grandpa, either in the apartment where you live or the house in Paris. I figured out that it wasn't the place as much as the feeling I had there."

She lifted the corner of one of the canvas covers and peeked at the breakfront underneath. "I thought of that same song when I was at my old house in Jefferson. That place built me, for better or worse—and it was the latter a lot of the time. But it made me who I am today, just like spending time with your grandfather made you who you are."

Benny raised the other corner of the cover so she could get a better look. "Are you getting past the feelings you had after you read that letter?"

"I think so—book club last night was good," she answered, running a hand over the breakfront. "When you build your house, you should make one wall big enough to accommodate this thing. It's too beautiful to be stored away. You could use it for a bookcase."

"What does book club have to do with the letter?" he asked.

"The book we discussed was about learning to trust your heart," she answered. "I always knew that something wasn't quite right where

186

Victoria was concerned, but I couldn't figure out what it was. I blamed myself: If I was a better person, she wouldn't leave me alone so much. If I did more for her, she would hug me. That breeds mistrust, and I'm not sure that I've ever trusted anyone but maybe Amanda and Dolly. And I never told them nearly as much about my past as I have you folks here in Sawmill."

Benny dropped the cover. "That makes me feel really special."

"You are very special, Benny," she said.

"Thank you for that," he said. "Now, back to this piece of furniture. I don't want a huge house. Maybe a ranch style with the possibility of adding a wing onto it if . . ." He paused. "If it becomes too crowded."

Libby wondered what he had been about to say. Was it if he had a big family and not just one child like his grandparents and his own parents had? "That sounds like a good idea. Start small and build big as you need it, but still leave one wall big enough for that gorgeous piece of furniture."

"Going back to your club meeting," he said as he crossed over to the other side of the warehouse. "What helped the person in your book learn to trust her heart?"

"Her friends," Libby answered, and wandered over to look at the pieces of wood he was stacking up on a dolly. "Kind of like you and Opal and Minilee are helping me. Sally and Ilene were helpful, too, so I shouldn't leave them out."

"So, you trust all of us?" Benny asked.

"I think maybe I do," Libby said and was amazed at her answer. How could she put her trust in people she had known for only a month?

Because you are trusting your heart! the voice in her head said.

"I'm glad," Benny said with a smile as he placed one last board on the dolly. "This should be enough. We can take them over to the store and draw out a pattern as to how we want to position them on the wall."

Libby wished she could position her life like that. Bottom shelves would hold past memories of things that didn't matter if they got broken. The top shelf would hold priceless items like her heart and soul, and it would have a railing around it for protection. In between would be the things that mattered but weren't as expensive or as important as the ones up above them.

"What are you thinking about?" Benny asked as he got the dolly moving toward the open door.

Libby answered with her thoughts about life.

"And where would I be?" Benny asked.

"At the very top," she answered with a smile.

"Thank you." He returned her smile. "We'd be there together, like the matched set of pink salt dips in one of those boxes we'll be unpacking tomorrow."

"You'd be willing to be pink?" she teased.

"My favorite shirt is pink." His eyes twinkled. "I'm very comfortable in my skin. I know who I am, and I don't intend to change for anyone."

"Me too," she said with a nod. "Thanks for being my pink other half."

"You are very welcome." He pulled the dolly out through the door and then locked it behind them. "Having someone who can talk the same language I do is pretty special, Miz Libby."

She grabbed the handle, and together, they pulled the dolly through the space between two trees and across the back parking lot to the store. "Having someone that I can talk to about the past—especially someone with listening ears and broad shoulders—is pretty special, too, Mr. Benny."

"That's just Benny to you."

"Then it's just Libby to you," she shot back.

He grinned. "Deal."

Chapter Twenty-One

"*I*'m surprised that you found so much more glassware," Libby said when she and Benny arrived at the store on Thursday morning. "If folks knew the value of what was on those three tables, they would be robbing *us* instead of going after banks."

Benny covered a yawn with the back of his hand. "This is supposed to be the day that we don't have to get up so early. Are you sure that your friend Raisa said she would be here at six thirty in the morning and not in the evening?"

"Yes, I am. She stayed over on the other side of the Red River with a friend in Valliant last night. She said she would swing by here on her way back to Jefferson this morning and check out what we've got. Our original plan was to have lunch together, but things changed," Libby answered. "She was very excited to get a look at the pink items."

The bell above the front door signaled that someone had arrived, and Raisa yelled, "I'm here. Where are y'all?"

Libby raised her voice. "We're over to your left."

The first table held the pink pieces, all the green antiques were on the second table, and the third one was covered with miscellaneous pieces that were anywhere from clear crystal to a deep purple hue. Raisa gave Libby a quick hug and then gasped when she looked at the first table.

"Good Lord! Where did you find this gold mine?" she asked. "I didn't know there were this many pieces still floating around out there."

"At a sale up in McAlester, Oklahoma," Benny answered.

"You will still give me the standard ten percent dealer's discount, won't you?" she asked as she picked up piece after piece, checked the prices, and carefully set them back down. "You've got them marked down from what I would consider retail for antiques like these, so I understand if you want full price."

"Ten percent always goes to dealers," he agreed.

His lack of greediness was just one more thing that Libby had come to appreciate about him. "I need to go get some more wood for another shelf. Have you got this, Libby?"

"I can take care of it," she answered and pointed toward the break table. "Raisa, why don't you hand me the pieces you are interested in, and I'll set them aside. Then you can go through them again and pick out the ones you really want."

"See y'all in a few minutes, then." Benny disappeared into the maze of furniture and antiques.

Raisa handed Libby a matched set of four pink Depression-glass bowls. "I want these for sure. One of my friends is doing her whole wedding in antiques, so I know she'll buy these to put mints and nuts in." She kept Libby running back and forth until the break table was covered; then she sat down in one of the chairs and looked over each and every piece.

"I'll take all of them," she finally said. "You've even got them all shined up for us, so they are ready for my friend to look at before we even put them out on the shelf. Now that the business is done, tell me about Benny. Are y'all dating yet?"

"No, we aren't," Libby answered. "Are you going to ask him out?"

"Nope." Raisa shook her head. "That ship has sailed. Right after I saw you the last time, I met this tall, dark rancher who lives up near Valliant. My friend introduced us, and I'm not rushing into anything, but there's a definite spark that could be telling me this is the one."

"Congratulations. I hope everything works out for you," Libby said.

Raisa stood up. "Thank you. Can I take some of the boxes you've got shoved up under that end table?"

"Sure thing. I'll get the roll of paper we use to wrap breakables in and help you get these ready to go."

"I'll wrap while you take the price tags off," Raisa offered. "And, honey, I'm not blind."

Libby drew her dark brows down in a frown. "What does that have to do with boxing this stuff up?"

"The sparks dancin' around between y'all are so plain, I can almost see them, and I can definitely feel the heat between y'all," Raisa whispered.

Libby could feel her cheeks turning red. "You are imagining things because *you* are falling in love."

Raisa slipped an arm around Libby's shoulders and hugged her. "Honey, I call it like I see it—and like I said, I'm not blind."

Before Libby could argue, Benny arrived with a board in his hands. "Did you decide which ones you want?"

"Yes, I have, but I may come back next week to look at what's left. I really like some of those rare pieces," Raisa answered, then winked at Libby and fanned her face with her hand.

"There's free water up in the front of the store," Benny said. "I'll bring each of you a bottle as soon as I lay this board down. I can take the price tags and tally up the total minus ten percent while y'all finish packing up."

"That would be great," Libby said.

"Thank you so much for letting me have first rights, and a bottle of cold water would be great." Raisa turned to Libby and whispered, "You might want to pour it on your head rather than drink it. The sparks just get hotter and hotter."

Libby gave her a dose of her worst stink eye and put a finger over her lips. "Shhh . . ."

"Might as well face up to the facts," Raisa told her.

"I might if it's the truth and not a figment of your overactive imagination," she said in a low tone.

When Benny returned with three bottles of cold water, Libby put all the tags in his hand. The tingle when her fingers brushed against his went all the way to her elbow. She told herself that the only reason she felt a little bit of chemistry was because Raisa had caused the feeling by the power of suggestion. Besides, Benny was her boss and pretty much her best friend these days. To get involved in a relationship with him would be downright dumb.

She caught Raisa's eye and said, "Tell me about this new man in your life."

"Y'all can talk about that," Benny said with a chuckle. "I'm going to tally these up and then hang that last shelf. That should be enough space to get what's left on those tables out for sale."

Raisa waited until Benny walked away before she lowered her voice and said, "He's tall and has dark hair. You wouldn't find him on the cover of a romance book, but he's got a wonderful personality. He treats me like I'm a queen. He opens doors for me and asks me where I want to go and what I want to do." As she talked, she wrapped the last bowl in paper and eased it down into the third box. "And he understands that I love antiques and that my job entails a little bit of travel."

"Your eyes twinkle when you talk about him," Libby said with a smile.

"Yours do the same when Benny is anywhere near," Raisa told her. "Call me when you wake up and admit it, and we'll talk about him instead of my Mr. Wright. You'll laugh, but his name is actually Allan Wright."

Benny came back with two sheets of paper listing the price of each item individually so Raisa would know how much to charge for the pieces in her store. "Here you go," he said as he handed it to her.

She whipped a checkbook from her purse and filled it in with the correct amount. "Thanks again for the discount—and like I said, I may be back for more by the end of next week. My aunt is going to be over the moon with all this, and my friend who is getting married will think she's hit the jackpot. Her wedding colors are shades of pink."

"We'll be right here," Benny said. "Let me get the dolly, and I'll load those for you."

"He's a keeper," Raisa whispered when Benny was out of hearing range.

"He's a very good friend, and I don't want to mess that up," Libby told her. "And besides, he's my boss, and I really like this job."

Raisa patted her on the back. "Call me when you need a bridesmaid. I'll go on out and get the back of my SUV ready to load up the merchandise. See you soon." She blew Libby a kiss and headed outside.

Libby giggled at her insistence and waved at her.

Benny came back, loaded up the boxes, and rolled them out the door. While he was gone, Libby arranged a few more pieces of glassware on the top shelves, alternating between different colors and patterns to give the pieces more visibility.

"Hey!" Benny returned, grabbed her around the waist, and spun her around until they were both dizzy. Then he fell back on the sofa and pulled her down beside him. "We just sold enough merchandise to your friend to pay for the whole lot. Every other sale is now pure profit. Libby, you are my good luck charm."

"Are you serious?" she panted. "How is that possible?"

"Ever since you arrived, my life has been easier, and the shop has made more money than it ever has—and besides all that, I got a good friend that talks about the same things," he answered. "As far as how it is possible, I did the same thing we did at the garage sale. I offered them a price to take all the glassware off their hands, and they took it. And while Raisa was picking out what she wanted, I got a call from another person in Clarksville. Her grandmother passed away, and that lady at the garage sale is related to her. She wanted to know if I would come take a look at what she's got and bid on the whole lot."

"Are you going to do it?" Libby asked.

"Oh, yeah, I am," Benny answered. "Want to go with me on Monday?"

"I'd love to. How far is it from here to there?" She turned toward him and their eyes locked.

No! she scolded herself. She blinked and looked away. She would not let Raisa's silly ideas ruin what she had going for her right here in Sawmill. Besides, Opal and Minilee would pitch a fit and unfriend her face-to-face, not on social media.

She glanced back at him to find him tapping out something on his phone. She couldn't force her eyes away from his mouth and wondered what it would be like to kiss him.

"Fifty miles, give or take a few," he said.

"What?" she asked.

"You asked how far it was to Clarksville. It's about fifty miles. We can go over there, take a look, and be back home by lunchtime," he replied. "Maybe you'll be my lucky charm that day, too. This might start off a new era in the way I buy merchandise. It'll require some sorting through, and maybe a bigger trailer. Or maybe I'll just buy a good-sized moving van."

Libby was a lot more interested in how it would feel to have his lips on hers than what he was saying about business.

"What do you think of that?" he asked.

"Might be a good idea," she said, jolted back to the subject. "But if you're going to start that mode of buying, we could open the store one more day a week—maybe Thursday—and close at five rather than working until seven."

Sounds like you are throwing the word we *around a lot here lately,* the pesky voice in her head whispered.

"I'm sorry," she blurted out.

"For what?" he asked.

"For saying *we* when I should have said *you.* This is your business, not mine," Libby answered.

"Libby, darlin'." He took her hand in one of his. "I'm the owner, but no one has ever worked as hard as you have, or put in as many hours"—he pointed toward the shelves on the wall—"or had such good ideas, including that garage sale that is putting me on the track to do things different."

"Will you be happy spending more time in the store and less on the road?"

He brought her hand to his lips and kissed the knuckles. "Yes, I believe I am, as long as we are working together."

Her breath caught in her chest. "Speaking of work, we've got shelves to get ready before we open the doors for business tomorrow, but . . ." She paused and wondered if she should even finish the sentence since it was so personal.

"But what?" He held on to her hand.

"But you make me feel special, so thank you," she told him.

"You *are* very special, Libby," he whispered, in an echo of her earlier words, and let go of her hand.

Chapter Twenty-Two

"Surprise!"

Libby recognized the voice even before she looked up from her work and saw the short gray-haired woman coming through the door into the office. She pushed back the chair so fast that it rolled against the wall behind her, and she rushed over to hug her old neighbor.

Dolly took a step back and eyed Libby from the toes of her athletic shoes to her dark hair that was done up in a ponytail. "You look happy. I knew coming up here would be good for you."

Libby took her by the hand and led her over to one of the wingback chairs that faced the desk. "Sit down and talk to me—and yes, ma'am, moving here is the best decision I've ever made. Thank you for talking me into doing it."

"I just gave you a little push." Dolly took a seat. "It's sure enough cooler in here than out there in the store."

Libby finally remembered her manners. "Can I get you a bottle of water?"

Dolly shook her head. "Thank you, but I just finished one. Giving away cold water is a great idea when the weather is like this."

Libby sat down next to her. "Are you on your way home or just getting started on an adventure?"

"My friends and I left Austin on Friday. We're on a road trip to Pawhuska, Oklahoma, to visit Ree Drummond's store, and we're hitting antique stores along the way. We stayed in Dallas that night. We spent yesterday in Jefferson, and tonight we'll be in McAlester. This is our last road trip, so we're making the best of it. By the end of next week, we'll be in Galveston to board a cruise ship."

Libby reached over and laid a hand on Dolly's shoulder. "Are you sick? Why is this your last road trip? And are you sure you'll have the energy for a cruise after a road trip like this? You didn't mention it in your letters."

Dolly's bright smile deepened all the wrinkles around her eyes. She covered Libby's hand with her own bony, veined one and said, "I'm not sick, and I plan to live to be a hundred—unless the good Lord has other ideas. But this is our farewell to big adventures for me and my friends. We are all going into an assisted-living place in Austin when we get home. We agreed years ago that when one of us started having problems, we would go together. The time has come. No looking back, other than to relive all our good times. No regrets about anything."

Libby picked up Dolly's hand and held it to her cheek for a moment before dropping it. "I want to grow up and be like you."

"Honey, don't set your goals that low. You get married and have a family. Everyone at the shelter keeps saying what good help you were, and the kids that are still there ask about you all the time." Dolly patted her hand. "Also, I want you to know that my friends are now volunteering at the women's shelter, too."

"Oh, Dolly, that is such good news, but how will—"

"Not to worry," Dolly said with a smile as she shook her head, "about how we'll get back and forth to volunteer. Pecan Grove—that's the name of our new home—has a shuttle van that will take us anywhere we need to go."

"That sounds wonderful," Libby said. "How *are* things at the shelter? I have missed the kids so much."

"Going very well," Dolly answered. "Jason and his mama are gone now. They've relocated somewhere up north. Nebraska, I think. The only trouble with volunteering is that I get too attached to the children and then they are gone."

"But more come in that need you just as bad. Thank you for bringing news of them to me. Getting to see you is like a breath of fresh air," Libby said after a sigh.

"Honey," Dolly said with a smile, "this is not the end of our visits. I've got your phone number, and when we get settled, I will text you my new address. If you are ever in Austin again, we can go out for dinner."

Benny opened the door without knocking and stopped right inside. "I'm sorry. I didn't mean to interrupt."

"No problem," Libby said. "Come on in and meet Dolly. She was my neighbor in Austin—the one who gave me a push to interview for this job. She loved the store the last time she was here."

Benny crossed the room in a few long strides with his hand extended. "I'm so glad to meet you, Dolly. Libby has mentioned you several times. Thank you so much for steering her up this way. She's really been an asset to the business."

Dolly shook hands with him. "I'm glad things worked out. I was just leaving. My friends will be ready to get back out in my air-conditioned car, and we've got two more hours before we get to our next hotel. Or maybe three, if we see a garage sale on the way." She winked at Libby, pushed up out of the chair, and raised her arms for another hug.

Libby bent slightly to embrace her, and Dolly whispered, "He's a keeper. Don't throw him back. His eyes light up when he looks at you." She took a step back and skewered Benny with a glance. "I told her I'd text my new address when I get moved into my new digs, and she will get my salt-dip collection. I ran out of room to keep all of them in my apartment years ago and had to put them in storage. None of my kids, grandkids, or great-grands want them, so they're being shipped to Libby. Keep her on track!"

"I couldn't . . . ," Libby stammered before Benny could speak.

"It's done," Dolly said. "You always admired them. Keep the ones you like and sell the rest. They should bring enough to make a little nest egg. This'll be a *see you later*, not a goodbye—oh my goodness, I was so excited to see you so happy that I forgot to give you something." She reached inside her tote bag and pulled out a manila envelope. "The kids all colored pictures to send to you. Even Jason did one before he and his mama left."

Libby hugged the envelope to her heart. "This is so special, Dolly. I may cry."

"No, you will not." Dolly shook her finger at Libby. "You will be happy and laugh at the pictures and color sheets. That's an order, young lady. Promise me?"

"I can promise to try," Libby said.

"That's good enough." Dolly blew her a kiss and left the office.

Benny opened up his arms, and she walked into them. She laid her head on his chest and did her best to keep the tears from flowing.

"I can see why you said Dolly was like a grandmother." Benny patted her back. "We'll have to go visit her this fall."

"I'd like that," Libby said. "And thank you for what you said to her."

"I meant every word of it," he whispered, and his warm breath on her neck sent tingles all the way down her backbone.

He moved one arm from around her, and she started to step back, but he tightened his hold with his other one. She moved away from his chest, and he tucked his free hand under her chin. She barely had time to moisten her lips before his mouth found hers in a long, lingering kiss. Her heart kicked in a few extra beats. Her pulse shot up so high that she could hear wind rushing in her ears. She didn't want it to end, and yet she wished it had never happened. Now things would be awkward between them, and she valued their friendship too much to ruin it.

Quit analyzing every little thing and enjoy the moment. Dolly's voice was as clear in her head as if she were still in the store.

She wanted to lean in, to feel more excitement in a whole string of hot, steamy kisses, but she took a step back. "Benny, we can't . . ."

He cupped her cheeks in his big hands and smiled. "We are two grown adults. We don't have to rush anything, but I've wanted to do that for several days now. I don't want to have regrets when I'm as old as Dolly."

Three things went through Libby's mind. The first one was Victoria scolding her about being a stick-in-the mud. The second was that Dolly had just said a similar thing. The last was the advice about how attractive Benny was.

She glanced up at him and agreed with all three things, but mostly with the last one.

"Are you going to finish what you were saying?" he asked.

Libby wrapped her arms around his neck. "No regrets," she said as she leaned in for another kiss.

"Not a bad week, considering this heat wave that we're having," Benny said on the way home that evening, but his mind was on the way Libby had felt in his arms rather than the total of sales when they closed out. His hand brushed against hers, and he laced their fingers together. He had felt the world stop when they kissed. That might sound silly coming from a man, but it was the truth. He'd never had such a strong reaction to just a few kisses—but then it had been months since he'd even had the opportunity for a good night kiss at the end of a date.

"We sold a lot of glassware from the new shelves," Libby said. "Those purple pieces really went fast."

Had the moment passed forever? Would she back away from even the idea of a real date? He wanted to voice the questions, but he didn't want to hear the answers.

"And the sale of those two four-poster beds made room for us to bring some more out of the warehouse—but I want to talk about us, not antiques." He dropped her hand when they reached the porch and opened the door for her.

"Benny, four people live here in Sawmill. Opal and Minilee made it clear when I first got here that you were off-limits. I know you are not a poor man and that you have a lot of money. How do you know I haven't been playing you all along?"

"You've never struck me as the dishonest kind, Libby. And besides, as a lawyer, I have dealt with some pretty sneaky people, and they all have the same traits."

Libby went inside and took off Fancy's leash. The dog flopped down on her belly in the middle of the cool tile floor.

"And those telling signs about devious people are . . . ?" she asked.

"Fancy has the right idea," Benny said.

"About sneaky people?"

"She could probably spot one of those kinds of people for sure, but I was talking about going in out of the heat," he answered.

"You want to flop down on the cool tile?" Libby teased.

"That's tempting, but I wouldn't go that far. I would like a cold beer, though, and to talk about us some more," he answered. "I can't describe the traits, but I haven't been fooled very many times. And, honey, you do not have any of them."

Libby kicked off her shoes and walked barefoot across the cold floor. "I might be one of those master manipulators who fall into the one percent that can fool even a smart lawyer like you."

Benny closed the door behind him and got two longneck bottles of beer out of the cooler. He twisted the top off one and handed it to her. "Are you in that one percent?"

"No," she answered and took a long drink. "But how can you believe me?"

"You've given me no cause not to."

"Hey, y'all!" Opal pushed her way through the door with a large watermelon in her hands.

Dammit! The word chased through Benny's mind, but he didn't say it out loud. He loved Opal and Minilee, but he didn't want to see them this evening.

"We harvested our best watermelon this morning, and we're here to share it with you," Minilee said. "We've chilled it all day in the refrigerator, and it's just what we all need at the end of this hot day. We had a potluck after church services this morning, but—"

Opal raised a hand and butted in. "The AC went out in the fellowship hall, so we didn't tarry long after we had eaten."

"It was an eat-and-run type day, and hot food on a day like this just didn't taste as good as it would have in a nice cool room. We just had a bologna sandwich at supper and thought we would share our melon with y'all for dessert," Minilee said and handed Benny a butcher knife. "You can cut it open for us. I figure me and Opal can dig into one half; you and Libby can claim the other one. We'll chunk up what's left over for later and use the rind to make pickles."

"I bet y'all could sell jams and jellies in the store," Libby said.

Her tone was cheerful. The smile on her face was genuine. *Does that mean she's glad for the interruption?* Benny wondered.

"We could never sell what we grow or make from our produce!" Minilee declared. "That would turn what we do into a job, and we retired years ago. We just make pickles and jam for fun. We've got lots of relatives and friends who always bring the jars back. When it gets to be a job, it's not fun anymore."

"I don't know about that," Benny said. "I think my job is a lot of fun."

"Me too," Libby said.

Minilee brought out four forks from her apron pocket. "Then you are a success. My grandmother told me when I was about to graduate from high school that I should find a job I loved to do. It didn't matter if it was digging ditches, being a stay-at-home wife, or campaigning to be the first woman president of the United States—I would be a success."

"Were you?" Libby asked.

"Yes. Me and Opal both were. We worked for Walter in the office for years and enjoyed our jobs. Now we are retired, and we love what we do in our old age," she answered.

"Life is good." Opal pulled a shaker full of salt from *her* apron pocket. "I like a little sprinkling on mine to bring out the flavor."

"Not me," Minilee said. "I take it just like the good Lord lets it grow."

Libby wondered if she shouldn't do the same—take it like the good Lord let it grow. Had the desperate times she had endured caused her life to ripen? Was she ready to let go of the past and move on without looking back?

Benny nudged her shoulder with his. "What are you thinking about?"

"Watermelons and life," she answered, but she wondered—if she split her life open like Benny had just cut that melon in half and looked inside, what would she see? Would there be rotten spots that could ruin the sweetness?

"How are those two things anything alike?" Minilee asked. "I can't imagine how *watermelon* and *life* can even be used in the same sentence."

"I'm not sure I can explain how my mind works, but the best I can do is, what's inside is not visible to anyone just looking at that green rind—somewhat like getting to know someone—and seeing the outside isn't like understanding their heart and soul," Libby said, then changed the subject. "I've never heard of watermelon-rind pickles."

"I hear ya on all of it," Opal said. "And we'll bring a jar of pickles out next time you kids eat supper with us."

"So, what's on the agenda for y'all this next week?" Minilee asked. "Libby has all the drawers cleaned out, and the office is looking like something other than a trash heap. I don't know where you are going to put any more merchandise if you bring home another trailer full, Benny."

Benny shrugged. "I'm going to an estate sale in Clarksville tomorrow. The owner of the sale wants me to make her an offer to buy what she's got—lock, stock, and barrel. I looked at the list of what they have, and there's quite a bit of glassware. What we had on the new shelves sold really well this weekend."

Opal dug into her watermelon and added a few grains of salt to what was on her fork. Before she took a bite, she looked over at Libby. "What about you? Me and Minilee thought maybe we could get you to go with us to the farmers' market in Paris on Tuesday."

"I'd love to," Libby said with a nod, glad that Minilee didn't want to talk about the watermelon-and-life subject anymore. "But tomorrow, I'm going to Clarksville with Benny."

"Want me to babysit Fancy?" Minilee asked.

"That would be great," Libby answered. "Some places won't allow dogs inside the house, and it's supposed to be another hot one, so . . ."

"So, she can stay with us," Opal declared. "And you should leave Elvis at home, too, Benny. It's not like you'll be gone overnight. We'll make sure his water bowl is kept full here on the station porch."

"Thank you," Benny said with a nod. "Elvis will appreciate that, I'm sure."

Libby caught the look that passed between Opal and Minilee and wished she could read minds. "What time should I bring Fancy over to you?" she asked.

"We get up early, so anytime is good," Minilee answered.

Benny used his fork to dig out a chunk of melon at the same time Libby did, and their hands brushed against each other. She hoped that neither of the ladies saw the instant surge of heat that passed between her and Benny. But then, why would they? It wasn't visible, and she doubted that Benny even felt what she did.

"I figured we'd leave at eight," Benny said.

"We'll have already picked the beans, cucumbers, and squash from the garden by then, so just bring Miss Fancy on over," Minilee said. "She can watch the game shows on television with me."

"After we read our chapter for the day," Opal scolded.

Minilee narrowed her eyes and frowned. "Of course, but you don't have to announce it so loud. Fancy might not be religious, and we don't want to scare her away by reading the Bible out loud."

"I think the lady who used to have Fancy might have gone to church," Libby said, biting back a smile. "She had a picture of the Last Supper in her dining room."

"That's good," Minilee said with a satisfied air. "But if she gets bored, we'll let her watch the birds and squirrels from the front porch."

Libby finished off one more bite of watermelon and then laid her fork to the side. "Y'all would be wonderful grandparents."

"Yes, we would," Opal said, and cut her eyes over at Benny. "But until we get a baby to rock and love on, we'll have to be content with Fancy. Elvis is too big to cuddle."

"You know what that makes us?" Minilee said with half a giggle. "We might not be grandmothers, but we are grand-bitches."

"Minilee Stephens!" Opal air-slapped her arm.

"The truth is the truth, whether it's served up plain or covered with salt," Minilee declared. "Looks like we've done enough damage with this thing. Let's take it home now and get the rest of it taken care of. We've only got half a dozen jars of pickles left in the cellar. Let's make preserves out of this one."

"If we're going to do that, we should get the rind cleaned and in brine to soak overnight," Opal agreed as she picked up what was left of the half that Benny and Libby had shared.

"Preserves?" Libby asked.

"The preserves are more like candied watermelon rinds. We use them in our fruitcakes at Christmas, and we use the sweet syrup in our tea," Minilee explained.

Benny placed a hand on her shoulder. "You'll get to taste one of their fruitcakes this winter. They are amazing."

"Thanks," Opal said as she started for the door. "Minilee, grab that other half—and don't stand in the open door, talking half an hour. Air-conditioned air ain't free."

"Don't you boss me. You might be two months older, but at our age, that don't matter," Minilee fussed as she followed Opal outside.

"On that note, I'm going to my trailer," Benny said.

Libby cocked her head to one side and frowned. "I thought we were going to finish the conversation about us that a watermelon and the ladies interrupted."

Benny dropped a kiss on her forehead. "I know where I stand, but I feel like you need to think about your position."

She could hear him whistling all the way from the station to his trailer and wished she knew where she stood.

Listen to my advice about not analyzing everything, Dolly reminded her. *Go with your gut and your heart.*

Fancy came out from under the table and meandered across the floor. Libby opened the door into her apartment. The dog's little toenails tapping on the floor told her that Fancy had gone straight to her food and water bowls. She cleaned the tabletop, washed up the forks, and laid them out on the cabinet.

Libby tiptoed into the bathroom when she saw that Fancy was asleep on the sofa. She adjusted the water, shed her clothing, and crawled into the tub. She slid down until her feet touched the far end and leaned her head back on the other end. Benny was right: she did need to get things settled in her own mind—not only about a relationship with him but also about what it would do to the friendship she had with Opal and Minilee.

Chapter Twenty-Three

"*T*his is our first trip without the children," Benny said as he opened the truck door for Libby that morning after she had delivered Fancy to Minilee.

"We're on our first *full* trip without children." She dropped her purse in the back seat and buckled her seat belt. "We adopted Fancy on our last trip together, so we can only count half of it. But we'll be home by early afternoon, so maybe they won't miss us too badly."

Libby didn't want to make small talk about dogs, the weather, or even the antiques they were going to Clarksville to look at. "Do you ever dream?" she finally asked when they were halfway to the paved road.

"Every now and then," Benny answered. "Rather than dreams, I often wake up discombobulated. It comes from sleeping in so many hotel rooms. Seems like it takes me a minute or two to figure out where I am. How about you? What do you dream about?"

"I've had dreams or nightmares almost every night since I was ten years old," she replied, keeping her eyes on the rearview mirror. The cloud of dust behind them obliterated the small community they had left behind. If only the past could be dealt with the same way—just get in a vehicle, drive away, and it was gone forever, never to return to haunt her again.

"Tell me about last night's dream," Benny said.

"Opal and Minilee brought over a watermelon, and you split it open. You ever seen those bubbles in cartoons that show people's thoughts?"

Benny nodded.

"Well, those little bubbles kept popping up—only instead of thoughts, they were things that happened in my past. I took the knife from you and stabbed them so that you wouldn't be able to read the words," she said, and suddenly, the whole dream made sense.

She had told her Sawmill friends about her past, but what had been showing in those crazy bubbles were the helpless feelings she'd had during those times of distress. She didn't want anyone to know she had been that vulnerable—most of all Benny.

You are not powerless now, a voice she didn't recognize whispered softly in her ear.

"What do you think the dream meant?" Benny asked.

"That I'm opening up enough to tell you about my past but I don't want anyone to know how it made me feel," she answered.

"Why?" He made a left turn out onto the paved road. "Your feelings are what make you who you are."

She turned and stared right at him. "Maybe so, but I've worked hard to become independent and self-sufficient. I don't want to see pity in anyone's face when they look at me."

Benny whipped his head around and locked eyes with her for a couple of seconds. "Do you see that in me right now? I hope not, because I have the utmost respect for you, Libby. I've never known a woman with so much fire and yet such a big heart as what you have. I want us to be more than just friends."

"Thank you," she said and finally smiled. "When did our friendship and working arrangement turn into something else?"

"When I realized that you were the reason I wanted to come home earlier than planned. When I found all that glassware and wished that I could have you beside me to see your excitement," he answered. "I really, really like you, Libby. I don't want to spend that many days on the road. I want to spend more time with you."

She remembered the kisses and the effect they'd had on her. She wasn't innocent. She had had a couple of relationships in her past, but she wasn't devastated when they had failed. Amanda had told her that was because neither one was right.

"We're together twelve hours a day," Libby whispered.

"Three days a week," Benny said with a nod.

"And sometimes I go with you on trips."

Benny smiled. "I want us to date, Libby, and to talk about something other than antiques and file cabinets. That day at the river was great. No one interrupted us with a watermelon or popped into the store when we were building shelves. We had the entire day to ourselves. I want more times like that."

She reached across the console and laid a hand on his shoulder. "I would like that, but I refuse to be sneaky. Are you going to tell Opal and Minilee, or am I?"

"Why don't we do it together?" he suggested.

"That would be smart—but what if we find that like is as far as it goes, and then it's awkward for us to work together?" she asked.

"We can't let the what-ifs control our lives. But I'll see your what-if and raise you another one. What if fate brought us together, and we look back in fifty years and regret that we didn't take advantage of our opportunities?"

Libby took a deep breath, let it out slowly, and smiled. "I'll dive into the deep water if you are willing to jump with me."

He reached over the console and took her hand in his. "I'm ready, and we can talk to Opal and Minilee when we get home this afternoon."

Could this be what I missed in my previous relationships? she wondered. *The openness? The honesty? The freedom to talk about the past and my feelings?*

"Sally and Ilene are coming today to help them can green beans and make squash relish. Let's wait until tomorrow and talk to them on the way to the farmers' market," Libby suggested.

Benny agreed with a nod. "What day each week will be good for our date night?"

"Sunday is out because we're wiped out from work," she answered. "Monday, we're playing catch-up with paperwork and straightening up from the weekend. Any of the other three is good for me. I don't have much of a social life, as you already know." On one hand, the idea of dating Benny was exciting enough to make her heart flutter. On the other hand, it terrified her to be taking their relationship to the next level.

"How about we keep it flexible and just go out whatever day or night seems right for that week?" He gave her hand a gentle squeeze.

"Or stay in and spend a day at the river, or maybe grill some hamburgers and watch an old movie. I'm a cheap date. I don't have to go to fancy restaurants," she said.

"Another reason I like you so much," Benny said with a grin.

"Good morning to y'all," Opal said as she hopped up into the back seat with the agility of a teenager.

"Ditto," Minilee groaned, using the handhold to pull herself up and ease into the seat behind Libby.

"Are you all right?" Libby asked.

"I'm just stiff from all the work we did yesterday. It'll work itself out when I walk around the farmers' market," Minilee answered. "Take my advice and remember to not just sit down when you get old. Keep going as long as you can because once you sit down, then you don't want to get up and go again."

"Yes, ma'am," Libby and Benny both said at the same time.

"You kids came home late last night," Opal commented as Benny put the truck in gear and started driving down the gravel road. "Did you find the note on the station door?"

"I did, and thank you for babysitting Fancy all day," Libby answered. "She was sound asleep under the table when I got home."

"She was a delight," Minilee said. "Sally and Ilene fought over who got to take her out for walks, so we all had to take turns. If she hadn't been fixed so she couldn't have puppies, I would have gladly taken a pup off your hands."

Benny looked at her in the rearview mirror. "Maybe you could find a little Chihuahua at the shelter in Paris. They're probably open today, so we could go by there."

Minilee shook her head. "No, thanks. I'll just steal Fancy when I want some doggy love. Did y'all find lots of good stuff yesterday?"

"We did, but not so much at the sale," Benny told her. "We hit several garage sales that were selling everything for half price and picked up a couple of things at each one."

"We brought home a lovely oak washstand that we got for five dollars and a couple of two-tiered tea stands from another one that we only paid ten dollars for both, not each. The auction had a barbecue wagon, so we got sandwiches for lunch, and then we found a little homestyle restaurant for supper," Libby said.

"Libby and I discussed a lot of things yesterday, but the most important one is that we like each other, and we are officially dating," Benny blurted out.

"Well, it's about damn time," Opal said.

"Hey, now," Minilee argued, "you were the one against them going out at all."

"Does that mean you think it's a bad idea?" Libby asked and felt like a teenager begging for Victoria's permission to go to the senior prom with Matthew Thomas.

"She can't say a word about a person dating or even marrying whoever they please," Minilee smarted off.

Opal shook her forefinger at Minilee. "You don't need to drag up old stories. Sleeping dogs are best left alone, or they might rise up and bite you on the butt. Remember, I know all about you, too."

Libby covered a giggle with the back of her hand.

"I'll spill the tea, as you kids say today for gossip," Minilee said. "Opal fell in love with Ernest, but her mama thought she could do better. He had been quite the ladies' man from the time he was about sixteen. He drew girls to him like flies to a fresh apple pie coolin' on the table."

"She came around after a couple of years," Opal protested.

"Yes, but you had to sneak around to date him for the six months before y'all eloped," Minilee reminded her.

Libby hadn't expected Benny to just blurt the news out and was surprised that Opal seemed to be okay with the issue. She had expected adversity from her, since she'd been the one who was so adamant that Benny wind up married to Tatum.

Opal crossed her arms over her chest and glared at Minilee. "Now that you've opened that can of worms, you might as well tell the whole story."

"It's your story, so you tell it," Minilee told her.

Opal sat up a little straighter. "Mama said that Ernest was flittin' around all kinds of young women that would make him a wonderful wife—like a fly or a honeybee. She expected him to finally light on a cow patty because all the good girls would figure out that he was what you kids call a player these days. But I loved him, and I knew he had a good heart."

She paused and stared out the side window for a few seconds. Libby took that time to study Benny's profile. From everything she'd seen, he had a big heart, too. He had refused to give up Elvis to go out with Tatum, and he didn't really care about being rich.

"So when he asked me to marry him, I said yes," Opal went on. "We knew we'd have trouble with my mama, so I told him we should get a marriage license at the courthouse in Hugo and get married by a justice of the peace. Then we would tell my mama afterwards."

"What about your dad? Weren't you worried about what he thought?" Benny asked.

"My father didn't say much, but he agreed with Mama when it came to Ernest," Opal answered. "I graduated from high school on a Friday. Ernest had been working down here at the sawmill for several months and had gotten a promotion up to supervisor, so we had a house to move into. On Monday, I rode into town with my dad with the excuse that I was going to apply for a job at the little grocery store. Ernest picked me up in his car out behind the store, and we went to the courthouse. The judge would have married us right there, but he was out sick with the flu. So we took our license and went next door to the justice of the peace. He had already left to go to Grant to go fishing with a couple of his buddies, but the lady there said we could probably catch him a couple of miles down the road."

"Did you ever think that those were two signs you shouldn't marry Ernest?" Libby asked.

"Nope," Opal replied. "I figured that I loved him enough to jump over the hurdles. We caught up to the justice and motioned for him to pull over, and he married us right there on the side of the road. Ernest had just kissed me when my father came roaring down the road and slammed on the brakes so fast that it made the dust on Sawmill Road seem like nothing."

Libby was totally engrossed in the story. "What happened then?"

"Daddy ranted and raved, and finally told me that I'd made my bed and now I had to sleep in it. We drove to Sawmill. Ernest went to work. I sat in an empty house the rest of the day and waited for him to come home. His folks brought us an old iron bedstead and a mattress that evening, along with some sheets and a quilt. The house had a cookstove and a refrigerator. Mama sent Sally down here with all of my personal things and said it would be best if I didn't come back to Grant for a while."

"How did that make you feel?" Libby asked.

"Deserted," Opal admitted. "But Minilee and Floyd were right next door. They saved us."

"Yes, we did," Minilee said. "But me and Floyd had already been through our first year, and we had had our folks' blessing. We've been taking care of each other ever since."

Libby knew what Victoria would say about her dating Benny. There would be no opposition. All she would see would be dollar signs.

"Thanks for telling us that story, but I've got a question," Benny said. "You were both against me going out with Libby when she arrived. What changed your minds?"

"She did," Opal said. "We judged the book by the cover when we should have waited to read the whole story. I'm fine with the two of you dating, but don't get in a hurry."

"And if you ever get married, we want to be there," Minilee told them.

"'If'?" Benny chuckled.

"Go slow, and we might change *if* to *when* in a few months," Opal said.

Libby had hoped that agreeing to go out with Benny wouldn't cause her to lose her friendship with Opal and Minilee. She was glad they weren't totally against the two of them dating, but talking about marriage this early in the game was downright scary. The very idea put her in flight mode. She reached for the door handle and began to tremble. She clasped her hands together in her lap and willed her pulse to settle down. Could she see herself committing to a lifetime with Benny?

"Maybe," she answered, so softly that the road noise covered up the word. Her hands stopped shaking, and the rush of adrenaline that had caused her to think about running away settled down. She had always thought she would never be able to trust anyone enough to commit to a relationship that involved a white dress and a cake, but living with Benny sometime in the distant future didn't sound too bad.

Chapter Twenty-Four

*L*ibby could hear music playing and children laughing long before Benny found a parking spot in the huge lot.

"Oh my!" she gasped.

"What were you expecting?" Opal asked.

"A pavilion where folks buy fresh produce—tomatoes, squash, cantaloupe," she answered. "This is more like a fair, and there's a carousel in the middle."

"We don't need to buy produce," Minilee said as she opened the truck door and slid off the seat. "Neither do you and Benny. We come here to buy honey for the most part."

"I've got allergies this time of year," Opal said as she picked up her empty tote bag and shoved her wallet into it. "Don't forget to lock the doors, Benny. I'm leaving my purse in the truck."

Benny opened the door for Libby and extended a hand to help her. She took it and wasn't even a little surprised at the chemistry that flowed between them at his touch. He kept her hand in his as they walked under the FARMERS' MARKET sign.

"What does honey have to do with allergies?" Her eyes darted around at the vendors, who were set up in a U-shape around the carousel.

"We mix a tablespoon of local honey with the same amount of apple cider vinegar in a glass of water and drink it twice a day," Minilee explained. "It helps with our arthritis and with Opal's allergies."

"Old home remedies are the best," Opal added as the four of them crossed the parking lot. "Sometimes we can even buy good homemade vinegar at this place, along with our local honey. How 'bout we meet y'all by the carousel at eleven o'clock? If we can stop at that little burger shop for lunch, me and Minilee will treat you kids."

"Sounds great," Benny said with a nod.

"What will they do for two whole hours?" Libby whispered.

"They know about half the vendors, so this is as much of a social day as it is business for them. They'll catch up on the gossip," Benny answered. "Which way do you want to go?"

"I want to ride the carousel before we leave, but I'd love to just take a look at all the stands."

He pointed to the other side of the lot. "Let's start over here, then. It looks like all the non-food vendors are over there, and we'll finish up with the produce sellers. I wouldn't mind taking home some of those peaches. That way we can buy them just before we leave and not have to carry them around."

"Sounds like a good plan."

They passed by vendors who sold everything from handmade jewelry to cotton candy.

"This is awesome. Do they have it every week?" she asked.

"Nope, just on the last Tuesday of each month. Grandpa brought me here a few times when I was a little boy. I loved the carousel back then—and of course, the cotton candy," Benny answered. "Grandpa always got one of the big cinnamon buns and a cup of coffee. We would sit on a bench not far from the carousel, have our treats, and then he would ride the ponies with me."

"Can adults still ride?" Libby asked and sniffed the air. "I smell the cinnamon."

"Yes, anyone can ride the carousel," Benny answered. "The cinnamon bun vendor isn't far away. Want to get a couple of buns and sit on that bench over there?" He pointed to the left. "We can watch the ponies go around while we have a midmorning snack."

"Yes, I would, to all of the above. I've never been to anything like this."

"Then our first official date is a winner?" he asked.

She smiled at him. "If this is a date, then it's the best one I've ever been on."

Benny squeezed her hand gently. "It's a date, and I agree with you."

He had dated a lot of women, and the ones from his past circles would never have gone to a farmers' market in the middle of a field. The ground alone would have ruined their expensive high-heeled shoes. Libby was one of a kind, and he loved that about her.

"Hey, what are you . . ." Tatum stopped in front of them and stared down at their hands. "I guess I don't need to finish that sentence, do I?"

"Nope, you do not," Benny answered, hoping her presence wouldn't sour the day.

"What are you doing back in this part of Texas?" Libby asked. "We heard that you had gone to the city to find a job."

"It didn't work out . . ." Tatum's full lips turned up in a seductive smile. "So I came back up here to spend some time with my grand-mother. I drove her and Ilene down here today. She has never been able to stay mad at me for long. How about you, Benny? Do you keep a grudge forever?"

"Nope," Benny said.

She laid a hand on his shoulder. "Then do I get a second chance with you if I play nice?"

"I'm not sure you ever had a first chance," he told her. "Seems to me like it was a choice between you and Elvis."

She took a step back and glared at him. "I wasn't asking for a date. That ship has sailed. *Evidently.*" She turned her evil stare toward Libby. "I just want a good reference. Everyone knows that Walter Taylor was a household name in Texas. A word from you would go a long way for me in landing a good job."

"I already said I wasn't comfortable with that, so the answer is still no." Benny tugged on Libby's hand, but she didn't move.

Tatum gave Libby a once-over, starting with the toes of her sandals and traveling all the way up to the messy bun perched on top of her head. "I could change your mind about that, and about your giant of a woman, if you'd give me a chance."

"Has anyone ever made you understand the word *no*, Tatum?" Libby asked. "I can understand your ability to talk your way around your relatives, but you were in the service. How did you spend so much time in the military and not learn that *no* means *no*?"

"Honey, if you have the right equipment and you learn to use it, you can get what you want any time," Tatum said with a fake smile. "Some of us have the goods. Unlike you."

"Bless your heart." Libby's words dripped with sarcasm. "Tell Sally hello from me and that I'm looking forward to seeing her at book club next week. Why don't you move along now and have a wonderful day with all your 'right equipment.'"

Benny bit back a chuckle. Libby was no pushover, for sure. That just made him like her even more. When he gave her hand another gentle tug, she turned and went with him. He led her to the cinnamon-bun wagon and ordered two, plus two cups of coffee.

"I should apologize," she whispered.

"What for?" He paid for the order and handed over her cup. Then he picked up the disposable basket with the pastries and his coffee.

"I butted into your conversation. That wasn't my business, and you were doing a fine job of handling Tatum," she answered.

"You don't owe me anything, but I owe you a thank-you," he said as he led the way to a bench beside the carousel.

Libby sat down on the bench and took a sip of her coffee. "Then let's just call it even, eat our cinnamon buns, and put Tatum out of our minds. Victoria's friend June used to say that whoever stirs the shit pile has to lick the spoon."

Benny burst out laughing. "I've never heard that, but I like it," he said when he could catch his breath.

She picked up her bun and took a bite. "This is an amazing first date, Benny. Can we come back again?"

"Every month, if you want to," Benny said. "Since I've been getting offers for buyouts, we can keep the stock up in the store and still turn a nice profit, and that means I'll be home more and more."

"Those kids are so cute," Libby said between bites. "I especially like the parents that are either standing or riding right beside them."

"You like kids?" Benny asked.

"Love 'em," Libby said. "I think I told you before that I volunteered at a women's shelter in Austin a few hours on Saturdays. Most days, I read to the kids or played games with them for a couple of hours to give their mamas a little time to go to therapy sessions."

"Miss it?" Benny asked.

Libby nodded. "Some of them were a lot like me at their age. They wanted to be loved so badly that they craved attention of any kind. I tried to fill in the gaps a little."

"Ever think about having children of your own?"

Another nod. "But, Benny, I don't know what my background is. What if I was a terrible mother? I have no idea if my mother would have had any mothering instincts. She died when I was born. Then, when you consider nurture . . ." She shrugged. "Victoria sure wasn't a good role model. I would rather never have a child than put one through the life I had."

"You could use all that as examples of how not to be," he said. He finished the last bite of his pastry and took a sip of his coffee.

"Never thought of that," she said. "I loved the kids at the shelter. Dolly, Amanda, and the time I got to volunteer were the reasons I thought long and hard about leaving the area. But my unemployment benefits had run out, and I was depleting what savings I had with rent and food. Dolly kept encouraging me to go somewhere else and get a fresh start . . . and here I am."

"I'm glad you decided to come up here," he said, and handed her a packet of wet wipes the vendor had put in the edge of the basket. "It's impossible to eat those things without getting sticky hands. Are you ready for that pony ride?"

"I'm ready," she answered. "This date just gets better and better. I can't wait to tell Amanda all about it."

"Where did you go on dates before?" he asked, leading her to the ticket booth.

"Dinner and the movies, usually," she said. "Two really boring places. I'd rather go to the river or come to a place like this."

Benny wondered if all women thought dinner and a movie, or maybe a play, was boring. He checked the time and found that they had a half hour before Opal and Minilee would be ready to leave. The carousel ride lasted fifteen minutes, so he bought extra tickets so they could ride until it was time to go. Libby was right. This was an awesome first date—but in all actuality, it was a second date if they counted the day at the river as the first one. And he certainly did.

Chapter Twenty-Five

"So far, so good," Libby said as she carried one of her no-bake pumpkin cheesecakes toward the door leading into the front room of the station. She was talking not about the way her dessert had turned out but about how dating Benny had been going. She reminded herself several times a day that a relationship with him wasn't smart, but then she would hear Victoria telling her that she was a stick-in-the-mud.

"No!" She shook her head. "I've faced that issue, and I'm not thinking about it anymore."

When she opened the door into the front room, she expected Fancy to hop down off the sofa, but the dog just opened one eye for a few seconds and then closed it again. Evidently, the long walk to the river that afternoon had exhausted the poor little thing.

Opal waved from across the room where she was putting ice in glasses. "You ready to discuss the book we read? It's kind of about you and Benny."

"Friends to lovers is the trope tonight," Minilee reminded her. "That's the story of you and Benny, for sure."

Libby set her cheesecake on the counter and nodded. They could think what they wanted, but the truth was that, right then, it was friends to *dating*. The lovers part had not happened yet. "I enjoyed reading the book a lot. Did y'all think it was a romance or a women's fiction?"

"Shhh . . ." Opal shushed her. "We can ask if you are ready to talk about the book, but we have to save the questions until after supper."

"But that's a good question to ask," Minilee said. "And we'll definitely dive right into that discussion."

"We're here!" Ilene called out.

Sally carried a box into the room and set it on the counter. "I brought a lasagna, a salad, and some of my famous hot rolls for supper."

"I made the salad," Ilene said, then giggled.

"She sprinkled the croutons on the top after I finished making it," Sally argued.

"That's the most important part of any salad," Ilene told her.

Libby peeled back the aluminum foil from the top of a long casserole dish. "Want me to carry this to the table?"

"Yes, and thank you," Sally answered.

Libby used two hot pads to carry the steaming-hot food. "This smells so good. I could eat Italian food for breakfast without even heating it up."

"So can Tatum," Sally said. "I made a small one for her to have tonight when she comes home from wherever she's going with her friends."

"I heard she had come back to Grant," Minilee said as she brought glasses of iced tea to the table. "What happened to her getting a job in the big city?"

"Benny wouldn't give her a reference," Sally answered. "At least, that's her excuse. They probably did a drug test and she failed it, if the truth be told. In my opinion—which doesn't matter one bit to her—she should have stayed in the service and made a career of it, but what do I know?" Sally shrugged. "I'm just an old lady who lets her come back whenever she has no place else to go. I realize her faults, but she's family."

Opal patted her on the shoulder and then sat down. "You got to do what your heart tells you to do or else you can't live with yourself. Looks like we all need a night of good food, a good book, and good friends."

"This is like a little Las Vegas," Minilee said. "What we talk about here stays here."

Libby wondered if that meant she shouldn't discuss anything that had to do with Benny, but she didn't ask. She pulled out a chair and took a seat. Opal said a short grace, then Sally served up squares of lasagna.

"How do you handle being so angry with Tatum and then welcoming her back into your home whenever she shows up on your doorstep?" Minilee asked Sally.

"It raises my blood pressure, for sure," Sally admitted. "But my granny often told me that my job was to do what was right, no matter what it costs me. I kept Tatum until she started school so that her mama and daddy could work. She was so cute back then that I didn't ever tell her no. Her parents felt guilty for leaving her, so they didn't discipline her. Then her parents sent her to live with me her senior year in high school because she got caught with whiskey on the school grounds and got expelled. She was a holy terror by then, but I believed her when she said that mean girls had put the liquor in her locker."

"Are you saying that you are to blame for her attitude?" Opal asked.

"If you are, I don't believe it," Ilene argued. "Tatum is a grown woman. She might have been a handful when she was younger, but she needs to hold herself accountable and not blame everyone else."

Libby listened to them disagree with Sally for a moment or two. Then she went into her own little bubble and thought about what Ilene had just said. Victoria had made sure that she was held accountable for every single mistake she ever made. But what kept looping back around to Libby was what Ilene had said about not blaming anyone else. She had just done that very thing when she told Benny she wasn't sure she would make a good mother because of her biological mother and Victoria's influence. She—not Victoria or Liza—could control the type of mother she would make.

"Is something wrong with the lasagna?" Sally asked. "You have only taken one bite."

Her question jerked Libby away from her own thoughts. "No, it's delicious. If you give out recipes, I'd love to know how you make it. I was just thinking about a conversation I had with Benny."

"They're dating now," Minilee announced.

"Oh, really?" Sally's face lit up in a bright smile.

Ilene laid her fork down. "Tell us more."

Libby quickly shoveled a forkful of lasagna into her mouth and held up a finger.

"She needs to get her supper eaten, or we'll be discussing our book until midnight," Opal declared. "So me and Minilee will fill you in on this case of friends to lovers while she cleans up her plate."

"Benny announced that they were dating last Tuesday when we went to the farmers' market. They've been on a couple of buying trips together—and they rode the carousel, not once but two times around," Minilee said and held up two fingers.

"He says that he's cutting down on the number of days that he travels and is spending more time at home. Last night after they came home from work, they took the dogs for a long walk near the river and didn't come home until after dark," Opal added.

"And they've been eating supper together almost every night," Minilee chimed back in. "We invited them over here for supper on Thursday, and they were holding hands all the way across the road."

Sally clapped. "Real-life friends to lovers."

Apparently, what happened in Sawmill did not stay in Sawmill. Not when Opal and Minilee were on watch-and-report duty. Libby wondered how much Sally would tell Tatum about what they talked about over the supper table that night.

She vowed that she would not let that woman or any other one cause her grief—not from her past, her bloodlines—or lack of them—or even the voices that popped into her head. She might still talk to herself on occasion, but she was a grown woman. As such, she would control her own future.

"Friends to *dating* right now," Libby said with a smile. "We are taking things slow. We've only known each other a few weeks."

Sally let out a long sigh. "I wish Tatum was more like you. She wants everything *right now*." She snapped her fingers.

"Instant gratification," Ilene said with a nod. "All this internet stuff has brought up a generation of kids that want everything right now, this minute." She snapped her fingers, too. "They don't want to learn to cook because they can pop a burrito in the microwave and have dinner in less than a minute."

"And forget about having the patience to garden," Opal said. "They won't even take time to open up a can, much less gather their own food and fix it."

"We won't live to see it," Minilee said, "but in the next couple of generations, I predict that they won't be taught to eat their vegetables at all. They'll just eat supplements, and folks will grow weaker from not having good nutrition."

Libby let their ranting go in one ear and out the other as she finished her supper. "Are y'all ready for dessert and then the book discussion?" she finally asked.

"Yes, we are," Sally said. "Let's put an end to this conversation about things we can't do diddly-squat about. I loved the book, but I couldn't decide if it was a romance or women's fiction."

Libby brought the cheesecake to the table and cut it into slices. "That was going to be my first question. I liked the romance, and that Lacey and Delmond went from being friends to lovers, but I felt like her friends helping her get through her past was also a key part of her growth and finding happiness."

"Yep, her friends were the ones who helped her see value in herself," Sally said.

"But she was the only one that could take that next step with Delmond," Ilene said. "This cheesecake is wonderful. A perfect dessert after a heavy supper."

"Did you have a favorite quote from the book?" Opal asked.

"Yep," Libby answered. "'When opportunity knocks, invite it in for cake and sweet tea. Don't wait until it's a mile down the road and chase after it.'"

"I liked that one, too," Minilee said, "but my favorite was 'Trust your heart.'"

"Mine was when they said their wedding vows, and Delmond told Lacey that she was the other half of his soul," Opal said.

They all turned toward Sally, who shrugged, sighed, and finally said, "I liked that part when Lacey told Delmond that she was afraid she would ruin their friendship if they took the next step into a serious relationship."

"Didn't the way the author described the love scene bring back memories?" Minilee asked.

Sally covered a giggle with her veined and wrinkled hand. "It made me think of the first time me and my late husband made love."

"Where was that?" Ilene asked.

"In the back seat of his car, down by the Red River. A full moon just about filled the whole back glass. I remember thinking that it was shining down on us both," Sally answered. "What did it make the rest of you think about?"

"My wedding night," Ilene answered. "I was scared out of my mind that I wouldn't do it right."

"Me too," Opal agreed. "But I wasn't scared."

"Floyd and I weren't married when we had sex the first time, and I liked it. I used to start an argument with him just so we could go to the bedroom and make up," Minilee said.

They all turned to Libby. She raised one shoulder and let the feeling of affection and warmth wrap around her like a thick shawl on a winter evening. "I love your stories and all the help you have given me, but I can't comment. The only thought I had after that scene was that it was such an emotional and beautiful time for Lacey, I hoped she and Delmond lived to see their fiftieth anniversary."

Own your sexuality. Dolly's voice was so loud that she jumped.

❖ ❖ ❖

Benny and Elvis watched the sun set from a lawn chair between his trailer and the station while the book club meeting was going on. For the past week, he and Libby had been together almost every day—either working in the store or simply enjoying each other's company over supper on the front porch. While she spent Thursday morning getting everything done in the office, he had brought several pieces from the warehouse into the store.

Dusk had settled and a few stars were sparkling in the sky when Sally and Ilene left the station. A few minutes later, Opal and Minilee walked across the road. He noticed that Libby and Fancy were standing on the front porch, so Elvis headed that way.

"Got any of that cheesecake left?" Benny asked as he walked up on the porch.

"They ate the one I took to the meeting, but the recipe makes two, so we have a whole one to ourselves," she answered as she sat down beside him.

He scooted his chair closer to hers, draped an arm around her shoulders, and drew her close to his side. "How did the meeting go?"

"Great," Libby said. "Enlightening. Thought provoking. At least, that's what I got from the book and from listening to all of the opinions the other four had."

"Didn't you tell me that it was a friends-to-lovers trope?" he asked.

She laid her head on his shoulder. "That's right."

"Think we'll ever get that far in our relationship?"

"Yep." Libby raised her head high enough to kiss him on the cheek and then snuggled closer to his neck. "I expect that we'll both know when the time is right for that step."

"I more than just like you, you know," Benny whispered close to her ear.

"Seems like what started off as like and respect has grown for both of us, hasn't it?"

Fancy strained at the leash, so Libby stood up. "Want to go back to the apartment and have a piece of cheesecake for a snack?"

"Yes, ma'am," he answered and took her free hand in his.

Elvis followed right along beside Fancy, as if he were protecting her from any evil hawks or snakes, until they reached the door, but then he stopped and lapped up some water. Benny opened the door for Libby, and she unclipped the leash from Fancy's collar. The little dog ran across the room and through the open door into the apartment.

Libby flipped off the porch light and the overhead lights in the front room. When they entered the apartment, she closed the door. "Cheesecake or kisses first?"

"Kisses win that question every time," Benny said as he drew her into his arms and found her lips in the semidark room.

"I feel like a teenager sneaking around for make-out sessions," she whispered when Benny backed her up toward the sofa and pulled her down onto his lap. "Opal and Minilee are right across the street."

Benny cupped her face in his hands. "We are consenting adults. It's no one's business what we do but ours."

Libby pulled away.

"Are you okay?" he asked. "Did I hurt you?"

"No, I just got a message that was loud and clear." She stood up and took his hand in hers. "Friends to lovers. I'm ready if you are."

"Yes, my darlin', I am," Benny said.

She gave his hand a gentle tug, and he stood up.

"But we don't have to hurry. We've got all night," he said.

"I guess we'll have dessert later?"

"Mmmm," he said as he buried his face in her neck. "Much later. Much, much later."

She tugged his T-shirt up over his head. "I like that idea."

Chapter Twenty-Six

The warmth of the morning sun flowing through the window warmed Libby's face the next morning and brought her out of a wonderful dream about her and Benny sitting on a porch and watching the sunrise together. She opened her eyes slowly and reached over to find the other side of the bed empty. She sat up so quickly that the room did a spin before things settled down. Benny came out of the bathroom with a towel wrapped around his waist.

He then picked up the leftover cheesecake and two forks. "Good mornin', gorgeous," he said as he dropped the towel and crawled beneath the sheets. "Breakfast in bed seems like a good way to start the day."

"I bet you say that to all the women you sleep with," she said.

"Nope, just the ones that have a cheesecake ready," he teased as he fed her the first bite, "and the ones I like well enough to give the first bite of pumpkin cheesecake to, which is my favorite."

"How many is that?" Libby asked, not really sure she wanted to know the answer.

"Counting you? One," he answered. "I have never spent the entire night with a woman, Libby. I have always left before daylight."

"What about when they stayed at your apartment?"

"Didn't ever happen, or in the house in Paris, either," he answered and fed her another bite. "How many men have fed you cheesecake for breakfast?"

"Not a single one," she answered, "until now, and that would be one—you."

"Okay, enough about that part of our past," he said. "I don't need to know numbers."

"Me neither," she told him, but she figured that his number would be way north of what hers was. "What's on our agenda for today?"

"I want to draw up a rough draft for a house," he answered. "And I'd like your input on the plans."

She took the pan from his hands and kissed him on the lips. "My only idea is that the big breakfront could be set on a foyer wall or even in the living room as an entertainment center. Other than that, it's your house, Benny. What made you decide to build a house now? I thought you were happy in your trailer."

"Mmmm . . ." He pulled her in for another kiss. "I like pumpkin cheesecake, but having the taste on your lips is even better than just eating it."

"That's both the funniest and the most romantic thing anyone's ever said to me," she said as she fed him a bite. When he had eaten it, she leaned in for another kiss. "You are so right. That makes for some good kisses."

"Oh, yeah," he said with a chuckle. "To answer your question— when I moved up here, I vowed that I would live in the trailer for a year to be sure I had no regrets about leaving the law firm. I haven't had a single one. Except that last week, when I was home for all those days, I figured out that when I'm in it for several days a week, the trailer feels pretty cramped. Out on the road for four days and working the other three seemed to work. Now I need a little more space."

"Well, then . . ." She crawled out of the bed. "After we eat a proper breakfast, I guess we will get busy designing a house. I've got a couple of rolls of Christmas paper we can use."

He raised an eyebrow. "Doesn't it have jingle bells or . . ."

She bent and kissed him on the cheek. "The back side is white, so we'll just flip it over and tape it to the table in the front room. I had no idea you were a draftsman."

"I'm not." Benny stood up and put on his jeans and shirt, which had been strewn across the apartment floor. He crossed the room and slipped his arms around Libby's waist and pulled her to his chest. "But I can make a rough draft and give it to an architect. I like the way you feel in my arms."

She turned and wrapped her arms around his neck. "I like having breakfast in bed with you."

"We could have lunch and supper in bed, too," he suggested with a wicked smile.

"Sounds good, but—" She barely had time to moisten her lips before his closed in on them. Her breath came in short bursts when he pulled back a few inches.

"What were you saying?" he asked and then grinned.

"That we need to—"

His lips found hers again. This time she forgot about everything until she heard Fancy whimpering at her feet. She put her hands on his chest and gave him a gentle push. "I can't think straight when I'm this close to you."

"Right back at you," he said and stepped around her to turn the bacon. "Can I steal a kiss or two while we are having breakfast and working on house plans?"

"Maybe a couple," she answered, hoping the euphoria that she felt right then—something she'd never experienced with any other man—wasn't just a flash in the pan but would last forever.

Forever! That's a really wonderful word. The voice in her head sounded happy.

"Hey, what are you kids doing?" Opal yelled as she entered the station.

"Building a house," Benny answered, but he didn't look up from the table, where he was using an old wooden ruler and a carpenter's pencil to make lines. "We went up to the warehouse and measured that antique breakfront that Grandpa bought when I was a little boy. I want to use it for an entertainment unit in the living room."

Minilee followed Opal and sat down at the table. "It's about time. I don't know how you've managed in that little bitty trailer for a whole year. It's even smaller than Libby's apartment. What kind of house is it, and where are you going to build it?"

Until that moment, he hadn't really thought about where he wanted to put the house. He laid down the pencil. "What do you think, Libby?"

"Depends on a lot of things," she answered. "How much land you own. How far from the road you want to put it. Things like that."

"I own six hundred acres." Benny went back to his work. "From here to the river. From the turnoff onto the gravel road to half a mile back behind the warehouses, and half a mile behind Opal and Minilee's houses. And I think we should build back away from the road to get away from all the dust."

"Oh! My! Goodness!" Libby gasped. "That's a lot of property."

Benny looked up with a smile. "It's all relative. Compared to the little bit of land that this station is sitting on, it really is—but compared to a ten-thousand-acre ranch, it's just a drop in the ocean."

Libby nodded. "Still, I guess that does offer more options."

"My opinion is that you should cut a road behind the store and warehouse," Minilee said. "Clear out enough that you've got good shade on three sides, and make it face the east."

Benny rubbed his chin. "That *would* make for privacy."

"Have a paved road built back to your place, so on rainy days you can drive to work," Opal suggested. "What made you decide to do this now?"

Benny drew another line on the paper. "Living in a trailer with Elvis for four straight days." He wasn't ready to tell them that he needed more room if he was going to have a family in the near future. Libby needed time to adjust to the idea of dating and then possibly spending lots of nights together before they became permanent housemates—and hopefully a married couple on down the road. She should be the one to decide about making the arrangement permanent.

Permanent! Benny stopped what he was doing and stood back to think about that word.

The idea of marriage had always put him in flight-or-fight mode, and the former usually won the battle. He felt like he couldn't trust a woman to love him for who he was and not because of his money. But that morning, the idea didn't terrify him, and instead of wanting to run, he wanted to take Libby in his arms and hold her there forever.

Elvis and Fancy were quite the pair in the back seat of the pickup truck on the Fourth of July. Elvis sat up proudly and looked out the side window. Fancy reared up on her hind feet and watched the world go past on her side.

"Don't worry." Benny reached across the console and laid a hand on Libby's shoulder. "Naomi has watched Elvis before. She's good with animals, and the backyard is totally fenced, so they can go outside and explore."

"I trust you," Libby told him.

She had worried that, in her excitement, Fancy might scratch a piece of priceless furniture in the Taylor mansion they were heading toward, but more than that, she was concerned about seeing Benny in a whole different element. Would he act differently in a house big enough to be considered an estate? Would she feel like a country bumpkin?

"Naomi is making lunch for us after the parade, and we'll have time to ourselves before the fireworks show tonight," he said. "But I'm rattling on. You already know the plans for today. Have I told you that you look beautiful in that sundress?"

"Maybe six times," Libby answered. "Why are you nervous today?"

"You don't miss anything, do you?"

"Not much," she replied. "It comes from having to read Victoria when I was young. Are you going to talk to me about what's going on in your head?"

Benny sucked in a lungful of air and let it out slowly. "You live at the station. I stay in a travel trailer. When you see Grandpa's estate, I don't want you to think I'm an entitled brat."

"I don't want you to think I'm a country bumpkin," Libby admitted. "I came to Sawmill with almost everything I own in my SUV. You are my polar opposite when it comes to wealth."

Benny chuckled. "If it's true that opposites attract, then we should get the prize, don't you think? Honey, I'm falling in love with a strong, independent woman who I want to spend time with, whether it's in your apartment, my trailer, or Grandpa's mansion. Those are all just places—some big, some small. It's the time that we spend together that's important to me."

Libby's breath caught in her chest. Benny had said the *L* word. Not actually *the* three magic words—*I love you*—but close enough.

"Right back at you," she said. "But—"

"There are no *but*s in a relationship like ours. Only *and*s," Benny told her.

"I like that." She smiled and hoped that there were never *but*s in their lives.

In order to have only *and*s, she felt like she had to get complete closure. A line in the self-help book she was reading for the club meeting for the next week came to her mind: *When you forgive those who have hurt you, you take away their power.*

Forgiveness was more than just saying the words, though. Still, the idea of no one having power over her appealed to Libby in a way that words couldn't explain. All that had gone on in her past had made her who she was that very day—someone who could fall in love with Benny and have a life of peace and happiness. He deserved a companion and a lover who didn't come with a load of mental baggage.

Closure might come in little bites, like another quote in the book said: *You can eat an elephant a bite at a time.*

They passed the WELCOME TO PARIS, TEXAS sign, and Libby decided that today, she was taking a big bite out of that elephant. After all, it was Independence Day.

Her resolve dwindled somewhat when she saw the house, but she felt better when a tall, plus-size woman waved from the rosebushes in the front yard. Benny opened the truck door for Libby and helped get Fancy's leash on her collar. Elvis bounded out of the back seat and ran right to the woman, who was dressed in jeans and a T-shirt.

"You are early," the woman said. "I wasn't expecting you for another hour and thought I had time to clean up a little. Who is this precious little thing on a leash?"

"Fancy is her name, and I am—"

"I am Naomi, and you are Libby," the woman said. "Benny has told me all about you and sent pictures. But you are much more beautiful than the photographs. Come on inside. I have a little snack laid out for you kids so you won't get hungry at the parade. We can have it in the kitchen while the doggies explore the backyard. I'll tell Claude to keep an extra eye on the little one since she's new here."

Benny ushered Libby into the house with his hand on her lower back. She covered a gasp with a fake cough. The credenza in the foyer was worth more than her SUV, and that was just one of the many pieces of antique furniture she could see from that angle. Evidently, Walter hadn't just *liked* antiques—he'd loved them. A few items were more modern but had been chosen well to fit in with the old ones. The deep burgundy leather sofa facing the massive stone fireplace looked inviting and well worn. Libby could well imagine spending hours curled up on it with a good book in her hands.

"Like I told you before, Claude is Naomi's husband, and they oversee this place together. There's also a cleaning staff and gardeners," Benny explained as they passed through the foyer, where two curved staircases led up to the second floor.

"We wish that Benny would live here," Naomi said over her shoulder as they passed through the dining room and went into the kitchen.

Libby had never seen such a huge, modern kitchen, not even in the home-decorating magazines she loved to glance through when she went to the bookstores in Austin.

"I made a few croissants this morning and stuffed them with chicken salad, and the macarons are leftovers from yesterday. They aren't as good as when they were fresh, but I'll make cream puffs for lunch. Claude plans to grill some steaks for supper, and then we can all sit up on the catwalk and watch the fireworks," Naomi said.

"It all looks delicious." Libby sat down on the barstool Benny had pulled out for her.

"Claude took his break early with the gardening crew, but he'll be in by suppertime to meet you and have supper with us," Naomi explained.

"I'm going to run to the restroom," Benny said and gave Libby a quick kiss on the cheek. "I'll be right back."

Naomi handed Libby a plate and motioned toward the food. "I'll pour a couple of glasses of peach tea. It goes well with the sandwiches and macarons."

"Are you going to eat with us?" Libby asked.

"Of course," Naomi answered. "Claude and I never had children of our own—we came here after we married in Paris, France, forty years ago—so we helped raise that boy, and we feel like he partly belongs to us. Benny's grandparents always treated us like family." She released a long sigh. "Poor Mr. Walter. He was never the same after Miz Katie passed away. He spent more time up at Sawmill. I think it's because he could feel her spirit here in the house, waiting on him to join her . . . I'm rattling on when you didn't even ask."

"Please, tell me more. So, you came from Paris, France, to Paris, Texas?" Libby asked. She wanted the kind of relationship Katie and Walter had had—one that was so strong that the one left behind could still feel the spirit of the one who had passed.

"That's right."

"How did you get all the way from France to Texas?"

"We didn't come here when we first came to the States," Naomi answered. "We spent a few months in New York City; then we were offered jobs in Tennessee, so we went there. Seemed like we were chasing a dream until we landed here. Once we got to Paris, we felt like we were home." Naomi looked up and smiled when she saw Benny coming back to the kitchen. "That's a story for another day."

He picked up a croissant and took a bite. "We're going to have to eat and run if we want to see the parade."

"I was about to tell Libby the same thing," Naomi said. "I'll wrap up the leftovers for you to take to Opal and Minilee. I wish they could have come with you. I haven't seen them in over a year now."

"I'll bring them next time," Benny promised.

Libby finished her first croissant and put another one on her plate. "Will you teach me how to make these?"

"I would love to do that," Naomi replied. "You kids come and stay with us a few days, and you and I will spend our time in the kitchen. Claude was just saying yesterday that there are things he needs Benny's opinion about—some remodeling on the gazebo out in the rose gardens."

"If Libby doesn't have anything else on the books, we might do that real soon," Benny said. "I'd like Claude's advice about the house I'm designing."

"Why would you build a house when this one is sitting right here?" Naomi fussed.

"This was Grandpa and Grandma's dream house. Mine isn't nearly this big or fancy," Benny answered.

"I can understand that," Naomi said. "Claude and I are very glad to go home to our cottage at night. If we lived in a place this big, we would spend all our time trying to find each other."

"My thoughts exactly," Benny said and nudged Libby on the shoulder. "Now that I've found Libby, I sure don't want to play hide-and-seek, trying to find her every day after work."

Chapter Twenty-Seven

"We didn't grow up with this holiday in France, but I have embraced it since we came to this country," Claude said when another burst of sparkles lit up the sky that night.

"I like it because it stands for more than just the United States winning independence. It reminds all of us of our own choices, doesn't it?" Naomi reached over to the chair next to her and patted Claude's shoulder.

Libby wondered if there was a story there to be told some other day. She took another sip of her wine and enjoyed the extra warmth that spread through her body. The heat that came from sharing a chaise lounge with Benny had nothing to do with the wine or the summer night. "Did you ever watch the fireworks from this spot with your dad?"

"No, just my grandpa," Benny answered. "My parents divorced when I was twelve years old. Mother didn't want custody, and Dad was busy with the oil companies up and down the West Coast that he owns. So I was sent to boarding school. I came here for holidays and the summers. Mother is somewhere in the UK with her third husband. Dad is still married to his work. I see him a couple of times a year, but like I told you before, Grandpa was my stability, and more like a father than a granddad. Opal and Minilee were my Sawmill grandmothers. Claude and Naomi were my Paris grandparents. I didn't hurt for love or attention."

"Do you ever hear from your mother?" Libby asked.

"I get a Christmas card almost every year, and sometimes she remembers my birthday with a card." Benny hugged her closer to his side even though it was a hot night.

No wonder he hasn't been in a permanent relationship yet, she thought. Although their backgrounds were very different, their upbringings still had the potential to produce mistrust and wariness.

"You do know the clock is ticking, right?" Claude asked. His silver hair shone under the lights.

"That's right," Naomi told him. "None of us—me or Claude, or your Opal and Minilee—are getting any younger, and we would love to have a baby to spoil."

"I hear the clock, but I'm still young," Benny answered.

"Yes, you are, but time goes fast," Naomi said. "It's been too long since we've heard laughter in this big, empty house."

"Who knows what the future might bring," Benny said and pointed to the sky. "That one is the biggest one yet. I bet it's the end of the show."

"They always save the best until last," Naomi agreed. "The trouble with it being the last one is that you and Libby will leave. Are you sure that you won't stay for the night?"

"It's tempting," Benny said, "but we have to open the store at seven in the morning, so we better go on home."

Home!

Libby loved that word more than ever before. Her little one-room apartment and the front room of the station felt more like home than any place she had ever lived.

"I'm glad that the best is always saved for the last." Claude patted Naomi on the shoulder. "That's why we enjoy our old age so much, *mon amour.*"

Libby wasn't sure what the endearment meant, but it had to be something like *my love* or *my sweetheart,* as they would say in Texas. She wanted a relationship with romance still in it even when Benny had sparkling gray hair like Claude's.

Oh my gosh! How can I be thinking about a lifetime with Benny after only knowing him a few weeks? She threw a hand over her mouth to keep the words from blurting out.

"Sleepy?" Benny asked.

Libby faked a yawn. "Little bit."

Benny stood up and extended a hand to help her. "It's time to take Cinderella home. Naomi and Claude, thank y'all for making this a special day for us."

She took it and loved the sparks that danced between them. The small amount of time they had known each other didn't matter at that moment.

"We should thank you for making it a wonderful day for us," Claude told him as he got to his feet and opened his arms for a hug. "Don't be a stranger. Come around more often and spend time here."

Naomi hugged Libby and whispered, "You are the first woman he ever brought home, and his eyes sparkle when he looks at you—but then, yours light up when his name is even mentioned. You have a good thing going."

"I know, and thank you for reminding me," Libby told her.

Libby awoke five minutes before her alarm went off on Friday morning. She rolled over and slung an arm around Benny's broad chest and snuggled up to his back. For the past two weeks, things had been the same: work with Benny several days a week and spend most of their waking hours together on the days the store wasn't open. They had been together every night in her apartment, and she loved it—but if she was truly honest with herself, sometimes she missed those days back in Austin when she could have some time alone. Even with her job and the volunteer work at the shelter, she could always carve out a few hours each week she could call her own.

Put it on the balance scale and figure out if being with Benny is worth the price of giving up your time alone, she told herself.

She couldn't make the decision when she was half-asleep, so she closed her eyes for another hour. She awoke the second time to a delicious smell in the air and steam on her face; Benny was waving a mug full of hot coffee under her nose. She sat up and he handed the mug to her, then went to the counter and poured himself one.

"We missed our run this morning, but that extra rest was pretty good," he said.

She sipped the coffee. "So was getting to snuggle up to you a little longer."

"When we get furniture for the new house, we are definitely buying a king-sized bed." He sat down beside her on the edge of the mattress.

"I was thinking that a twin-sized would be better," she said with a grin. "That way you'll always be close to me."

"Darlin', I'm never going to be very far from you," he declared. "We should grab a protein bar and get dressed. The store opens in half an hour, and there's already more than a dozen cars in the parking lot."

"Have I got time for a quick bath?" she asked.

He wiggled his eyebrows. "It would be quicker for us to go over to the trailer and get a fast shower together. But"—he paused and chuckled—"it is so small that it will be like sleeping in a twin bed."

She set her coffee mug on the bedside table and slung her legs out of bed. "Give me time to grab some work clothes."

He grabbed the shirt he'd worn the day before, jerked it down over his head, and kissed her on the cheek. "I'll go on ahead and get the water adjusted."

"Be there in five minutes, tops." Even though she was excited about the prospect of taking her first shower with a man, she took a deep breath. Overwhelmed with all the emotions that were chasing through her mind and body, she still smiled and looked forward to what was about to happen.

At midmorning, Benny took half a minute from waiting on customers and grabbed one of the cookies Opal and Minilee had brought in that morning. "Did y'all have a good time yesterday at the birthday party for Sally?" he asked before he bit off a chunk.

"Wonderful, for the most part," Minilee replied. "But you're too busy for us to tell you the whole story right now. This is sure a hoppin' day for the middle of the month. The first weekend usually brings everyone out to shop, not two weeks later."

"Must be because Independence Day was so close to that weekend," Opal said. "Folks were off traveling or staying home with the family and friends that came to see them. Why don't you and Libby come over after work tonight for a game of dominoes?"

"Sounds great," he said and hurried over to greet another group that had just come into the store. "Hello, and welcome. Take a look around, and call me if you need help finding anything. Feel free to help yourselves to the cold water bottles." He nodded toward the cooler. "It gets a little warm in here this time of year."

"Thank you." An older woman headed across the room and passed out half a dozen bottles of water to her friends. "This is a really nice thing you are doing. There's no way you could keep a big place like this cool. I'm looking for antique glassware, and I see a bunch over there on the side wall, so that's where I'm headed."

"Holler if you need me to get anything down from the top shelf for you," Benny said, picking up two water bottles. He chuckled at the thought of the shower he and Libby had shared that morning. Two tall people in a tiny space had created a lot of heat, and even more giggles, but there was no time for sex—at least not that morning. He imagined what it would have been like and rolled the cold bottle over his forehead to cool him down, but it didn't do much good.

The line of people waiting to pay for their items and get an invoice was backed up to the door so far that he could barely get it open. When he did, he took a step to the side. Libby was good with the customers, talking to each one about the item or items they were in the process of buying. Yet she was efficient and fast when she entered numbers, ran credit cards, or slipped the cash payments into the register drawer.

Simply standing back in the corner, watching her, made him so happy that he wanted to push everyone out of the way and take her in his arms for a long kiss. The only time he could remember being this excited was when he left boarding school on holidays and could spend time with his grandparents. He really should send Dolly a thank-you gift for talking Libby into coming to Sawmill.

When the last person in line finished paying out and collecting their invoices, he stepped away from where he'd been standing and set a bottle of water on the desk. "Thought you might need this," he said, and bent to kiss her on the forehead.

"Thank you." She smiled up at him, and that made him even happier. "Business has been steady from the time we opened the door this morning," she said as she twisted the lid off the bottle and took a long drink.

He hiked up a hip on the edge of the desk. "I guess everyone is making up for that slow weekend we had right after the holiday. If this keeps up, we'll be dog tired by Sunday evening, so no date night then."

"Nope—but then, we agreed that date night would be sometime in the middle of the week, didn't we? We'll have to drag our tired butts home tonight, fall into bed, and go to sleep."

He raised an eyebrow. "Or maybe do something that will ensure a good night's sleep?"

"Hey, y'all ready to play a game of Moon?" Opal called out from the porch when they walked past her house that evening.

"Can we take a rain check?" Benny answered. "Exhausted tonight."

"Sure," Opal answered. "No problem. We've got leftovers from supper. We'll bring them over so neither of you have to cook. We can visit while y'all eat."

"Thank you," Benny said.

"That didn't sound very heartfelt," Libby whispered. "I had no idea that we were planning to play dominoes with the ladies tonight."

"It wasn't heartfelt at all. I would rather eat a grilled cheese sandwich and have the rest of the evening with you," he told her.

"Do you ever think that we need a night apart?" she asked.

"Do you?" he fired back as they went inside the station.

She kicked off her shoes at the door, and as usual, Fancy went to her favorite spot under the table. "Sometimes I do. Don't you?"

"Has this got anything to do with me forgetting to tell you about Opal and Minilee inviting us to play dominoes?"

"No," she answered, "it does not. We had a lot of customers. I understand how you could have forgotten about something that small. But we've always been honest with each other, and I'm just asking if we're together too much. Are we rushing things? Will what we have fizzle out? Will we both want what we had in the beginning so much that we hang on just to be hanging on?"

"I've been alone four days a week, except for Elvis's company, for the past year." He pulled out a chair and sat down at the table. "I thought we were happy spending time together—and besides, today we only saw each other twice all day. That was only for a few minutes."

Libby sat down across from him. "I'm happier than I've ever been in my life, Benny. I never dreamed I could be in this place. You've helped me so much . . . But I was alone most of my life. You know the story with Victoria. Then I got a job where I lived in a cubicle by myself, went home to spend most evenings alone. I volunteered at the shelter, but even with that, I had a lot of hours when—"

"We're here!" Minilee called out. "And we brought a big old ham bone for Elvis to gnaw on. He wagged his tail so hard when we gave it to him that I thought he would lose his balance and fall over."

Opal uncovered a casserole dish and a bowl. "We brought some burgers that were left over from yesterday's cookout at Sally's house."

"And my potato salad," Minilee added. "Judging from all the cars and dust they stirred up, I figure y'all didn't get much of a break today."

"We sure didn't," Libby said. "Thanks for supper. It all looks delicious."

Minilee brought two beers from the refrigerator and disposable plates to the table. "We had quite the day at Sally's, and I could have wrung Tatum's neck for spoiling it for her grandmother."

"Oh?" Benny opened the floodgates with that one word.

"Tatum got drunk and was using foul language. Sally told her that she should have stayed in the military and that she should settle down. She used to have a tantrum when she was a little girl and didn't get what she wanted, but what she called her grandmother made me so mad that I grabbed her by the arm and dragged her around to the back of the house," Opal said.

"We could hear some of what was said but not all of it," Minilee explained. "I didn't realize that Opal had such a temper. Poor Sally was weeping and apologizing to everyone. I was trying to smooth it all over. I decided to step up and start everyone singing the birthday song. I can't carry a tune in a galvanized milk bucket, but I really tried to drown out the dressing down that Opal was giving Tatum."

"That poor girl needs a lot of help, and I hope that some of what I had to tell her sank in deep enough that she goes to someone who will tell her she needs to grow up and change her attitude," Opal said. "Now, that's enough spilling the tea on our part. You didn't tell me what you thought when you visited the estate, Libby. I was in a state of shock the first time me and Ernest went to the Christmas party at that place. But it wasn't so intimidating the second time we were there."

"It's beautiful, but I figured out that the size of a place doesn't matter. A tiny apartment can be a mansion if there's happiness and love in it," she answered.

Opal almost smiled. "I sure wish Tatum would learn the same lesson."

"Maybe you should invite her to book club," Libby said. "That and having y'all to talk to has sure helped me."

Benny wondered if maybe he should go to their club meetings, too. Was he smothering Libby? Was that why she needed some breathing room? He thought about the questions and decided he didn't want to spend time away from her, but if she needed space, then she should have it.

Half an hour later, Opal covered a yawn with her hand. "We're all talked out now, and my energy is still zapped from the heat and all the visitin' yesterday. Let's go on home, Minilee, and let these kids get some rest. I bet they're worn out, too, and they've got to get up early and go to work tomorrow."

Minilee stood up and carried the plates and empty bottles to the trash can. "Y'all have a good night."

"Thanks for supper," Libby said.

"And the visit," Benny added as he stood.

As if on cue, Fancy went to the closed apartment door and yipped. Benny let her in and then turned to face Libby. "I'm going to the trailer, darlin'. I'll see you in the morning for our run."

"Are you angry with me?" she asked.

"I don't really know what I am," he answered. "Maybe disappointed is more like it, but if you need some alone time and some space, I'll give it to you. We are evidently in two different places in this relationship, but I'm a patient man."

"Thank you," she whispered.

He kissed her on the forehead and walked out the door.

Chapter Twenty-Eight

Libby's heart felt like someone had wrapped a rock around it with heavy chains when Benny was gone. Sure, she would like some time alone, but she hated the heaviness in her chest. She ran a warm bath and even put in vanilla-scented bath salts to relax her. The smell made her think of the shaving lotion Benny used—that woodsy stuff with a hint of vanilla in it. She got out of the tub before the water was even lukewarm and dressed in her rattiest old sleep shirt—the leftover one from her college days that was almost threadbare.

She picked up the book she was supposed to finish in time for book club at their next meeting, but after she'd turned the page several times, she couldn't remember a word of what she had read. Her mind kept drifting back to the day she and Benny had gone to the river and the conversation they'd had about the stories they had been reading then.

Finally, she gave up and went to bed. She expected to fall right to sleep like she always did when Benny was beside her. She felt as if she had not made him understand why she wanted them both to have time alone: so they could be sure that the arrangement they had fallen into headfirst was right for both of them. What she'd said had apparently come out all wrong and made it sound like *she* was the one who needed space, when she really wanted to be sure of what they *both* wanted before they went any further.

"I don't want this to be a fleeting romance that puts us both in too deep, too quick to get out of without regrets," she told Fancy.

The dog hopped down from her place on the sofa and trotted across the floor. Libby picked her up and set her on the bed. The animal stuck her nose in Benny's pillow and whimpered.

"Whose side are you on?" Libby grumbled and moved over to bury her own face in the pillow, inhaling deeply to get a good solid whiff of his scent. There was no getting to sleep, so she got up and paced in circles for a few minutes.

All the color sheets and pictures from the shelter kids that Dolly had sent her were taped to the broad side of the refrigerator. She stopped and looked at each of them, imagining their little faces as they worked on the special gifts for her. Someday, she wanted to hang things like that on a very different refrigerator—pictures her own children had made for her. And she wanted their father to be Benny.

"I can't let this alone until tomorrow," she whispered.

She went into the front room, peeked out the window, and saw the trailer's lights were still on. She shoved her feet into the shoes she had kicked off earlier. "How do I know that my feelings are real? That this isn't all just . . ." She stopped midsentence when the lights in the trailer went out.

Before she could talk herself out of what was in her heart to do, she walked outside and closed the door behind her. Elvis raised up from the porch, but when he saw that it was Libby, he went back to sleep.

She took a deep breath, walked halfway across the distance, and lost her nerve. She couldn't knock on his door. She had been the one who wanted space.

"I've changed my mind," she said, and took another step.

She made it all the way up the steps to the trailer door and froze again. She had never made the first move in any relationship. Elvis's cold nose prodded the back of her leg and scared her so badly that she almost tumbled backward. She had barely gotten her balance when the dog yipped a couple of times and scratched the door.

"I'm coming." Benny's voice sounded like it came from the back of the trailer.

Light suddenly flowed from the windows again and left a yellow path to the station. The door creaked when it opened, and Elvis raced inside. Benny was silhouetted by the light behind him inside the trailer and was wearing nothing but a pair of sleep shorts. Libby had seen him in far less clothing, but she stood there, speechless, before him, not knowing what to say or even where to begin.

"Did you get hot out there on the porch?" he asked the dog, and then his expression changed when he saw Libby standing on the other side of the top step. "Libby, is everything all right?"

"Not right now," she answered. "Can we talk? On the porch?"

He stood to the side and motioned for her to come in. "It's cool in here," he said in a flat tone. "Come on in."

Libby stepped into the tiny living area. Elvis took up most of the space on the small love seat that sat against one wall. She heard a noise and glanced to her left. Benny had pulled out a chair at a table for two. She sat down in it, and he brought out two beers from a refrigerator under the cabinet only a few feet away. He twisted the top off each of them and handed one to her.

She took a long drink and asked, "Are you going to say anything?"

"Not until you do. You're the one who is calling this meeting," Benny answered and sat down in the other chair.

She wanted to move over and sit in his lap and lay her head on his broad chest. She wanted to listen to his steady heartbeat the way she had done so many times before. But she knew that that wasn't going to happen when his face was set in stone. She realized, without hearing any voices in her head, that she had caused this situation, so it was up to her to fix it.

"I was wrong." She shifted her gaze from his face to the bottle of beer in front of her. "Having space means loneliness. Not trusting you, when you haven't given me a single reason not to, is wrong. I'm sorry. I love you, Benny. Please, come back to the apartment."

He reached across the table and took her hands in his. "Why? We've got a perfectly good bed right here."

Her eyes darted up to his face, and the smile she saw there erased all the tension in her body. "Are you inviting me to spend the night here?"

"I'm asking you to spend every night from now on with me—either here or in your apartment. I want us to live together, but we really need to build a house so that we aren't shifting from one place to the other all the time," he answered. "It'll confuse our dog children."

"Don't we need to talk this through some more?" she asked, fighting back a small smile of her own.

"Do you love me?" he asked.

"Yes," she said without blinking.

Benny stood up, still holding both her hands. "I love you, too. That's the beginning of making a foundation in every relationship. We'll build on that." He walked backward until they reached the edge of the bed. "One brick at a time, but love is the cornerstone." He sat down and pulled her onto his lap.

"What if we argue? Will that destroy our foundation?"

He tilted up her chin and kissed her—long, lingering, and heat producing. "No, darlin', we'll just have makeup sex."

Libby thought of what Minilee had said about starting fights with Floyd so they could go to the bedroom and make up. After the way she had felt when she and Benny were apart for a few hours, she vowed that she would never deliberately start an argument. If she had a valid opinion, she would stand by it, but if she wanted to have sex, she would just take Benny by the hand and lead him into the bedroom.

"What are you thinking about?" he asked as he strung kisses from her neck to her lips.

"Makeup sex," she whispered. "And, Benny, I really do love you with all my heart and soul. I have fought with my feelings and with my trust issues, but I truly believe I've found closure, thanks to you."

"And, Libby, I love you, too. We are going to be so happy together."

Epilogue

Two years later

Libby didn't need to see the Sawmill Antiques freebie calendar hanging on the kitchen wall to know what day it was. Tuesday, the first day of September—Benny's thirty-fifth birthday and their daughter Katie's first one. Opal and Minilee had declared she was the spitting image of Benny's grandmother Katie.

Libby was dancing that morning with excitement. Several times over the last few days, she had almost blurted out the secret she had been keeping from him for a whole week.

Benny came into the kitchen, wrapped his arms around her, and drew her close to his chest. "Good mornin', darlin'."

"Happy birthday to you. Your present is on the table." Her arms snaked up around his neck and pulled his face to hers for another kiss.

"Last night was amazing enough to be my birthday gift," he whispered.

"For me, too," she agreed. "Katie's present to you is that she stayed asleep while we made a little noise last night. We have been together more than two years now, and I love you more today than I did the day we got married."

"Right back at you," he said with a grin, and like he did every morning, he went over to Katie's high chair to give her a kiss. "Good mornin', baby girl. It's still hard to believe that your mama gave you to me for my birthday present last year."

Katie patted her daddy on both cheeks and then held up her arms. Benny took her out of the chair and carried her over to the kitchen window. "Look, sweetheart!" He pointed toward the trees that grew out beyond the fenced yard. "The deer have come up this morning, and there's a little fawn who came up here to wish you a happy birthday. It's going to be a wonderful day. You will have a little birthday party with Naomi and Claude in Paris. Opal and Minilee will be there with us—and afterwards, we will come home and have our own party right here."

Libby's thoughts went back to the evening they had gotten married and moved into the house together. Benny had offered to close the store and take her for a honeymoon anywhere in the world, but she had chosen to spend the time in their new home. It hadn't been completely finished then, but there was a big four-poster, king-size bed in the right room. Benny had put a patio set out on the back porch, and they'd had their meals out there every day—when they weren't having them in bed.

Benny broke into her memories with a question. "What is your mommy smiling about?"

Libby poured a cup of coffee and set it on the table. "Our honeymoon."

"Would you have changed anything about it?" he asked as he put Katie back in her chair.

"Not one thing about those four days—or about anything since I first arrived in Sawmill," she answered. "How about you?"

He gave her a quick kiss on the cheek and took a sip of his coffee. "Not one single moment. My life started when you came to Sawmill, and the way I figure it, we're still on our honeymoon and will be until Katie is a grandmother and we are watching the deer in the backyard with our great-grandchildren."

Libby made herself a cup of decaf coffee. "Are you going to open your present?"

"I told you not to buy me anything," Benny said. "I've got all I need or could ever want right here in this house."

"Open it," she insisted. "I promise I didn't pay much for what's wrapped up in that Christmas paper. I hope it's a surprise and you haven't guessed what's in it."

"Okay. Let's open this up." He picked up the long, slim box and shook it. "Sounds like a new pen. I hope it has a GPS locator on it so I can find it anywhere in the store. You know how I am always losing mine. I don't think you can beat last year's present of Katie."

"Oh, really?" Libby raised a dark eyebrow and pointed to the picture hanging above the kitchen table. She had rescued the rough draft of the house they had designed on the back of Christmas paper and had it framed for him the first Christmas after they were married. "I thought you really loved that."

"I do," he said with a nod. "I don't know how you managed to keep those plans, but I love that we still have them up there to remind us of our first rough draft of this house." He smiled and lowered his voice. "And I really like that you've wrapped most of my gifts in Christmas paper ever since then."

"Most?" Another eyebrow shot up.

"Last night's present was wrapped in something silky and sexy," he teased.

"You do realize that the time is coming when Katie will be old enough that I'll have to be more discreet in what I wear around this house?" she asked, wishing he would hurry up and unwrap the present before she blurted out what was inside the box.

"Then you will be sexy in a long flannel nightgown." He pulled the tape off the ends of the present carefully.

The box had once held a letter opener. Libby had found it in an old dresser drawer, and since it was definitely not an antique, she had claimed it.

Katie began to fuss, so Libby put a few pieces of cereal on her tray. She was planning to make chocolate chip pancakes for their birthday breakfast—both Benny's and Katie's favorite—but she didn't want to miss Benny's expression when he opened his present.

"Is something going to pop out and startle me?" he asked when all the paper was gone.

"I hope not!" She clasped her hands together in her lap and held her breath.

He eased the lid off and peeked inside. His eyes got wider and wider, and his smile grew bigger and bigger. "Is this for real? You aren't teasing me, are you?"

"It's real!" Libby answered.

"When?" he asked.

"I won't know the exact date, but sometime at the first of the summer, just a couple of months before Katie's second birthday," she answered. "Are you—"

Benny jumped up so fast that his chair fell over backward with a loud thump. He picked Libby up out of the chair and danced around the room with her. "Yes, I'm happy, if that's what you were going to ask me. I've always wanted a big family, and Katie needs a sibling."

They were both panting when he finally took her back to the table. "Can we tell everyone today?"

"I'd rather wait until the first trimester is over," she answered, "like we did with Katie. I liked having it to ourselves for a little while."

"Then we'll announce it at Christmas," he agreed and laid a hand on her still-flat stomach. "This is a wonderful birthday present. Thank you."

"We'll have double diapers and high chairs, and we'll have to put a second crib in the office," she reminded him.

"I wouldn't care if we had twins or triplets and had to do more than that," Benny assured her. "I love you so, so much." He planted kisses all over her face and then held her close to his chest.

Benny's whole personality, strong and steady, was right there in his heartbeat—just like it had always been.

"I love you right back. You might get a son this time," she told him.

He pulled back enough to push a strand of dark hair from her face. "I don't care if I get a son or another daughter. Either one is fine with me."

Claude waved from the porch that used to be part of the Taylor estate when Benny parked the truck in the circle drive. He had a book in his hands, and several small children were gathered around him. Benny got out, rounded the front of the vehicle, and opened the door for Libby.

Naomi came out of the house and made a beeline for the truck. She flung open the back door, unfastened Katie's car seat belts, and picked her up. "Happy birthday, sweet baby girl—and happy birthday to you, Benny."

"Thank you," he said and draped his arm around Libby's shoulders.

"You gave me and Claude a new lease on life when you turned this into a women's shelter," Naomi said. "The house is filled with laughter, and we're helping needy women get new starts all over the place with the contacts you have around the country. Walter and your dad both would be so proud of you."

Claude reached up for Katie, but Naomi shook her head. "You can have her later."

"Claude, I could finish reading the book to the kids if you want to go inside," Libby offered.

Claude handed the book off to her and followed Naomi and Benny into the house. "That's a good woman you've got," he told Benny.

"Yep, and I'm one lucky man to have her," Benny said.

A safety gate blocked the bottom and top of the staircase. Four women—some still with fresh bruises—waved at him from the living room, where toys and babies were everywhere. When they reached the kitchen, where Opal and Minilee were having coffee at the table, he noticed three more women in the backyard. Two were pushing their children on the swing set, and the other one was sitting on a blanket under the shade of a big pecan tree with a set of twins.

Benny had teased Libby about having twins this time around, but he really wouldn't care if they did have more than one baby this time around.

"I'm taking Katie out in the yard to push her in the swing. Claude did good when he built a special one for her and hung it in the tree," Naomi said without stopping. "I'm glad she doesn't mind sharing with the other little ones that come through here."

Benny went to the window and watched the mothers and children enjoying a day out in the yard. A few minutes later, he saw the children who had been on the front porch rush into the back yard, with Libby right behind them. She stopped and visited each mother as she crossed the yard to the pecan tree, where Naomi was pushing Katie in the swing. Benny couldn't hear his daughter's squeals or his wife's laughter, but he could tell from their expressions that they were happy.

"It's been a good two years," Opal said.

"We are so proud of you for all this, Benny," Minilee added.

"Thanks, but like I told Naomi, this was Libby's idea."

"But it was yours to do, and there's no telling how many women will be helped by it in the future. Exactly where have you been sending them when they leave here?" Opal asked.

"I can't say where they all end up, but my dad has helped a lot, with his contacts in the oil business," he answered without taking his eyes off his wife and child.

"It's better that we don't know," Minilee said.

"Probably so," Benny replied.

Libby left the swing and crossed the yard. Benny thought she was even more beautiful in her sundress, which was the exact same shade of blue as her eyes. A gentle breeze blew her dark hair away from her face, and when she looked up and saw him in the window, she smiled and waved.

He met her at the back door and drew her to his chest in a tight embrace. "I love you so much, Libby Taylor."

She whispered the vow she had made to him on their wedding day. "I will love you with my whole heart and my soul, forever and a day."

Acknowledgments

Libby and Benny both came to me several months ago and needed someone to tell their story. Libby's part was so emotional that I wasn't sure I could do it justice, but with Benny's help, I decided to give it a shot. My characters are as real to me as my next-door neighbors—in some cases, even more so. I lived with Libby and Benny in my head for a long time, and we had such interesting conversations. Some made me giggle, and others put tears in my eyes. I hope all you readers enjoy meeting and getting to know the people in Sawmill as much as I did.

As always, a lot of work goes into taking a book from an idea to the finished product that you are holding in your hands. I would like to thank everyone who had a part in that process. A special thanks to Amazon/Montlake and Alison Dasho for continuing to believe in me, and to Krista Stroever, my developmental editor. Thanks to my agency, Folio Management Literary Agency, and to my agent, Erin Niumata. And to my family, with special thanks to my husband of fifty-seven years, Mr. B. It takes a special person to live with an author, and he doesn't mind take-out food or dust bunnies under the beds when I'm working on a deadline.

Most of all, I want to thank my readers. Your support means everything to me. I've said it before, but I want you all to know again that, without you, we authors would be an endangered species. I really, really do not want to find my name on that particular list.

Until next time,
Carolyn Brown

About the Author

Photo © 2015 Charles Brown

Carolyn Brown is a *New York Times, USA Today, Washington Post, Wall Street Journal,* and *Publishers Weekly* bestselling author and RITA finalist with more than 130 published books. She has written women's fiction, historical and contemporary romance, and cowboys-and-country-music novels. She and her husband live in the small town of Davis, Oklahoma, where everyone knows everyone else, knows what they are doing and when, and reads the local newspaper on Wednesday to see who got caught. They have three grown children and enough grandchildren and great-grandchildren to keep them young. For more information, visit www.carolynbrownbooks.com.